VIKING WARRIOR RISING

ASA MARIA BRADLEY

sourcebooks
casablanca

Published by Sourcebooks Casablanca, an imprint of Sourcebooks, Inc.
P.O. Box 4410, Naperville, Illinois 60567-4410
(630) 961-3900
Fax: (630) 961-2168
www.sourcebooks.com

Printed and bound in Canada
MBP 10 9 8 7 6 5 4 3 2 1

To Mamma and Pappa for always believing in me and for encouraging and enabling my love of books.

Chapter 1

NAYA'S HANDS SHOOK AS SHE CLIPPED THE LAST alligator clamp over the electrical wires, short-circuiting the power and the security alarm.

"Get it together," she muttered to herself.

As she crouched and peered down the darkened corridor, her infrared goggles helped her see the contours of the barred doors. Her brother was behind one of those. Alone.

She jogged down the hallway to the only cell giving off a heat signature.

"Scott," she whispered through the bars of the cell door, but the man lying on the cot didn't move. Her fingers recoiled when she touched the cold metal, remembering how often she'd been trapped in a cell just like this. She had to get her brother out. He'd suffered enough at the hands of Dr. Trousil and the rest of the lab's scientists. They both had.

The door swung open silently and she entered the cell. She shook her brother's shoulder, keeping her hand hovering over his mouth in case he woke up screaming. He remained lying limply on his side. When she turned him onto his back, his arm flopped over and dangled down the side of the cot.

Holding her breath, she leaned closer to his mouth. A weak puff of air fluttered against her cheek. Relief flooded her body. She joggled him again. "Scott, you need to wake up."

He still didn't react.

Naya hoisted him in a fireman's carry so that her much smaller frame could transport his six-foot body. Another five minutes and the security guards would return to patrol this end of the building. She'd figure out how to wake him later.

Her brother had weighed almost two hundred pounds when she last saw him. It had taken her eleven months and six days to return. Hanging across her shoulder now, his body barely slowed her down. She headed for the closest exit. The door closed softly behind her and she jogged across the field. When she reached the perimeter fence, Naya carefully lowered her brother to the ground and slid the bolt cutters out of her backpack.

"Hold on, Scott. Just a few snips and I'll have you out of here." She glanced down, trying for a hopeful smile, but her lips quivered. She remembered his nervous, yet excited, laugh as they raced toward this same fence that night almost a year ago. They had been so close to getting out together. He'd boosted her up on top of the fence, smacking her behind. "Let's finally get the hell out of here," he'd shouted.

She'd just reached down to help up Scott when the first shot rang out. The second pierced her brother's thigh and he fell screaming to the ground.

She blinked. *Can't think about the past now.* She couldn't fuck this up. There might never be another chance. Her sharp cutters snipped the wires like they were string instead of high-grade reinforced steel. A normal human wouldn't be able to bend back the ser-rated wire, but Naya was not normal. Ten years in the lab and weekly serum injections had created a super-soldier out of the twelve-year-old girl she had once been. Now she was the ultimate weapon. The ultimate freak.

She doubled over the folded metal to keep her brother from getting caught on any rough edges. Her baby brother. The only family she had left.

She slid Scott's unconscious body through the hole, hoisted him over her shoulder again, and then headed to the rental car parked in the woods. The smell of fresh pine permeated the air as her combat boots pounded the needle-covered ground. The crisp forest cleared her mind of things she no longer wanted to remember.

Now that Scott was out, she could build a life and never think about the years in the lab.

Soon, the dark-green Jeep glittered in the moonlight filtering through the trees. Without slowing, she punched a button on the key remote. Behind her, a powerful boom of an explosion drowned out the double beep of the doors unlocking. A kaleidoscope of red and orange illuminated the night sky. She heard shouts and commands carry through the woods from the compound. A bitter smile stretched her lips. That would keep them occupied for a while.

Growing up in the compound, she'd spent countless hours honing her combat skills, but the government-sponsored black ops program had also trained her in electronics, cyber technology, and weaponry—including explosives. "I used everything you taught me," she whispered at the flames.

She cradled Scott's head as she slid him into the backseat. His eyelids fluttered. For an instant, indigo-blue eyes so like hers focused on her. A slow smile spread across her brother's face before his eyelids fluttered closed again. "I knew you'd come for me, Neyney."

The childhood nickname pierced her heart. "I told you I would," she whispered. She kissed his forehead and brushed back his ink-black curls—the same color as her own spit-straight hair.

He mumbled something incomprehensible before his body fell limp against the seat. She clicked his seat belt in place and allowed herself to touch his face once more before she slid into the driver's seat. A glance in the rearview mirror told her the lab security forces were too busy fighting fires to come after her—for now. But they would eventually. And when they did, she'd better be ready for them. No way she'd let them imprison her brother, or her, again.

She threw the Jeep into four-wheel drive, hit the accelerator, and pushed the car as hard as she could down the rutted old logging road. Scott's head bobbed back and forth in the rearview mirror, but he didn't wake up. She swallowed the lump in her throat and pressed harder on the gas. Once they reached the main arterial, she eased off the pedal. No reason to attract attention.

She tuned the radio to the classical music station. Getting to Dr. Rosen's clinic in Colorado was the most important thing now. The doctor and his team had been sampling her blood for the last six months. Hopefully whatever he had learned would help Scott. Dr. Rosen was the best in his field. More importantly, he was her only hope for curing her brother. She settled in for the fifteen-hour drive from North Dakota to the exclusive medical facility.

—◦—

Two days later, Naya struggled to keep her expression neutral as Dr. Rosen leaned forward in his chair, concern glimmering in his emerald eyes. He pushed up the rimless glasses perched on his nose and addressed her by the alias she'd given when they first met. "Ms. Driscoll, I'm afraid there has been no improvement in your brother since his intake."

"Maybe we need to give it a little longer before the drugs will work." She resented how her voice sounded. Pleading. She hated not being strong.

Dr. Rosen paused, his eyes kind. "I don't think waiting will help. I'm afraid we're going to have to try a different approach."

Naya's gaze drifted from the doctor's as she allowed his words to sink in. A bank of windows behind his desk revealed breathtaking views of snowcapped mountains. The clinic's exclusive clientele included media-shy movie stars and foreign dignitaries. It was the perfect place to hide her brother. She also needed it to be the perfect place to cure him.

"You said the modified formula your team developed based on my blood looked promising." All that research for nothing, but she refused to give up. There had to be a way to save her brother.

Dr. Rosen pushed up his glasses. "We had some promising nerve reactions after the first doses, but Scott reverted back to his vegetative state—"

"Don't say that." Naya burst out of the chair. "He's not a vegetable. He holds himself up, supports his body without help." She clenched her fists. "He spoke to me, damn it."

He held up his hands, palms facing her. "That may have been a temporary reprieve from his condition."

She slowly sat down again. "Are you saying he's getting worse?"

"At this point, I don't have a clear diagnosis. However, unresponsive and bedridden patients run a higher risk of infection, which can lead to respiratory complications, even organ failures. I can remedy that with antibiotics, but I'm not sure I can repair the extensive neurological damage Scott has sustained."

To avoid the pity in the doctor's eyes, Naya looked out over the mountains again. "Why are the drugs in Scott's blood shutting him down when I'm functioning just fine?" Better than fine, but the doctor didn't need to know that. He lived in the normal human world, blissfully ignorant of monsters and freaks like her.

"What do you propose?" Naya gripped the armrest of the chair and eased up when she heard the wood creaking. She had to rein in her emotions or she'd treat the doctor to a full freak show.

"We can continue to tweak the formula and hope for better results. I'd also like to explore your brother's vascular system and test how it differs from yours." He put his hands on the desk. "At this point, I must caution you about the high cost of therapy that may ultimately not produce the outcome you want."

"Let me worry about the money." Nothing was too costly if it helped Scott. Besides, she earned enough. As one of the best cybersecurity experts in the world, her services did not come cheap.

She stood. "I'd like to visit with my brother again before I leave."

The doctor rose as well. "Of course. He'll be well cared for until you come back."

"Until then, please keep me updated."

Dr. Rosen nodded. "I will personally send you a weekly report."

Naya thanked him before leaving the office.

She didn't want to leave her brother, but living near Scott in Colorado was too risky. If the handlers found her, they might also find him. Naya harbored no illusions about their outcome if the handlers caught them. They would be neutralized, or worse, returned to the lab for more experiments.

Naya wouldn't let that happen.

Her heavy boots beat a dull staccato as she strode down the hallway. Smells of antiseptics and disinfectant wafted through the air. Naya shivered. Those same scents had permeated the lab in which she had spent most of her life.

Taking a deep breath, she opened the door to her brother's room. He sat unmoving in a wheelchair, staring into space with empty eyes. "Scotty, it's me, Naya." She crouched before him, taking his limp hands in hers. His skin was dry and warm. He had spent the last two days sitting or lying, depending on which position the nurses put him, and always unnaturally still. He hadn't spoken to her again.

"I know you can hear me." She paused, waiting for a response. Naya touched her brother's cheek and hair, but he didn't react. She stood and averted her face to hide the tears about to spill. "Shall I read to you a little? How far did we get this morning?" She crossed the room and picked up the astronomy book she'd bought, his favorite subject. At least it had been when he still talked and walked and laughed.

She wouldn't let her thoughts continue down that depressing path, as if he was already beyond saving. Instead, she began reading to her brother about distant nebulas and galaxies. For another hour, she would pretend they were back in their childhood home, their parents still alive and watching TV while she read her little brother a bedtime story.

Chapter 2

Two months later

LEIF SKARSGANGER STRODE ACROSS THE POCKMARKED asphalt of the alley, his footsteps echoing against the brick walls. His berserker paced, clawing at the mental cage Leif had created to stop it from taking control over his body. The fierce warrior spirit lived inside each of the *einherjar*, Odin's elite Viking warriors. Calling forth the berserker made them undefeatable in battle, but the inner warrior required a steady supply of human energy or it got out of control. Leif should have left the fortress before his berserker got this restless. The berserker lunged and growled, resembling its namesake animal, the bear, forcing Leif to stop. Breathing heavily, Leif rubbed his chest then continued walking.

At the back door of the nightclub Desire, Leif opened his senses to the energy created by the people dancing inside. Outside the walls, he couldn't see their gyrating bodies or sweat-soaked skin. He didn't need to. The frenzy of their sexual arousal as they ground against each other washed over him. His berserker howled in hunger. Leif's nostrils flared as the humans' energy swirled around him in an invisible maelstrom that he pulled deep within himself. Wave after wave washed through Leif's body, and the berserker gulped it down, absorbing it all.

The human energy from inside the club worked like
the frenzy that arose from battle, and since the twenty-
first century's warfare didn't include large-scale battle,
the Vikings and Valkyries had found new ways of feeding the berserkers or *feberandas*.

Leif sighed deeply when his warrior spirit was finally
sated and lay down in slumber. Hopefully it would
remain dormant for a while. He pulled his cell phone
from the back pocket of his jeans and checked the time.
Two hours past midnight and plenty of time to sneak
home before any of his warriors noticed him gone. If
his second-in-command knew where he was and what
he was doing, Harald would haul his ass home, king or
no king. As the ruler of a band of Vikings and Valkyries,
Leif broke a number of rules by leaving the fortress
without backup in the middle of the night, but with his
berserker growing more and more restless each day, he
had no choice. This was the only way he could remain
in control of his warrior spirit.

He took a step toward the alley entry, but feet scuff-
ing on pavement made him slowly turn around. Behind
him, four creatures were lined up for attack. Their faces
were narrow and pointed, vaguely resembling wolverines. They could pass for human, except their eyes were
black voids and sharp claws extended from the ends of
their fingers. Through his connection with the resting
berserker, Leif recognized them for what they were—
Loki's minions. So far, Leif and his warriors hadn't
been able to gather the proof Odin and Freya needed
to outright prove that the half god was behind sending
these creatures to the human realm, but they had an oth-
erworldly glow only found in Asgard.

He'd been too preoccupied with feeding his berserker to notice these freaks sneaking up on him, but he wasn't worried. Four against one were odds he'd beaten before. Still holding the cell phone, Leif widened his stance and relaxed his shoulders.

Bring it on, you bastards.

A good fight would help calm his warrior spirit even more. So far, none of his soldiers had noticed how much more of an effort it took Leif to control his warrior spirit. He meant to keep it that way. But he should take a picture of this new threat so his warriors knew what to look for when out on patrol.

"What can I do for you…men?" He curled his lips on the last word.

"Greetings, king," wheezed one of the creatures. "Such a coincidence to run into you tonight." He leered at Leif and all four took a step forward.

Leif remained still. "What do you want?" he challenged.

He snapped a picture with his cell phone to show his warriors this new tasteless creation of Loki's.

The minions hissed and snarled as the flash went off. One of them fiddled with something behind his back and brought out a long pipe and a shorter black cylinder. The creature's satisfied smirk indicated he'd armed himself.

Leif snapped another picture, earning another snarl. Not that he cared.

"We want so much from you, king," answered the apparent leader, his smirk broadening into a nasty smile.

Leif grinned back. He'd remained largely undefeated through the centuries. This was one of the reasons why Odin had appointed him as the leader of one of the Norse warrior bands sent back to Midgard, the human realm. The Wise One also believed Leif was the king predicted on ancient rune stones to prevent the final battle, Ragnarök.

Leif sighed. He was awful at strategic planning and diplomacy, never mind saving the world. But he was a damned good warrior, which these monsters would soon find out.

Slipping the phone into his back pocket, he tilted his head from side to side, loosening the kinks in his neck and shoulders. "Let's get this over with." He faked a step forward and then tripped the two creatures that lunged at him. A duo of swift kicks sent them careening across the asphalt, shrieking.

"Who's next?" Leif asked and couldn't keep a satisfied grin off his face.

The wolverine with the tube glared at him.

"Put down your toy and face me like a man," Leif taunted him.

An odd smile graced the creature's face as he lifted the weapon to his lips.

Leif frowned. Misgivings prickled at the back of his neck. He tapped the connection to his berserker.

Immediately alert, the warrior spirit roared a battle cry. Leif willed it to stand down, but remain prepared should he need it. His gaze focused on the pipe at the wolverine's mouth.

A door clicked open behind him and he turned slightly, alert to any potential new enemy entering the alley. A human woman slipped out and descended the stairs soundlessly with the grace of a dancer. She kept her head down, her features hidden by a curtain of black hair.

Leif watched the wolverines out of the corner of his eye, but his main attention swung toward the woman while he positioned himself between her and the creatures. He had sworn to protect all of Midgard's humans, including this one.

Suddenly, a prick similar to a bee sting pierced Leif's neck.

"What the—?" His hand shot up and found a small protrusion just below his ear. He pulled it out and his vision blurred.

The two creatures on the ground stood up and brushed off their trousers, approaching him. One of them poked Leif in the chest with sharp claws, piercing his T-shirt. He swatted, but his arm moved in slow motion as if underwater. A stream of color followed its wake.

The wolverine leader laughed. "Not so cocky now, are you, Viking king? We won't even need an advantage to take you down." The four creatures retracted their claws and charged en masse.

Leif tried to block their attack, but his limbs wouldn't cooperate and the creatures moved too quickly. A blow to his kidney hurt so badly he saw stars. Desperately, he reached for the mental connection to his berserker. Instead of the familiar heat of his warrior spirit waking and rushing to battle, he found a deep, achingly empty space where Leif's call to the other half of him echoed into a vast black void.

Male grunts and the thuds of fists connecting with flesh reverberated through the alley as Naya left the nightclub through its back entrance. She kept her head down, concentrating on getting to the parking lot and reaching her car undetected.

Halfway there, a shout of pain pierced the foul night air. She faltered, muttering a curse. The fifty thousand dollars in the messenger bag slung over her shoulder almost overrode her curiosity—*almost*.

She turned to see who was fighting behind her new client's hot spot.

A blond giant of a man fought against four opponents. Their advantage in numbers made up for their smaller size, as did their agility. Ducking most of Blondie's blows, they danced around him and delivered sharp punches and kicks, focusing their blows to the kidneys and lower spine. They fought dirty, like Naya.

The shorter guys were dressed in black with identical cropped dark hair and small pointy noses, giving an impression of ferrets from the same litter.

Blondie had tied back his shoulder-length hair. Dressed in faded blue jeans and a plain blue cotton T-shirt, he looked like he'd been on his way home to spend the evening with the remote control and a beer.

So far, the blond held his own, but it wouldn't last. A normal human would not have detected Blondie's decreased speed and agility, but his slight hesitations before punching were obvious to Naya. She shook her head as he announced his intentions before each strike by moving before he was ready to commit. Only rookies made that mistake.

A particularly vicious cross-counter to the right kidney felled Blondie like a chopped pine in the forest. She sucked in her breath.

The four ferret-like men swarmed on top of him, kicking and stomping his massive body.

Naya muttered another expletive. It really wasn't her business, but the ferrets were literally kicking a guy while he was down. She'd always had a soft spot for the underdog. Besides, dead bodies brought cops, which was not something her client desired. Once the law showed up, there was no telling what they'd poke their noses into.

She was less than twenty-five yards away from the fight scene. The ferret-men paid her no attention. She must not look like a threat.

The blond wasn't getting up. He lay on his back, arms unmoving by his side, eyes closed. His body rippled as kicks shook his massive bulk. Well, not that bulky—his sweaty T-shirt showed off some impressive six-pack abs. Not that his amazing physique did him any good. Those dark little fighters would eventually kill Blondie.

In one swift movement, she pulled the shoulder strap over her head and slid the bag across the parking lot grime. It skidded to a stop just under her car.

She turned and ran back through the alley, her boots pounding the asphalt. The four halted their assault, heads raised toward her.

She leapt mid-stride, twisted in the air, and hook-kicked first one then a second chin. The heel of her boot vibrated as the sound of necks snapping reached her ears. She tucked and rolled her landing.

Shit, she hadn't meant to kill them. Her combat training had taught her to immediately neutralize a threat, not how to incapacitate an enemy. Nothing she could do about that now. She pushed the guilt aside and narrowed her focus.

Pivoting, she faced her remaining opponents. Adrenaline surged through her body. Her lips curved as she blew black bangs out of her eyes. It had been a long time since she'd had a good fight. The morning's news from Dr. Rosen had been discouraging. She was ready to blow off some steam and take out her frustration on these guys. Hopefully she wouldn't have to kill again, but she'd find a way to get rid of the bodies before the cops showed up.

Crouching down, she kept her arms loose but ready.

The men's eyes had no pupils or irises. They were just eerie black orbs. A little freaked out, Naya kept an eye on their hands. They held them loosely in front of their bodies. Slowly, their nails elongated into vicious claws.

Well, that's new. Shit!

Naya silently berated herself for getting involved. The guys had looked normal. Now they were freaky monsters with jet-black eyes.

"Want to play, little girl?" one of them growled, clicking his claws.

"You're not much bigger than me." She tilted her head, keeping an eye on the one who hadn't spoken. He inched to the side and toward her, but she wasn't worried yet. Her enhanced strength was always superior in any human fight.

Key word: *human.*

She swallowed and willed her pounding heart to slow down. *Steady.*

The two freaks rushed her, and she concentrated on

not getting impaled. Even with her ultrafast reaction time, she had to work hard to avoid their slashing.

The guy on the left executed a vicious overhand swipe with his claws. She parried and found herself in the perfect position for a reverse roundhouse.

Her boot made contact right in the sweet spot. The creature whimpered, hands instantly pressed to his balls—lucky for her, he was human enough to have a set of those. He hunched over and slowly sank toward the ground face-first.

She quickly gripped his neck and forehead and twisted in opposite directions. Movement out of the corner of her eye made her lurch to the side. She was too late to completely avoid the ferret's right hook.

Claws pierced her waist, puncturing her skin but thankfully missing her liver. The searing pain was almost worth it when she heard the first guy's spine snap in her grip.

And then there was one.

Naya and the remaining monster circled each other, looking for an opening.

"You're bleeding." The ferret smirked. "And outside the lab, you'll find no healing accelerant to help you."

What? Naya sucked in a breath. How did this creature know about the lab? "It's just a scratch." Her side might hurt like hell later, but right now Naya had enough adrenaline pumping through her body to mask the pain. "I'll need a rabies shot though," she said. "Can't be too careful when fighting rats."

With a furious roar, the guy lunged for her.

She twisted, barely avoiding him tearing her eyes out. Shit, he was definitely as fast as she was.

He grabbed her hair. "You will regret those words." Pulling her head back, he smelled her neck. "Sweet," he purred. His arm encircled her waist, claws inching up her rib cage toward her breast. "I recognize the smell of you."

Naya twisted to get free. "You know nothing about me."

The monster tugged, setting her scalp on fire. "Quiet, little girl. We are the same, created in the same place. And now that we've found you, your brother's next."

Ice-cold panic shot through Naya's body, paralyzing her. Mentally, she shook herself. Emotions had no place in a fight.

"I don't have a brother."

"Brave girl, but lying won't save you." He shook her savagely. "But let's have some fun first."

Gritting her teeth, she forced her muscles to relax. When the ferret automatically loosened his grip in response, she flexed her knees slightly. Naya shot up, arching her back. Her skull smacked into her captor's nose with a satisfying crunch. Turning, she smirked at the gushing blood.

"You fucking bitch," he gurgled. He tilted his head back, pinching his nostrils, and backing away from her.

She didn't bother to reply. Instead, she delivered a three-finger stab straight to his throat.

Slumped forward, he wheezed his last breaths through a broken windpipe.

She looked around the alley. She'd have to clean up these bodies before anyone else showed up. But first she needed to check on Blondie.

Naya limped over to the big man on the ground.

He was still breathing.

Looking for some kind of identification, she patted down the front pockets of his jeans. The denim fabric outlined lean hips and muscular thighs. Her search found only keys.

His eyelids fluttered but didn't open.

Rolling him onto his side, she discovered the shape of a phone in a back pocket. Jackpot. This should have contact information. Most recently called or maybe there'd be an entry for *Home*. Heck, she'd use the number under *Mom* if she had to.

Making a point of not noticing how nicely his butt curved, she slid her hand into the pocket and retrieved the cell. Naya had just unlocked the display when she looked down and found a pair of ice-blue eyes staring at her.

"Hi there, big guy. I'm one of the friendlies. Just hang on. I'll see if I can reach one of your friends." She licked her lips. Even lying down the man intimidated the hell out of her. He was huge. She desperately hoped his eyes would stay blue and not fill with black.

"No doctor," he growled, grasping her hand holding the phone.

"Ease up there, Blondie. I'm calling someone you know." Her wrist felt like it was trapped in a vise. She wiggled her arm to loosen his grip. No luck. Maybe he wasn't human either.

"No doctor." The cold stare was unwavering. He had an accent. From the short sentence, she couldn't quite place it. A strange half-finished snake tattoo on his bicep bulged as his grip tightened, cutting off her circulation. Definitely not human. Her lips were dryer than gunpowder, but she refused to lick them again. Show no fear.

"No doctor. I get it," she snarled. "Who do you want me to call?"

He held on to her wrist, his icy eyes willing her to do what he wanted. "Harald," he finally said. "Call Harald."

"You're going to have to let go of me, or your phone is toast, and we won't be calling anyone."

Blondie gave her a measured look before releasing her wrist, but as he did, lightning-fast fingers curled around the back of her neck and pulled her face to his.

The kiss seared her lips, melting her insides. Their mouth-to-mouth contact lasted only a few seconds, but long enough for Naya's bones to liquefy. When he released her, Blondie sighed deeply as he sank back down, closing his eyes.

Naya shook him. "What the hell was that?"

He didn't react. She gave him a hard shove and concentrated on the phone again. The kiss had scrambled her brain. She had to scroll through the contact list twice before the letters stopped jumping around and she found the name he wanted. Keeping the big guy in her field of vision, she pressed "send."

Before it even rang, a male voice answered. "My king, where are you? Fuck, how could you leave unprotected?"

Too stunned to speak, Naya managed only a croak in reply. This guy had a similar accent. Dutch? Danish?

"Leif?" The voice sounded suspicious. "Are you there?"

She cleared her throat. "Are you Harald?"

"Who the fuck is this?" the man roared.

"I need to know if your name is Harald." She sounded pissy, but enough already with these demanding men.

"Why do you have Leif's phone?"

"If Leif is a big giant blond dude with a snake tattoo on his arm, he can't talk right now. He's too busy recovering from getting the shit kicked out of him."

"What have you done to him?"

"Look. Just tell me if you're Harald."

Blood still oozed out of her side and the injury burned like a bitch. She wanted to get home to stitch up the wound. She refused to think about the kiss, and concentrating on her injuries kept her from freaking out about the ferret recognizing her scent and knowing about the lab—and Scott.

She hissed out a breath. If the guy on the phone wasn't Harald, then he needed to find that dude. *Fast.*

Muffled cursing came down the line. "Yeah, fine. I'm Harald. What the fuck do you want? If you're responsible for Leif's injuries, I'm going to flog you until there's nothing left of you. Do you hear me? I'm going to—"

Naya groaned. "Look, I'm the one who saved his pretty eyes from being permanently shut, so just calm down."

"Where are you?" Harald's voice turned considerably softer.

"In the alley behind Desire. It's a club on Main."

"I know it. Be there in a few."

She hung up and checked on Blondie again. His pulse was weak but steady.

She studied the ferret guys for movement. They lay where they'd fallen. Naya got up and touched two fingers to the neck of each body. None of them had a pulse.

Since they weren't human, she'd keep an eye on them. Hopefully she'd have enough strength left to dispose of the bodies. Right now, she had to monitor Blondie and make sure he didn't go into shock.

She returned to his side. Exhausted, she sat down and studied him. Blond stubble covered a square jaw-line and continued up and around full lips. He had a strong straight nose, except for a small kink that looked like a break that hadn't set properly. She blushed when her fingers itched to trace its ridge and quickly moved her gaze to the black ink of the snake tat on his bicep. Strange symbols intertwined to form the serpent head and part of the body, but the snake had no tail. The tattoo just ended abruptly on the inside of his arm.

Naya shifted on the cold ground. She touched her shirt where the ferret freak's claws had pierced her skin. Her fingers came away wet and sticky. Shit.

The leather jacket that might as well be permanently grafted to her body had scratches on the arms and slashes down one side. She buttoned it to keep out the frigid night air. The blood loss made her feel colder than normal. She turned and checked on the monsters again. Not so much as a hair had moved.

She'd killed before, but only while on missions ordered by her handler in the lab. This felt different.

She'd ponder that later, soaking in a warm bath back in the safety of her apartment. That would also be when she figured out how the monster had recognized her scent. She shuddered.

If the ferret guy was right, his supernatural abilities came from the same chemical formula that contaminated her circulatory system. Their cocktails must differ by more than a few ingredients, considering the claws and the black eyes. She should take a blood sample.

Before she was able to act on the thought, a car's headlights swept the dirty brick walls of the alley. Naya got up and limped to a recessed doorway. She'd make sure this was Blondie's friend, but then her stint as Good Samaritan was over. Even though the reward had been enjoyable—she quickly squelched the memory of their hot kiss.

When the beams revealed the big guy on the ground, the black Escalade stopped. Two guys got out, slamming the doors behind them. The sound ricocheted against the alley walls.

They both kneeled next to Blondie. One of them slapped his face.

"Leif, you fucker. Wake the hell up." Wiping a palm over his bushy red beard, he cursed again. She recognized his voice from the phone—Harald.

"He's got a pulse," said the other one. His hair was as blond as the man's on the ground, but styled in a crew cut. "What are these freaks?" He surveyed the alley, eyeing the ferret bodies.

Harald looked up. "Looks like Loki has engineered a new threat. These fuckers look like wolverines. If they are as wily as the actual animal, we're going to have to be extra alert."

Naya peered out through the shadows. The creatures did look more like wolverines than ferrets.

Crew-cut leaned back on his heels. "Whatever they are, I can't believe they got the drop on the king." His eyes swept the dark alley. "Where's the woman who called? Maybe she can tell us what happened."

She held her breath and crouched down lower against the door.

"We don't have time. We need to get Leif home." Harald stood.

Together, they lifted their comrade and put him in the back of the SUV. Closing the doors, they looked around the alley.

Harald sighed. "We should do some housekeeping."

They picked up two wolverine bodies each and slung them into one of the Dumpsters as if they weighed nothing.

Naya's jaw dropped. If Leif's strength matched theirs, she was glad he was weak while gripping her wrist. She'd hate to be a one-armed freak.

"Should we cover them?" the blond asked.

"They're Loki's monsters. They'll disintegrate by morning." The men got in the car.

As soon as their taillights disappeared, Naya limped to her own vehicle. She'd be lucky if she made it home before passing out. Forget Dumpster-diving for blood samples.

She groaned as she retrieved her bag from underneath her car. Her teeth chattered. Another hot kiss would warm her up. She shoved the thought aside. She needed to concentrate on staying safe, not making out with giant blonds.

Black spots danced across her vision as she drove. She bypassed her regular safety precautions and just went straight to her front door after parking the car.

She dumped her leather jacket on the chair inside the entry. It made a loud clunk and she paused. She'd put the giant's phone in her pocket. Nothing she could do about that now, except dump the battery without hitting the off button. It was a weak security measure, but at least the device wouldn't ping any nearby cell phone towers.

Stumbling into the bathroom, she tugged on her shirt. The fabric stuck to the wound and she clenched her jaw as she peeled away the cotton. The wolverine freak's claws had swiped four parallel inch-long tracks just above her hip. Her good ol' Levi's had stopped them from progressing lower.

The injury flashed angry red and already oozed yellow pus. The claws must have been coated with something to accelerate the rate of infection. At least it didn't look like she would need stitches. She washed the wound with soap and water. The sting sent out tendrils of icy-hot pain. She had to white-knuckle the rim of the sink to keep from passing out.

When she could stand without support, she opened the faucets of the large claw-foot tub. Lowering her body into the tub, she hissed as the water lapped at her wound. Breathing deeply, she commanded her shoulders and arms to relax.

She should have left Leif to fend for himself. There was too much at stake to get involved in other people's problems.

The wolverine creatures she'd fought were not like her. She raised her hand and watched the water drip from her skin. As far as she knew, she couldn't change her fingers into sharp weapons. She'd never seen anything like them in the lab. Had the creature lied to her? Either way, it freaked her out that he knew about the lab and Scott. She needed to be more careful. She couldn't afford to be discovered now. Not when she'd finally gotten Scott to safety and hopefully a cure.

Leif and his friends were obviously also enhanced. She slicked back her hair and winced. She gingerly probed her scalp with her fingertips. In the alley, it had felt like the creature ripped out chunks of her hair, but she couldn't find any bald patches.

She pulled herself upright and climbed out of the tub. It was time to get some work done. Her client hadn't given her a fifty-thousand-dollar down payment for her to linger in the bath. Although the pus had oozed out, her skin still pulsed angry red. She cracked open a bottle of hydrogen peroxide, cleaned the injury, and then taped it. She wrapped herself in her favorite blue terry-cloth robe and padded into the living room. Instead of a sofa and a coffee table, a large steel and glass desk occupied the space: central command.

She grabbed her bag from the chair by the front door and extracted the money. The dial on the safe under the desk turned easily as she clicked through the combination. Naya added the new bundle of bills to the stacks inside.

Sitting down, she grimaced when the wound smarted. The mystery chemicals in her blood should be able to heal the injury in a few hours. Another perk of being a freak. Meanwhile, her new client had ordered a complete cybersecurity plan due in two days, including secure email communications, web traffic, and money transfer. He also wanted wireless surveillance cameras throughout his club. Naya hadn't asked why he needed such an over-the-top system. She didn't care.

She never did.

All she worried about was whether the customers could pay their invoices. She signed up anyone referred by a previous client, if they cleared Naya's thorough and slightly illegal screening.

Booting up the computer, she keyed in the passwords to unlock the hard drive. A quick glance at the firewall log told her there had been no attempts to breach the system. She opened the files for Desire's floor plans.

Three levels of dance floors, hidden nooks, and private rooms required a lot of cameras. The club servers processed several gigabytes of data traffic each day, all of which needed virus and security scanning. This was going to be a lucrative project.

Her fingers flew over the keyboard as she focused on the work, trying to ignore how the wound throbbed and itched.

Chapter 3

War drums pounded painfully inside Leif's skull. He slowly cracked open an eyelid and, as light pierced his pupil, the drummers increased their torment. It felt like they were now stomping their feet as well.

He tested his sword arm by lifting it just a fraction. No restriction. His legs too were unbound. The sheets underneath him were soft and clean. All good signs.

Ignoring the drumming in his head, he searched his memories for clues as to what had happened. A vision of a pale face framed by black hair emerged. A woman. He remembered dark indigo eyes and beautiful lips. He'd kissed those lips. Why?

More memories surfaced. He'd been out to feed his berserker behind a nightclub when four of Loki's creatures cornered him. There was something important to remember. He'd taken photographs with his cell phone, but the details were unclear. The wolverine monsters had charged. He remembered kicking feet. A lithe body dressed in black leather. A flurry of expertly executed chops bashing the creatures' bodies. After that things were too hazy.

The woman had fought the monsters for him? Why? She wasn't a Valkyrie. His berserker would have alerted him to another Norse warrior. Something else niggled at the back of his mind, but before he could grasp it, a door hit the wall and heavy boots thundered across the floor. "Are you awake, *min kung*?"

Leif winced. "Harald." It hurt to talk.

His second-in-command bowed, touching his forehead to Leif's knuckles as a sign of deference to his king.

Leif tried to clear his throat so he could say the appropriate greeting, but his mouth and throat were dry as deserts. An arm slipped under his shoulders and gently lifted him up. The cool smooth lip of a drinking glass pressed against his mouth.

"Drink."

He drank until the glass was empty and heard Harald fill the vessel again. After two more pours, Leif found his voice.

"What happened?" Harald liked to speak their native Swedish, but Leif usually kept to English. That way he didn't forget they were supposed to blend in.

"I was hoping you could tell me." His second-in-command pulled up a chair but quickly adjusted its position to give Leif's sword arm free range.

Leif waved his hand to make him continue.

"All I know is that I got a phone call from some female. She told me you had the shit beaten out of you and where you were. I grabbed Ulf and we hauled your tattered ass home."

He should take issue with Harald's tone, but left it alone when he noticed the worry in his friend's voice. "What did she say when you got there?" He lowered his eyelids to ward against the bright light in the room and to hide the memory of the kiss from heating his eyes.

"Nothing. She wasn't there."

She'd fled the scene after calling his battle brother? What had happened? It was too complicated. He could only concentrate on one thing for now.

"I felt a pinprick in my neck. I couldn't access my berserker during the fight. They must have poisoned me." He frowned. There was something else he was supposed to remember.

"The healer found the small wound when she examined you." Harald sounded bitter.

"What did they drug me with?"

"Irja is working on it now."

Irja—their medical officer's skills were superior. If anybody could identify the poison, it would be her. The thought of Loki's minions having the power to defeat the Norse warriors' berserkers chilled Leif to the core. Loki had sent creatures that had tried to poison them before, but the Vikings' immortal bodies had always purged their toxins without any harmful effects.

Harald succinctly summarized Leif's thoughts. "Fuck, Leif. Just…fuck."

Leif silently agreed. It was bad enough Loki had sent monsters who looked like an animal they revered. Now they had to worry about the monstrous wolverines defeating them.

Leif sighed. He had tried many times to tell Odin about the evils of Loki, and still the Wise One wouldn't take action against him. The runes told clearly of Loki causing Ragnarök, and the half god, half giant was doing everything he could to fulfill the prophecy. According to the ancient sagas, the Norse gods' enemies would band together and trigger natural disasters of epic proportions, including a huge flood that would drown all gods and humans. There were many interpretations of the final runes. Some said there would be no survivors but one man and one woman. A few predicted Loki as the sole surviving deity. And still Odin wouldn't—or couldn't—ban the half god from the Norse gods' council, which would weaken Loki's power considerably. Loki got away with a lot because he had once saved the life of Odin's beloved wife. Or maybe the ruler of Asgard preferred to keep Loki on the council so he could keep an eye on him. As long as Loki belonged to the Norse gods' ruling body, he had to obey their rules, which included staying in Asgard and not entering the human realm.

The pounding had subsided. Leif opened his eyes again. Harald's red hair stuck up in tufts all over his head. The beard he was so proud of was uneven and snarled.

"How long was I out?" Leif asked.

"Long enough, my king."

Leif raised his eyebrows and tried one of his more commanding glares. It backfired. He blinked furiously when pain shot through his brain.

Harald grimaced. "Three days. The first two, we didn't know if you were going to make it." Clouds chased across his face and he fiddled with the pitcher in his hand. "I need to check if Irja has isolated the poison." He rose abruptly and then hesitated. "Why were you alone by the club?"

Leif closed his eyes. "I was just out for a walk." He could feel Harold's eyes boring into him, but refused to open his own. He understood Harald's worry. The man was his friend, but also his *stallare*. And as the marshal, the second-in-command, it was his duty to make sure that Leif remained fit to rule. If Harald found out how close to the edge his king's berserker was, it was his duty to report this to Odin.

"Were you there to *feberandas*?" His friend's voice was stern.

"I went for a walk." Leif's tone matched Harald's. He opened his eyes. If he couldn't control his inner warrior, he'd be trapped in permanent battle fury. He didn't know which was worse, losing the connection with the berserker or losing control. Without the connection to his inner warrior, he felt as if part of him was missing. How would he be able to protect his people now?

The two stared at each other until Harald nodded, turned, and strode out the door.

Leif watched him leave. They had known each other for more than a thousand years. Fought side by side in too many battles to count. Saved each other's hides in tavern brawls and stickier situations. But sharing their feelings was not something they had ever done. Nor would they.

He sighed and closed his eyes again. The wolverine poison made him weaker than he'd been as a small boy. Maybe sleep would help. Judging from how he felt right now, it would be many days before he was back to regular strength. Flexing a few of his muscles and a brief conversation had tired him out. He let sleep embrace him as visions of ink-blue eyes in an expressive face framed by black hair danced at the edge of his consciousness.

When Leif woke again, twilight dusted the room in peaceful grays and pinks. The familiar sights of heavy oak furniture and dark burgundy drapes comforted him. This was the longest he'd spent in this bed since they'd built the stronghold. His body felt weak, his mind muddled, but rested. Only at home in the fortress did he ever really relax. Nestled deep among the evergreens in eastern Washington, the dwelling was protected from intruders by an impenetrable forest. And the exposed ancient basalt volcanic rock unique to the region enhanced the powerful magic seeped into the fortress walls. He thanked Freya every day for allowing them to use elven illusions that made their dwelling invisible to humans.

His gaze finally rested on the chair next to his bed. A figure loomed in the shadow. His sword hand automatically flexed until he recognized his visitor. Irja, their healer, sat in the chair, one long leg crossed over the other. She watched him with an inscrutable expression. Her dark eyes, high cheekbones, and translucent skin bore witness to ancestry far from his. Unlike Leif's blond Anglo-Saxon forefathers, Irja traced her roots to the Saami people, nomadic Laplanders who followed huge herds of domesticated reindeer.

Even though she was six feet tall, she moved her body with an unearthly grace. She was also able to sit absolutely still for hours. He wondered how long she'd been in the chair.

"*Min kung*," she said finally, her voice low and melodic, the accent particular to Finish-Swedish. She too followed Harald's example and touched her forehead to the top of his hand.

"*Hur mår du*, Irja?"

"A lot better than you, it appears." Her lips formed a small *Mona Lisa* smile. "I don't think you've ever rested in this bed for more than a few hours."

"I was just thinking that I am finally making good use of this beautiful piece of furniture." He stroked the bedcovers.

Her smile widened and she shook her head, as if he was a little rascal making trouble. "*Min kung*, I've been able to isolate the poison in your bloodstream."

"I had no doubt you would."

Irja glanced down at a sheet of paper on her lap. He doubted she needed the reference. More likely, she had every detail of that document memorized.

"The injection you received was extracted from *Aconitum napellus*."

"Swedish or English, please." His head hurt too much to translate Latin.

"*Stormhatt* or monkshood, sometimes called wolf's bane."

Of course she knew the names in both languages. Leif recognized the Swedish name, his father had used the herb to kill sick livestock. The blue flowers were deceptively beautiful.

Like the woman who saved you.

He squelched the voice in his head and instead checked the connection with his berserker. Still nothing but a deep emptiness.

He stared at the ceiling. "There is no cure for this poison." It was a statement, not a question.

"No," Irja confirmed. "All we can do is wait for your body to purge the poison."

"And will it?" Panic increased his heart rate. He willed the vital muscle to slow down.

"Yes," Irja said. Her confidence in her king unshaken, it seemed.

"How do you know?"

She looked away.

It wasn't confidence he'd heard in her voice. Wishful thinking? Hope? He swallowed. Odin had promised the Vikings and Valkyries he sent back that it would be very hard to kill them. He hadn't said it would be impossible. Nobody knew what happened when a warrior of Valhalla actually died, because nobody had seen it happen. "You don't actually know, do you?"

She hesitated, but then shook her head.

"Shit."

"Precisely."

Her terse agreement brought a quick smile to his lips despite the seriousness of the situation. "Why would the poison quiet my warrior spirit?"

Irja raised an eyebrow. "You spoke of this, but I hoped it was your fever talking."

"The fever has nothing to do with it. When I reach for my berserker, there's a void." Leif closed his eyes. Being disconnected from his inner warrior wounded his very essence.

"*Min kung*, I searched the old healing books for poisons affecting the berserker. I found nothing. Loki's minions must have found a new way to manipulate the herb. Maybe added some kind of toxin that our bodies are not immune to."

He sighed. "We have to find an antidote. We cannot allow Loki to weaken us."

"I'll have to do some more tests." Irja stood to leave.

He grabbed her hand and tugged on it to get her to look at him. "Irja, thank you. You are very valuable to us."

Dark eyes regarded him solemnly. "Thank you, *min kung*." She slid her hand out of his grip and walked out the door.

Before Leif had a chance to mull over his potentially imminent death, he heard Harald grill Irja in the hall. It wasn't long before the red-haired warrior bustled through the entry.

"What is this crap about no antidote? Of course there is an antidote. All poisons have one." Leif held up a hand to stop the tirade, but Harald looked away, making a point of not noticing. "The witch just doesn't want to make one."

"Don't call her that." It pleased Leif that his voice wasn't as weak as his body.

Harald sank down into the chair Irja had just vacated. "You know I don't mean it."

"Yes, but she doesn't."

His red-bearded friend shrugged. "She should know better than to take me seriously by now."

"Irja takes everything very seriously."

"True that."

Leif flinched at his friend's words. The man resisted learning any of the new technology these last centuries had brought. He claimed his fingers were too large for a computer keyboard. And yet, the big brute had not met a slang word or pop-culture phrase he didn't like.

"What do you want?" Leif's voice was gruffer than intended, but expunging poison was tiring. He needed more sleep.

"I came to ask if you want us to track down the girl."

An image of dark blue eyes rose in Leif's mind, and

he realized it had been there all along, just hovering in the background. "Yes, we need to find her. She saved my life."

A sly smile played at the corners of Harald's lips. "So, a human woman saved your ass. Never thought I'd see that day coming."

"Just find her." Leif sighed.

Harald nodded and then studied his hands.

"What?" Leif finally barked when the man continued his irritating quietness.

"Out of curiosity, how many of the little bastards did she bring down?"

Leif didn't like the gleam in his friend's eyes. He glared at him. Harald calmly met his eyes. "All four of them," Leif bit out between clenched teeth.

His *stallare* grinned. "Well, isn't that something."

"Not. One. Fucking. Word."

Harald held up his hands in mock surrender. "I would be the last person to talk about how the mighty king got his ass kicked by four wolverine creatures. Or that a woman defeated them all and saved his hide."

Leif groaned. Harald would be the *first* person not only to tell the story, but embellish it and then regurgitate it for centuries. "I was drugged." Both the excuse and his voice sounded feeble.

"You hold on to that small comfort." Harald clasped his hands and a megawatt grin spread across his face. "Hold on tight with both hands."

Leif glared back, but his friend's grin didn't diminish. "Don't we have more serious business to discuss?"

Harald's face fell. "It's true," his *stallare* said quietly. "If Loki's minions are adding poison to their arsenal that can affect *you* like this, we need to step up our game."

A hazy memory floated up from Leif's subconscious. He looked around the room. "Where's my phone?"

Harald frowned. "It wasn't in your pocket when we cut your clothes off." He swallowed and shook his head, as if to clear his mind of unpleasant images. "Did you get it back from the girl?"

"I don't know." Leif mentally reached into his mind, ordering his brain to help him remember. "I know I took pictures of the wolverines. There's important data on there, we need to find it." He pressed a hand to his forehead when his head throbbed again. "Shit, I can't remember what I did with it." An image of his hand engulfing a slender wrist holding his phone rose in Leif's mind. "The girl must have it."

His *stallare* stood. "Fuck, Leif. You don't think she would have stolen it? Do you think she's working with the wolverines?"

"If so, why would she save me?"

Harald paused. "She wasn't on the scene when we got there. Maybe she took it with her."

"Even more reason to find her."

"I don't like this." His friend tugged at his facial hair. "If the wolverines have other toxic weapons, we may be beyond well and truly fucked."

Leif slumped back in the bed, his immortal body carrying the unfamiliar weight of old and tired. They had battled Loki and his creatures for a century and they had always been one step ahead of the half god's monsters. Leif thrived on battle and had done so even as a mortal. It was what he was bred to do. Everything about him—his body, his physical strength, his analytical mind—contributed to an almost unstoppable warrior. This battle would be no different.

Since Odin had sent him back to Midgard to dwell among humans once more, he had not lost a single one of his warriors. He looked at his oldest friend. They had grown up together. Harald had been there when Leif took a wife, when his children were born.

When he had lost his entire family.

He could not accept losing Harald, or any of the others. "We will find a way to defeat our enemies. We always do." He met his friend's gaze until Harald nodded.

"You rest. I'll go speak with the others and see what they have to say. Maybe the youngsters will have some suggestions." He rose. "I'm too old for this crap." Harald marched out of the room, slamming the door behind him.

My sentiments exactly. Leif settled deeper in his bed. Loki's wolverines were just the latest in the half god's demented arsenal. They had fought weird lizards that walked upright, unusually large wolves, and humanlike creatures that were strong but dumb as battle-axes. These wolverines were intelligent and used a dangerous poison as their weapon. It should have cost Loki a lot of magic to create them. Somehow the half god had figured out how to enhance his powers. Leif wanted to tell his Vikings and Valkyries to not patrol alone, but their numbers were small. Sending them out in groups would limit the area they could cover.

Once again he tried to remember what he'd seen the wolverines do in that alley. It had something to do with the poison. He needed to find the woman so he could get his phone back. He ignored how much the thought of seeing her again pleased him and forced his thoughts back to fighting Loki and his minions.

The information on that cell phone might be crucial. If Loki's creatures defeated Leif and his warriors, the human realm would be vulnerable to the half god's manipulation, leaving the world ripe for Ragnarök—the final battle destined to destroy both Asgard and Midgard.

Chapter 4

SOMEONE WAS FOLLOWING HER.

Naya didn't yet know who, but the fine hairs standing up on the back of her neck were never wrong. Walking down the sidewalk, careful not to increase her pace, she glanced over her shoulder under the pretense of flicking her hair. The quick jerk of her head made her dizzy.

She hated how weak she felt. Fever still hummed through her body and spiked at inconvenient times. Like during the meeting with her new client that morning. Luckily, he had been distracted by the security plans she'd presented. She was confident in her work, although it had taken her two days to do a simple preliminary recommendation. Something she usually whipped out in five hours. Her illness had forced her to take frequent breaks and long naps.

In her mind, she processed the scene of the street and sidewalks behind. With her photographic memory, she logged each detail and then zoomed in on the pertinent ones. The silver Escalade had been behind her for three blocks. She'd be more worried if it was one of the gray or black sedans the black ops handlers usually drove, but she hadn't seen any of those while using this identity. Of course, the wolverines had known who she was. Were there others like them looking for her? Maybe they drove silver SUVs. She had to be vigilant.

Last time the sedans appeared, she had gone underground and relocated to a new city with a new name. She didn't have time for that now. The nightclub account was too lucrative. The money for this job alone would cover Scott's upkeep and therapies for a year.

Dr. Rosen had emailed her about some promising research looking into artificial hormones. She just hoped they didn't interfere with the massive amounts of junk already swimming around in Scott's body. Why had the cocktail that made her a comic-book freak fried her brother's circuits so completely? She reined in her thoughts. She had to concentrate.

Blondie's friends had driven a black Escalade. Could this be them again? Her aching leg muscles distracted her and Naya slowed down. This must be what normal humans felt like. So many times she'd wished for normality. A body without superstrength and a brain that didn't constantly draw optimization graphs and possible outcomes charts. Now, she wasn't so sure.

She sank down on a bus stop bench and made a show of digging around in her bag for her MP3 player. While popping in the earbuds, she surreptitiously checked her surroundings. She need not have bothered. The Escalade slowly crept up the street and she could now see the two men in the front seat. Both of them stared straight ahead.

They may have changed from a black luxury SUV to a silver one, but she recognized the red beard and the snow-white blond crew cut from the night in the alley. Why were they following her? She'd saved their friend. They should be on her side. Blondie had liked her enough to kiss her. Naya slumped down on the bench but winced as the injury in her side made itself known. It still throbbed angrily.

A series of human emotions flooded her senses: smallness, loneliness, tiredness—all completely useless. Maybe she'd get on the bus for a while and just ride around, a great way to get in a nap and confuse the men in the car. And she'd get out of her own head. It was never a good place in which to spend a lot of time.

"Ms. Brisbane, there you are," a smooth voice on her left said.

Shit, where had this guy come from?

Cheap brown shoes, off-the-rack blue suit, bland tie, dark sunglasses, basically a complete government-agent-wannabe kit. Naya hadn't even noticed him approaching, never mind sitting down.

"Here I am," she singsonged, blinking away the fevered haze clouding her vision. It was pointless to pretend she was someone else.

Where was that freaking bus? Cops and buses, never there when you needed them.

Although this guy probably *was* law enforcement. Some under-the-radar, supersecret black-ops branch. She'd long suspected the lab had connections deep in the government, or in fact was a branch of the government. They seemed to have unlimited resources and access to information beyond even the best civilian hacker. She'd narrowly escaped their cyber tracers eight months ago, when she lived in Seattle. She turned to face the man.

"You were very hard to find." The handler's lips stretched in a smile. She didn't need him to remove his sunglasses to know it didn't reach his eyes.

She shrugged.

"Where's your brother, Ms. Brisbane?"

Naya shrugged again.

The guy stared at her and then popped the muscles in his neck. "I don't like playing games," he said, his voice ice-cold.

Well, neither did she, but she wasn't the one who insisted on this rabbit-and-fox game. She was sick and tired of being the rabbit. And now she was a sickly rabbit. Forced to run from the fox, she had to fight the wolverines too. Her cheeks flushed and she could feel her scalp tingle. Actually, her whole skin tingled and ached. Being injured really sucked.

Out of the corner of her eye, she saw the silver Escalade still crawling up the street toward her. The two men inside faced straight ahead, but their eyes were as far to the right as they possibly could be.

Amateurs.

"Ms. Brisbane, what do you think of my proposal?"

Oh shit. What had he been rambling about? She glared at him.

His right hand moved toward his coat pocket. "I think it's time the two of us took a walk. Don't you?"

Naya popped her earbuds out and dropped the MP3 player in her bag. The SUV was almost in front of the bench now. She stood.

The suit did as well.

She turned toward him and partly opened her mouth as if she was going to say something.

His hand hesitated on the way to the pocket that most likely contained a gun.

She pretended to drop her bag and leaned down to retrieve it.

He leaned over as well, reaching for the bag.

Swiftly, she punched her elbow into his nose. A loud

crunch and a deep male groan made her smile. She twisted and drove her heel into his groin.

His moaning shifted up several octaves. *Nice falsetto.*

The Escalade stopped. Both men forgot to pretend they were not looking at her and stared openmouthed. She opened the backseat door and slung her bag in before catapulting her body after it.

Two heads swiveled toward the backseat in unison, their mouths still open.

"Drive!" she shouted as blackness embraced her.

~~~

Leif stared at the small woman lying in the middle of the four-poster bed. They'd put her in one of the fortress's guest bedrooms. According to Ulf and Harald, she'd demolished a guy's nose before kicking the sausage between his legs into hamburger meat. If he didn't know firsthand that she'd defeated four wolverines, he'd have accused his men of lying.

She mumbled something and turned over, exposing a bare shoulder in the process.

His loins immediately tightened.

Leif sighed. Why did his body—why did he—find this woman so fascinating? She wasn't a Valkyrie, and although he liked human women, he'd never been drawn to one like this.

Long black lashes swept over lustrous cheeks as she slept. In his mid-teens, he'd accompanied his father and other warriors on a raiding trip to Langbardaland, which people now referred to as Italy. As a randy teenager, he'd found the dark-haired beauties sensually exotic compared to the blonds at home, but even then his body had not responded as it did now.

Her build was slight, but there was strength in every sinewy limb of her graceful body. And in her face.

He thought of the angry lacerations above her hip and for the first time in days, his berserker stirred. Leif let his head fall back as his inner warrior's anger rose. It wanted to find whoever had done this to the woman—find and kill them. Leif quickly secured the mental bonds that tied his berserker to himself. The connection was frail, but at least it was there. He allowed a small amount of relief to trickle through his veins.

He watched the woman in the bed again. Her wounds were deeper than his, and weakness still plagued his body.

Irja had applied an herbal tincture to the woman's wounds. It wouldn't counteract the poison in her bloodstream, but it would speed up the healing of her skin. At least her body would be able to fight the poison better if it didn't also have to deal with an infection.

He owed her his life, but could only stand by and watch as she fought for her own. There had been another time he'd kept vigil by a woman's sickbed, feeling equally useless, watching his wife, Solveig, die. Before the dark memories surfaced completely, the door behind him opened quietly.

Irja glided across the carpet and nodded once, a quick dip of the head, the standard way his people informally greeted their king. "How is she?"

Leif much preferred it to the whole head-to-knuckles thing. Just as he much preferred being upright. A warrior couldn't protect his people when he was flat on his back in the sickbed.

He turned toward her. "I don't know. She's resting peacefully, but that may be because the poison has shut down her body."

The Valkyrie laid her palm against the small woman's forehead. "Her fever is down. Her immune system is purging the poison quicker than yours." She pulled the bedcover a little higher. "Her body is unusually powerful."

"She doesn't look powerful." Which was why his loins' interest puzzled him. Except for the teenage trip to Langbardaland, he had always favored tall, muscular women, usually blond. Nordic women.

He should ask Irja if this weird attraction could be a side effect of the poison, but not in front of the woman. "How can a mere human survive a poison that had me recovering for days?"

Irja looked up and frowned. "She's different."

Leif startled. "Different how?"

"Something inside her is helping the process. Almost like with us. But not the same." She hesitated. "I won't know until I run more tests." She quietly walked out of the room.

Leif returned to watching the sleeping woman. Why did she save him and then keep his phone? They'd found the device in her bag. Ulf was working on retrieving the images.

She sighed contentedly and his cock twitched, betraying its attention. Maybe he'd just been without a bed partner for too long. Sex helped calm the berserker, and he desperately needed a way to better control his warrior spirit. In full battle fever, he wouldn't be able to distinguish between friend and foe. Leif would most likely kill those closest to him, and Odin would be forced to reclaim him and induce the eternal sleep.

Leif scratched the inside of his arm. His bicep itched like crazy. Frowning, he checked his tattoo. The head of the serpent grinned maliciously. He twisted to inspect the inside of his bicep. The rune right above the unfinished tail glowed brilliant gold. That couldn't be right.

He sucked in a deep breath.

None of the Valkyries under his command had ever tempted him. He had not made any new female acquaintances. Except for—

His mind refused the thought.

The dark-haired woman could not be his *själsfrände*, his true mate. He shook his head and turned his arm back over to stare at his hand. It was faint, but he could make out the tail of a serpent just above the wrist.

It couldn't be. The poison must be playing havoc with his system.

As if she knew he was thinking about her, the female sighed and rolled over. The covers glided down, revealing delicate clavicles and the upper curve of her breasts.

Leif's groin tightened again. He cursed and quickly walked out of the room.

After retrieving a long-sleeved shirt from his chambers, he took the stairs down to his office to meet with his warriors. The office was a place where he spent more time than he would like. When he'd first come to Midgard a century ago, being king meant organizing hunting parties and defending the fortress from invaders. Now he had to write reports on security threats and communicate with liaisons and the kings of other bands of Norse warriors. There were five other main outposts in the world, plus scattered Vikings and Valkyries working by themselves in areas that Odin and Freya considered too sensitive to risk drawing attention to.

Loki's creatures popped up in a variety of places, but Odin and Freya had learned to predict where Loki would next form an outpost by looking for ancient artifacts or geological formations. Something about ancient rock enhanced the half god's power. The gods' council was unstable due to political infighting, and Odin and Freya couldn't risk confronting the half god without solid evidence. That would shift alliances and weaken the council further. But they could send their own warriors in secret to protect the humans from Loki's creatures. When the monsters were sighted at a location in Midgard, the two gods established a more permanent band of Vikings and Valkyries in those places. Leif communicated mostly with the North American warrior tribes around Steep Rock Lake in Northern Ontario and Taos in New Mexico.

At least now they stayed in touch electronically. The mounds of papers he used to have to deal with were thankfully obsolete. He much preferred typing on a keyboard to scratching parchments with a goose feather or tracing ballpoint pens on paper. Modern times weren't all that bad. He was a big fan of indoor plumbing too.

In the office, his band of warriors were lounging or standing in various positions. Those seated quickly stood when Leif strode through the room. He pulled the cuffs of his shirt down and then gestured for them to return to their previous positions.

Harald had claimed one of the chairs in front of the desk. Ulf usually took the other, but today he'd lost out to Astrid.

She crossed her legs, one booted foot jiggling up and down. How she managed to fight in those spiked heels was a mystery only the God of War would know. He'd have to ask Thor when he saw him next.

The blond Valkyrie sat contentedly while throwing triumphant glances at Ulf, who leaned against the wall by the large fireplace. Defiantly crossing his arms, he pretended not to notice her taunting or Harald's grin.

Torvald and Sten sat on the sofa. Torvald leaned forward, elbows on knees, resting his chin and grizzly gray beard in his palm, unsuccessfully covering a grin.

Sten studied the ceiling, shoulders twitching. Leif wondered how long his youngest Viking would be able to hold on to the laughter that was so obviously trying to escape.

"Now this is one comfortable chair." Astrid made a show of stretching her arms above her head.

Ulf ignored her.

"You better explain to our king why Ulf and you are switching seats," Torvald said.

Leif walked to his desk. "Tell me." He often found the rivalry between Ulf and Astrid tiresome, but today he could use some cheering up.

"Ulf lost a bet," Sten interjected and then burst out in laughter. Except for Ulf, the rest of them joined in.

Leif shot Ulf a look, quirking a brow.

"I was hungover," the buzz-cut Viking said. This merited another round of laughter from the others.

Leif sat down behind his desk. He shifted his gaze to Astrid.

"He bet he could beat me at any sword sport," she explained.

Leif shook his head.

"How was I supposed to know she would pick sissy swords?" Ulf exclaimed.

Astrid was a champion fighter with any sword, but with rapiers she was unbeatable. She claimed a former lover, a noble Frenchman, had taught her. Apparently, Ulf had not paid attention during battle practice.

"Decent enough to make a pincushion out of you," Torvald shot in. More laughter erupted.

Leif waited a short while before holding up his hand. One by one, his warriors calmed down. "You better have a seat, Ulf. This might be a long meeting."

Throwing one last petulant look at Astrid, who grinned and winked at him, Ulf sat in one of the loungers next to the couch.

"Where's Per?" Leif asked.

Harald frowned. "He went to pick up the new weapons. He should be here by now."

"I'll text him, *min kung*." Sten fished a phone out of his pocket.

The door opened just enough to allow Irja to slip in. She quietly took a position in the back of the room, leaning against the far wall.

Leif considered telling her to have a seat, but changed his mind. She wouldn't like him calling attention to her.

Astrid nodded to Irja, as did Ulf. The healer returned their greetings. The rest of the men ignored her. They respected her preference for her own company.

"Let's start," Leif said. "Per will have to catch up when he gets here." He looked at Irja. "Tell them what we know about the poison."

As the Valkyrie explained her findings and how the

poison broke the connection to their berserkers, his war-riors' faces displayed shock, then disgust, and finally outrage. Even Harald, who already knew the details, looked ready to kill.

"Those little fuckers," Torvald said. "How can a man fight honorably against an enemy who uses trickery?"

"The point is," Leif said, "our enemy has altered their combat style, and so must we."

"I refuse to fight with poison." Torvald slapped the armrest of the sofa. "It's bad enough we use guns instead of a decent *svärd*." The older Viking always grumbled about their swords being used in training and ceremonies, but rarely in battle. It was hard to blend in with a broadsword strapped to your belt, or in Astrid's case, to her back.

The rest of the Vikings voiced their agreement.

Leif bellowed to be heard over the ruckus. "I'm not asking you to carry poison around." At the sound of his voice, his warriors quieted down. "I'm asking you to be vigilant. Our enemies are getting stronger."

"Those cowards wouldn't know strong if it bit them in the ass," Harald said. "Why won't Odin rein in Loki? His creatures are getting out of hand." He directed the last comments to Leif.

"You know Odin's position already. He sent us back to Midgard to prevent Ragnarök and he can aid us in our quest, but he cannot take the fight to Asgard without solid proof that these creatures belong to Loki. Freya excepted, his alliances with the other gods are not strong enough yet, and Loki has a lot of allies among the half gods."

Astrid uncrossed her legs and clunked her boots on

the floor. "The rune stones predicting the battle are so vague, they could mean anything."

"But the Icelandic *Prose* and *Poetic Eddas* are not vague," Irja said.

The whole room quieted. The Finnish Valkyrie rarely offered a strong opinion.

Leif broke the silence. "The Icelandic sagas and the Nordic rune stones say the same thing. Loki will take away mankind's free will and trick them into instigating Ragnarök. But only a few of the Norse gods believe the rune stone that predicts Loki to be the only surviving deity. Unfortunately, Loki is one of them. Stop arguing about things we can't change. Plan for things we have control over."

A murmur of agreement spread through the warriors.

Leif turned to Ulf. "What was on my phone?"

The man shook his head. "You took some pictures, but the images are too dark and blurry to tell what's going on. I can clean them up, but it's going to take a while."

Leif nodded. "Keep working on it."

"Can you remember why you took these images?" Harald asked.

"I wish to the gods I did." Leif pinched the bridge of his nose. "I wanted to show you the wolverines, but there's something I can't remember about the poison." He looked up. "Until we've figured out the details of this new threat, nobody leaves the fortress by themselves. Whenever you go into town or on patrol you do so in pairs, preferably in groups of three."

He heard muttered protests.

"I'm not insulting your strength or your courage," he said. "I'm giving you an order to keep yourselves safe."

"So that you may keep your king safe," Harald interjected.

The Vikings sat up straighter, and Leif sent his second-in-command a grateful look. Leave it to his *stallare* to know the words that would appeal to his warriors' honor. Although he hated the idea of staying behind. He should be out there fighting with them, protecting them.

"I want to find out where these wolverines sleep and eat. We'll strike on their turf next time. I'm not waiting for them to attack us."

His warriors nodded.

"Use any resources you have to find their dwelling. I want these creatures extinct."

Harald turned toward Irja. "Is there anything you can tell us about the poison that would give us a clue to finding their home?"

"The plants grow only in spring and summer."

"That doesn't help us," Harald said.

Irja wasn't finished. "But the poison has a short half-life. They need permanent access to the plants." She flushed when heads turned her way. "They will have a greenhouse or grow room where plants can survive in winter."

Excitement rose in Leif's chest. "If we find their grove, we find them."

"Yes," Irja confirmed. "But these plants can grow in artificial light, so they could cultivate them anywhere, in any house."

Harald rose. "We look for dwellings with higher than normal energy consumption. If we eliminate the illegal pot growers in the area from the list, we'll have a decent starting place."

Finally a plan of action. The warriors filed out, talking loudly among themselves.

Leif asked Irja to stay.

"What can I do for you, *min kung*?" she asked as she stood in front of his desk.

"Please sit." Leif gestured toward the chair Astrid and Ulf had fought over.

Irja sat, watching him calmly. She looked like she could wait for hours. She might have to. The words would not come to him. The black-haired woman with the midnight eyes could not be his *själsfrände*. She was human. The gods—the universe—were playing evil tricks.

Leif cleared his throat. "Some tea maybe?"

"No thank you."

He rose and went to the sideboard opposite the fireplace. If this wasn't a side effect of the poison, he had to complete the *själsfrände* bond—soon. As if wolverines and poison were not enough to worry about, now he had to seduce this woman. She had to come to his bed willingly in order for the bond to complete. If not, Leif's berserker would take over and he'd be overrun by battle fury. He had enough trouble controlling the berserker already; he didn't need a woman to agitate his inner warrior further.

Various decanters and a large pitcher of water stood on a tray. Another tray contained large crystal tumblers. He felt like whiskey, but opted for water instead. "Would you like some?" He held up the pitcher.

Irja sighed. "Please just tell me what's on your mind."

Leif returned to his desk. "Is it possible—" He took a drink of water. "Could the poison have side effects?"

"Are you in pain?" Irja leaned forward.

"No," he hastened to assure her. "I have other... symptoms."

She waited for him to continue.

"I am unusually restless."

"Can you reach your berserker?" she asked.

Leif nodded. "The bond is weak, but it's there."

"Is your berserker hungry?"

Leif swallowed. "It is more of a...a sexual appetite." He had no trouble seducing women, but committing to them was another story. His duty did not allow time for romance. The *själsfrände* bond required complete surrender and trust from both parties. The last time he thought he could handle both love and duty, it had ended badly. He forced the images of Solveig's and the twins' broken bodies out of his mind.

Irja studied him for a moment, her dark eyes unreadable. "Is there a particular person you are drawn to?"

"The female who rescued me." He couldn't look at her. "The berserker has never taken an interest in a human woman. Perhaps the poison is to blame." To meet your soul mate was a rare occurrence, and Leif had never heard of it happening when one of the partners was not a Valkyrie or Viking. He raised his head.

Irja watched him with calm eyes. There was nothing to do but show her. He pulled up his shirtsleeve and exposed his wrist. The black ink of the serpent's tail now showed clearly against his skin. The tip curved toward his smallest finger and then widened into two lines that faded into nothing before reaching his wrist. Between them, faint runes appeared, not yet clear enough to be read.

Irja didn't react as he'd expected. "It's going to be beautiful," she said.

"Can you cure it?" His tone was sharper than he meant.

She blinked a few times. "You think the poison caused this." It was a statement rather than a question.

"Of course," Leif said. "What else can it be?"

"It will be awhile before the tail travels up your arm and completes the serpent. You will have some time to get to know your new true love." Her eyes were soft.

"Don't call her that." The hardness of his voice surprised him. This couldn't be happening. "How long?"

Irja shrugged. "One never knows. This happens so rarely, and each couple is different."

"Guess," he demanded.

"Two weeks? Maybe a month?"

No time at all. "Thank you. Don't tell anybody else."

She stood. "Of course. You didn't have to ask."

"I know." He met her gaze.

She nodded once and walked out of the room. As she opened the door, Harald came through.

Harald bowed to Leif and then planted his butt in a chair. "Did she have more information?"

Leif didn't look up from the tumbler he was turning in his fingers, swirling the water inside, creating a maelstrom. Just like the one he was getting sucked down into. "No, not as such."

"Something's been bothering me since your attack."

Leif sat up straighter. "Yes?" Leif needed to pay attention or Harald would figure out something was wrong.

"How did Loki's wolverines know you would be out and unprotected?"

Leif studied the man opposite him. "What are you saying?"

"You told me they knew you'd be in the alley. On your walks, do you always go to the same club?"

Leif considered lying about how often he went walking at night, but now was not the time. "No, and I make sure there are several weeks between visits. I don't want the humans to become suspicious."

Harald scratched his beard. "Those bastards would have known you were on your own only if they were watching the fortress, or if someone fed them the information."

"We would know if someone broke through the enchantments."

"Exactly. The creatures would have to wait by the main road and then follow you."

Leif sat silent as the enormity of what Harald was telling him sank in. The roads to and from the fortress were magically obscured. The road from the dwelling intersected the main road at a different point each time. And the end of the road only appeared when someone left the fortress.

The wolverines had gotten to one of his warriors. But which one?

"Whom do you suspect?" His friend wouldn't have raised the issue if he didn't have a culprit in mind.

"I don't have any evidence." Harald didn't look him in the eye.

"But there is someone on the top of your list." He waited.

"You know who I suspect. I've always questioned her loyalty."

Leif stood. "Irja."

Harald sprung out of the chair. "*Min kung*, listen to me before you dismiss what I have to say."

"You are wrong." Leif thumped his knuckles on the desk and leaned forward. "She is loyal to all of us."

"She is the only one who was here when you left the fortress that night," Harald protested.

Leif stopped mid-stride. When he'd left that evening the warriors had been out on patrol, but Irja had been in her lab. She'd stopped by his office on her way to the kitchen and he'd told her he was going out. "I only told her I was heading downtown."

"Although there are many bars downtown, only two offer dancing and have back alley access. I've checked." Harald's eyes darkened.

Leif still couldn't believe what Harald was saying. "She would not betray her people."

"We are not her people," Harald said quietly. She's not Norse, he meant.

"She is a Valkyrie. She was sent back to Midgard by Freya and Odin. They would not have picked some-one unworthy."

The other Viking wouldn't meet his gaze. "You know she is not as we are."

She had not betrayed them, of that Leif was sure. Harald was convinced of the opposite. Until they had concrete evidence of her innocence, arguing would serve nothing. But somehow the wolverines had known where he would be that night. "I don't want anybody else to know of your...our suspicions."

Harald opened his mouth, but Leif interrupted him. "It's unthinkable. We're discussing treason."

Harald nodded. "Yes, that's exactly what we're talking about."

Chapter 5

ALTHOUGH SHE'D BEEN AWAKE FOR A WHILE, NAYA kept her eyes closed and forced her breathing to remain even. The last thing she remembered was a man with a bloody nose. Then some confusing stuff about a silver Escalade. Maybe she'd been drugged.

Metal clinked against metal, then glass against metal. She opened her eyes just enough to detect shapes and movement. All she saw was a bright window next to the bed and the whiteness of the walls and the sheet.

She could be in a hospital, or maybe a clinic.

Sniffing the air, she tested for antiseptic and disinfectant. There were none.

"You don't have to be afraid. It's safe here," a female said in a melodic accent.

"I'm not afraid." Her voice sounded exactly like that of a petulant twelve-year-old. She cringed.

"Good."

Naya opened her eyes fully, turning her head toward the voice. A striking woman stood at the foot of the bed. Her black straight hair ended at her waist and she had eyes darker than coal. High cheekbones and a strong nose hinted at Native American ancestry, but not quite. "Who are you?" Naya asked.

"My name is Irja." A shroud of calm surrounded the woman, but her eyes belied the stillness of her posture. In them, dark shadows swirled.

"What is this place?"

"A safe place where you can rest."

"Talk in riddles much?" Naya regretted the bitchy comment as soon as it slipped out. The woman was not only tall, she was muscular. Pissing off the amazon would be wiser when Naya was back to normal strength.

The woman, Irja, cocked her head. "Why does your body react differently compared to regular human biology?"

Talk about cutting to the chase. "I have no idea what you are talking about." Naya looked her straight in the eye.

The corner of the woman's mouth twitched for a microsecond. "You are a bad liar."

"Why would I lie?"

"I don't know. You are a stranger to me."

"As you are to me."

The woman held Naya's gaze for a few beats, but then she walked to the dresser opposite the foot of the bed and picked up a tray with some gauze and bottles. "I've put on a clean bandage and will be back later to check on your injuries. The poison is almost purged from your body. Since your fever broke and you seem to have stopped sweating, I took the liberty of dressing you as well."

Distracted by Irja, Naya hadn't noticed that she no longer ached with fever or that the maddening beat in her side had stopped. She slid a hand down to check the wound. Underneath an oversize T-shirt, a new bandage covered most of her hip. Lower down, her fingers met her own cotton panties. "Thank you," she said and actually meant it.

The tall woman paused and regarded her solemnly. "What is your name?"

"Naya." Shit. She'd given her real name instead of the one on her driver's license. "Where are my clothes?"

"We had to cut off your jeans and your shirt was ruined when your wound opened up again. We'll find you new clothes." Irja walked to the door and turned before opening it. "Eat the soup. It will give you strength."

Naya looked at the bedside table and saw a big bowl of delicious-smelling broth. She turned to offer thanks, but the woman had slipped out without a sound.

The soup tasted of herbs and chicken, filling without being fatty. Naya gave up on the spoon. She picked up the bowl and drank deep mouthfuls. Her stomach purred contentedly.

Next to the bowl she found a pitcher of water and a glass. She drank half the water straight from the pitcher. Her bladder quickly protested. Her eyes swept the room and settled on a door in the corner. She prayed it was an en suite bathroom.

As she tried to get out of bed, her feet went out from under her. Using the bed for support, she pulled herself up and focused on a nearby chair. Holding the chair, her next target was the window seat, and then she finally reached her goal. She twisted the handle and exhaled in relief when the door opened to reveal a bathroom.

What a ridiculous way to cross a room. She'd never been this weak.

After her round-trip to the bathroom, she had to lie down to catch her breath. To distract herself, she sorted through disjointed memories, piecing together where she'd been before this place.

She'd been hot, burning hot. One of the handlers from the lab had found her at a bus stop. A silver SUV stopped.

Before she figured out the connection between the two, exhaustion claimed her. She relaxed into the soft pillows and forced her racing mind into slumber.

—⁓—

When Naya next opened her eyes, the room was bathed in twilight. Another bowl of broth stood on the table next to the bed. Her mouth watered. She wanted the nourishment but briefly wondered if it could be drugged. She felt better than she had since the fight in the alley. If they were slipping her chemicals, at least they were making her better.

As she sipped the broth, she looked around the room for the first time. The king-sized bed took up only a quarter of the space. A dresser, a vanity, and a pair of sky-blue plush armchairs occupied the rest. The minimal white walls and pine furniture screamed decor by IKEA.

She looked around for her clothes but didn't see them or her bag. She needed her laptop. Nobody could break her secure login, but it was annoying to not have it near. Even more annoying that she couldn't go look for it.

She flung the covers off her legs and lifted them straight up. Five leg lifts exhausted her. So much for superhuman strength. Maybe she'd lost that strength forever and would now have to live her life as an average human.

She shuddered. How would she keep her brother safe?

Surveying the room, she concentrated on each separate piece of furniture then closed her eyes. She had no problem piecing together a three-sixty image in her head. Her cognitive powers remained strong. She was too tired to try her reaction speed.

The door opened. Naya hastily covered her body with the comforter as a man entered.

Blondie, or Leif, as she had learned that night in the alley.

The last time she'd seen him, he'd been lying flat on his back.

Correction, the last time she'd seen him, he'd seared her lips with the hottest kiss she'd ever experienced *and* he'd been flat on his back.

A flush crept up her face, making her scalp tingle. She waited for him to speak.

He approached the bed in a loose-hipped saunter, showing off lean legs and broad shoulders. His skin glowed as if freshly showered and shaved, his hair pulled back and gathered at the nape of his neck. Ice-blue eyes pierced hers. She swallowed and ignored the unfamiliar heat flushing her body.

She liked a good-looking man as much as the next girl, but she'd never before reacted to anybody the way this blond hot-bod made her nerves tingle.

Damn, that kiss had scrambled her brain.

He stopped a few feet away. "Irja says you are feeling better."

She watched him warily, trying not to stare at his lips. They were full and delicious. What would it be like for them to kiss while he was fully conscious? She quickly turned away to hide the deepening blush.

Leif pulled one of the blue chairs closer to the bed and sat down. "You look a little better, but still feverish." He leaned forward, hand raised as if to touch her forehead.

She jerked away and then cocked an eyebrow, giving

him the death stare she used to give Scott when they were very young and he wouldn't do as told. It didn't work on this man.

He chuckled, tracing a finger down the side of her cheek. "Why does your driver's license say Daisy?"

Her nerve endings burned in the wake of his touch. She swatted his hand away. "Because it's my name."

He smiled. Dimples appeared.

If the wolverines had been female, he could have just flashed those and they would have swooned to the ground in no time.

"Irja tells me it's Naya."

"That's my middle name," she said after a long pause. The dimples distracted her, so did the killer smile.

His grin grew broader. "You're a bad liar."

Naya looked past him at the dresser opposite the foot of the bed. She was an excellent liar. She'd been doing nothing but lying for more than a year. "I want new clothes and my computer back. My bag too."

He nodded. "I'll have them brought to you."

That was easy. A little too easy. "Why am I here?"

His forehead creased. "You jumped into my men's car."

Ah yes, the silver vehicle. Now she remembered the drivers. "Your men are not very good at following people."

He chuckled. "Nobody ever accused Harald or Ulf of being subtle." He leaned forward and put his hand on her forehead.

She flinched again, but his other hand cradled her cheek, immobilizing her head. The tenderness of the touch stunned her. Although the coolness of his hand soothed her skin, electricity crackled where he made contact. Did he feel it too? It was more than a little disturbing.

His fingers lingered, caressing her face lightly before he pulled his hands away. "Your fever is gone. I worried you'd be out for longer. It took me almost three days to purge the poison."

So that was why the wolverine guys got the drop on him. They must have laced their claws with toxins, which explained why her wound didn't heal. "What kind of poison did they use?" She looked away from his piercing eyes.

"An herbal extract that shuts down your circulatory system. It basically suffocates your organs. A dose as large as yours should be fatal to a human." He put extra emphasis on the last word.

She fiddled with the comforter. When the silence lasted, she finally looked up and found him studying her. "What?"

"Why aren't you dead, Naya?" Her name sounded too intimate on his lips. His eyes saw too much. Again, she truly regretted sharing her name with Irja, but insisting on her alias now would be counterproductive.

"How am I supposed to know?" she asked, offering a tight smile.

Leif remained silent.

"Why did those guys jump you?" Naya asked. What she really wanted to know was if he knew why they were hunting her and her brother.

"They are our enemies."

If he found out she might have been created in the same lab as these creatures, would he consider her an enemy too? "And that's why the wolverine monsters want you dead?" *And why did the poison not kill you?* She would save that last question for when she had a better idea of how safe, or unsafe, it might be to ask.

"You noticed they weren't human."

"I noticed their freaky long fingernails. Talons really."

His dimples distracted her and she missed his cool touch.

She reminded herself of the blows he had delivered to the wolverines before succumbing to the poison. He was not a gentle guy. Quite the opposite, she could feel the checked strength emanating from his muscular body even in his lightest of touches.

And the way her body responded was distracting. Her hormones needed to quiet down.

He watched her for a second. "I'm sorry you were hurt, but grateful for your intervention. I owe you my life."

That was unexpected. Heat blossomed on her cheeks. "What did you do to piss them off?"

"It's a long and tiresome story. I will tell it to you another time. You should rest now." Standing abruptly, he smoothed a hand over his glossy hair and down the short ponytail at the nape of his neck. "If you need me, ask for Leif. As long as you are my guest, I will provide you with anything you require."

She felt more like a hostage than a guest but decided not to argue. "I still need clothes and my bag." Naya watched his reaction.

"I will have them brought to you." He flashed those dangerous dimples. "Harald said you broke a man's nose at the bus stop. Why?"

An image of clocking the agent's schnoz with her elbow flashed through her mind. She shrugged. "It's a long and tiresome story."

He chuckled. "Fair enough. I'll tell you my tale when you tell yours." He moved his hand as if to touch her again, but changed his mind and dropped it to his side, clenching it into a fist.

She berated herself silently for wishing his fingers had made contact.

"Why did you take my phone?" he asked.

"I didn't know I had it until I got back home. I was pretty out of it after the fight."

He nodded slowly. "We found it in your bag."

"Great, now you have it back." Was the phone important?

"Rest well, Naya. You are safe here." He walked out without looking back.

She tried hard not to notice how nicely he filled the seat of his jeans or remember what that ass felt like when she had searched for his phone.

Irja had also said this place was safe, but that's how the handlers had described the lab compound. And that experience had shown her not to trust people who used that word.

She scrambled out of the bed. This time the destination was the door through which Leif had just exited. It felt like hours by the time she crossed the room. An eighty-year-old woman with a walker could have overtaken her.

Slowly, she twisted the handle and pulled on the door. It swung wide on well-oiled hinges. She poked her head out. A long hallway stretched to the left. Several shut doors lined it. Turning right revealed a large stained-glass window. Like the ones in churches, but instead of saints and lambs, the top half showed mighty Vikings sailing huge ships as sea serpents leaped out of the water. In the lower half, a giant wolf attacked a woman on a horse. The rider was about to pierce the wolf's flank with her broadsword.

Naya considered exploring the closed doors but couldn't find the strength. Also, padding around in a strange place in nothing but panties and a T-shirt was not the best idea. Instead, she shuffled back to bed and crawled under the covers, waiting for her belongings to be returned. She'd have a little nap until they arrived. As long as she wasn't locked in the room, she could relax enough and rest until she regained her strength.

<hr />

Leif's berserker was trying to crawl through his skin. During his conversation with Naya, it had insisted on skin-to-skin contact and sent mental images of Leif and Naya naked, entwined, and sweaty.

Mine, the berserker whispered to him now. *Go back. Mine.*

Never had it spoken in words to him or sent images. Their communication lay in the emotional realm. Anger, rage, revenge were what he felt through the bond. Not attraction.

Irja had better figure out how to get rid of this poison side effect soon—he couldn't think of it any other way right now—or he'd have a hard time controlling himself around Naya. Until he had more answers, he'd head for some physical sparring to control himself and his berserker. The repetitive exercises should distract him from the diminutive woman lying in his…in the bed in the guest room. Technically, it was also his bed, but not the one he and his berserker wanted her in.

Leif almost made it to the training center in the big barn behind the fortress before someone called his name. He groaned softly and turned to see Sten jogging up to him, his usual happy face tight and stressed. "*Min kung.*" The warrior bowed and kept his head low. "I can't get ahold of Per. He's not answering calls or texts."

"Maybe something's wrong with Per's cell phone." Leif touched the young Viking's shoulder.

Sten briefly leaned into his grip. "Then he would have found some other way of contacting us. He's been gone for six hours on a job that normally takes two, maybe three." He averted his eyes.

Leif still caught the flash of despair. "You're worried." He studied his youngest warrior. Sten had died in battle and gone to Valhalla at the age of eighteen. The time he'd spent with the gods, and the hundred years passed in the mortal realm, added maturity to his demeanor and eyes. His body and face, though, were still those of a young man.

"Something feels wrong." Lines of worry marred the normally smooth skin of his forehead.

Leif didn't waste time on second-guessing. Sten and Per were battle brothers. As such, they'd developed a sixth sense about each other. They knew the other's location in the midst of combat, just as Leif and Harald knew where the other positioned himself during a fight. "Grab Astrid and go see what's keeping our brother."

Sten's shoulders sagged in relief. "Yes, my king." The young Viking ran off at full speed.

If something had happened to Per, Harald needed to know. Leif went in search of the marshal.

The berserker paced impatiently. *Fight.*

Gritting his teeth, Leif ignored the silent command.

He found the red-bearded warrior in the kitchen, lifting a sandwich the size of his forearm.

"I've sent Sten and Astrid to find Per."

Reluctantly, his friend halted the sandwich halfway to his face and closed his mouth.

Good thing, it would never have fit.

"He's not back yet?" Harald asked, placing his food back on the plate.

Leif shook his head. "Sten can't reach him on his cell and he hasn't checked in."

"I'll ask Ulf to see if he can use the gadget that tracks the cars." They'd installed GPS in all their vehicles.

"Sten has a bad feeling."

"Fuck." Harald rose. "I'll go right away." He looked longingly toward the pile of bread and meat, then shook his head and left.

Leif waited a few moments before getting out a knife and cutting a chunk off the sandwich. It was Torvald's night to cook. Quite a few of the warriors went on "night patrol" to the Chinese restaurant when Torvald had dinner duty.

He cut another chunk and brought both of them with him.

~~~

Naya woke to find a pair of sweats and three brand-new pairs of pink lacy panties on one of the blue chairs. She frowned at their frilliness, but they would have to do.

Her bag lay on the floor next to her black motorcycle boots. She pulled on the clothes. Her familiar heavy leather footwear made her feel more like her usual badass self. She was ready to explore the fortress.

She found five other bedrooms similar to hers. At the end of the hallway, a staircase led down to the lower floor. The banisters shone with polish and a rich Turkish runner ran down the center of the steps. The staircase opened up into a massive foyer with gleaming hardwood floors and large oil paintings of lush landscapes and violent battle scenes on the walls.

Tall oak double doors at one end of the foyer were big enough to drive a pickup truck through. They swung open to a cobblestone courtyard that looked about half a basketball court in length. Beyond that, tall pine trees rose majestically.

She closed the doors and went in the opposite direction, discovering a restaurant-sized kitchen. Recessed lights reflected warmly off stainless steel appliances. A rectangular pine table stood in the middle of the room, surrounded by ten chairs. On the table lay a massive pile of bread and meat. Someone had made a sub sandwich. Her stomach growled. A knife rested beside the plate.

She cut off a large piece and placed it on a napkin she found and sat down to eat. The meat tasted salty and tangy, like wild game. Not your average Hickory Farms. After she finished, she dug around in the cupboards to find a glass and filled it with water. She drank two glasses before wiping her mouth with the back of her hand.

Naya hesitated in the doorway. That was one ass-kicking good sandwich. She stepped back to the table, cut another chunk of sandwich, and wrapped it in a napkin.

At the end of the hallway a door opened into a

glass-covered walkway flanked by gardens. Brilliant flowers in primary colors grew everywhere and a fountain sprayed the air with water droplets. She opened the door at the other end and stepped into a big open space. Familiar smells of chemicals and metal hit her nostrils. A counter with microscopes and test tube centrifuges covered one wall. Large fume hoods competed for space with tall glass-door refrigerators.

Naya wanted to scream. A lab. A freaking lab.

Safe, they'd told her. No wonder Irja knew her biology was different. She had pulled Naya's blood and studied it under one of these microscopes, probably had a pint stored in one of the refrigerators for future experiments.

Bile rose in Naya's throat. The lab walls undulated. She sank to her knees, dropping the sandwich.

A door opened somewhere. Heels beat on the floor as someone ran toward her.

A woman called her name.

A man shouted in surprise.

Hands held her shoulders. She tried to get away, scratching and hitting desperately, but slipped. Her head hit the floor and everything went black.

Chapter 6

LEIF HAD FINALLY MANAGED TO GET A WORKOUT. STILL too weak to do any serious weapons or fight training, he'd opted for the treadmill, but lasted only forty-five minutes before his legs threatened to buckle. At least the berserker had calmed down. After the gym, he'd grabbed another piece of Harald's sandwich, which was slightly smaller than before, and then headed to the office to catch up on emails. He needed to ask the other Viking tribes if they had information about a poison affecting berserkers and if they'd encountered creatures like the wolverines.

But thinking about administrative duties annoyed him. He'd rather go see Naya. He forced down those thoughts before the berserker woke up. This newly alert warrior spirit he'd experienced by Naya's bed might be able to wrestle complete control of Leif's body.

Suddenly a dull nausea rose in his gut. He heard heavy boots run past his office door, followed by lighter steps. Leif flung open the door and saw Harald and Irja disappearing down the hallway. Harald had something in his arms. Leif's gut clenched and the nausea increased. He followed.

"Put her in the bathroom first so I can wash her off," Irja said.

Harald took the stairs two steps at a time.

Leif's berserker jumped to attention. "What's

going on?" Leif roared as he followed them into Naya's bedroom.

Harald turned. Naya lay limp in his arms.

"She had some kind of episode," Irja said. "I think she's okay. She just ate too much too fast. Her body can't handle solid foods yet."

"Fucking waste of a great sandwich," Harald muttered.

Leif felt a momentary stab of guilt, but it disappeared when he saw the paleness of Naya's face. The nausea in his stomach gave way to fright. What he felt was connected to her. Naya was upset and afraid. He stepped closer to Harald. "I'll take it from here."

"I got her," Harald said.

Leif's berserker jumped to attention. Another male was *not* going to undress Naya. "Get out," he growled and pulled the slight body into his arms.

Harald stared at him, mouth wide open.

Irja wedged between them. "Actually, I've got her." Carefully edging Naya's body out of Leif's grip, she carried her into the bathroom, closing the door firmly behind them.

Harald's face flushed. "Is there a problem, *min kung*?"

Leif ignored the question. "What happened?"

"Fuck if I know. I went looking for the thief who ate my sandwich when I heard a commotion in the lab." He paused.

Leif tried not to punch him to get him to continue.

Harald caught sight of Leif's face and raised his brows. "Naya had fallen down. Irja and I tried to help, but she fought like a wildcat. She slipped and hit her head."

Leif rubbed the back of his neck. He wanted to go to

her. He needed to make sure she was okay. The serpent tattoo on his bicep throbbed. He scratched it.

"What are you not telling me?" Harald's voice rumbled low.

"Nothing." Leif glanced away.

"So, tell me what she is," Harald insisted. "No normal human defeats four wolverines."

"I don't know. Her blood reacts differently than other mortals', or she wouldn't have been able to purge the poison, but that's all we know."

His marshal took a step forward. "Were you going out to see her that night in the alley?"

Leif frowned. "No, I'd never met her before."

Harald quirked an eyebrow. "Never?"

"I swear to our mother Freya that before the fight in the alley, I'd never seen Naya." He raked a hand through his hair. Harald's questions would lead to things he didn't want to think about or even ask himself.

"Do you not find it curious that a girl you have never met all of a sudden saves you from four of Loki's wolverines? Creatures who managed to drug you? And then she jumps into our car?"

Leif clenched his jaw. "You said she fought with someone."

"That could have been staged too."

Leif shook his head. "She's not staging anything."

"How can you be so sure?"

Leif met Harald's gaze straight on. "I'm not, but I owe her my life, and so she has earned my trust."

"You are very trusting, my king. Too trusting."

"Watch what you're saying." He took a step toward Harald.

He responded with one of his own. "Are you speaking as my friend or as my king?"

"Whichever will make you shut up."

The berserker roared. *Fight*.

Harald opened his mouth, but then closed it again. Anger flickered in his eyes, and something else. Hurt.

Leif's stomach clenched. He'd never come to blows with his best friend, but his warrior spirit itched for a fight and he didn't know if he could rein it in. He breathed deeply through his nose, nostrils flaring.

Without another word, Harald shook his head. Looking straight ahead, he walked out of the room, slamming the door behind him.

The berserker urged Leif to pursue the fight. He fisted his hands, struggling to remain in control.

Irja returned from the bathroom. She had Naya wrapped up in an oversize towel. He reached for her, but the Valkyrie shook her head. After putting Naya to bed, tucking the comforter around her, she watched Leif for a long while. "You will have to tell him eventually."

Leif avoided her gaze and instead studied the unconscious woman in the bed. "I don't want to talk about it," he said, distracted. Naya was too pale.

"Harald is your *stallare*. He can't do his job effectively if he has to worry about you becoming unhinged, losing control of your berserker."

His head jerked up. She knew about the serpent's tail showing up, but did Irja also know how restless his warrior spirit had been even before he met Naya? His nostrils flared again.

Irja tilted her head. "Harald knows you very well. He's worried about you."

"I don't want to talk about it." He knew he was going to have to tell Harald eventually, but he needed to control this strong attraction he had to Naya before he could deal with questions from his *stallare*. "How is she?" he asked instead.

The tall woman watched him for a few heartbeats more before she answered. "I checked for a concussion, but she's fine."

"What happened?" Leif wanted to touch Naya. The need to feel her skin against his scared him. He forced himself to take a step back.

"I don't know. I found her in the lab. She was distraught and then became ill."

"That sounds like more than just a reaction to solid food."

Irja nodded. "Something upset her."

He lowered his voice. "I felt her anger and something else, maybe betrayal, when I caught up with you."

The Valkyrie looked surprised. "Your berserker connects with her emotions? I didn't realize the bond was that strong already."

"Me either," Leif said through clenched teeth.

"You are going to have to tell Harald, whether you like it or not."

"I will," he grumbled. "I just need a little more time."

"Do it now, before that macho posturing goes any further and you cause permanent damage to your friendship." Irja's firm voice had a bitter edge.

Surprised, Leif stared at her. He'd never heard that tone from her. She always treated him with reverence.

Lowering her eyes, she bowed her head. "I'm sorry, my king, but these are bad times. We cannot afford a rift between you and your *stallare*."

Leif stepped closer to the Valkyrie.

She looked up, fear clouding her eyes.

He grasped her chin gently and touched his forehead to hers in the ancient custom of a king honoring a trusted advisor. "Never be afraid to tell me your opinion, Irja. Your advice is always welcomed." He released her. "I will speak to Harald."

Irja nodded.

"Please stay with her. She may still be afraid when she wakes up." He turned to leave the room.

"I will watch over your queen."

Irja's quiet voice tripped him, but he recovered and left the room without falling flat on his face. Once the door closed, he sagged against it. *Fuck.*

When they completed the bond, Naya would be queen of his people. A non-Valkyrie ruling ancient Nordic warriors. That would not sit well with them—or with the gods. There was nothing he could do about that now. And to gauge how his people might react to their new queen, he might as well start by breaking the news to his second-in-command and best friend.

—⁓—

He found his marshal at the training center. Harald's massive pectorals glistened with sweat as he went through the paces, quick-stepping forward while thrusting with a wide double-edged sword. When he saw Leif, he straightened up, expanding his chest as he quickly dipped his head. "Have you come to fight me, my king?"

Leif's inner warrior relished the challenge, but he ignored it and forced it to calm down. "Cut the crap. I've come to talk."

Harald shot him a sour look but put away his sword and shield. He grabbed a towel and wiped the sweat from his brow and shoulders. "I need something to drink."

The two walked into the house and to the kitchen in silence. Leif sat at the table, where the remains of Harald's giant sandwich still sat. Harald pulled two pilsners from the fridge. Popping off the caps, he handed one to Leif.

Leif raised the bottle. "*Skål*." He took a long swallow.

Harald pulled from his own beer and sat down at the table, seemingly patient to wait until Leif spoke again.

"There's something I haven't told you."

"No shit." Harald took another drink.

Leif glared at him.

The thickhead just quirked an eyebrow and raised the bottle to his lips. It had always been hard to intimidate his battle brother.

"This is difficult. Stop busting my balls."

Harald nodded.

"I have never met Naya before." Leif held up a hand when he saw that Harald was about to interrupt. "The alley was the first time I saw her, but I know we can trust her."

"How, my king?"

Leif studied his *stallare* for a long time. Their friendship might not survive what he was about to say. Harald's loyalty would be split between kinship with a battle brother and his duty to the Wise One. Finally he sighed. "You've already suspected that my berserker is unusually strong these days."

Harald nodded. "You're the king. Your berserker has

always been stronger than any of the warriors'. You're formidable in a fight. That's one of the reasons your troop follows you without question."

Leif startled. He knew his inner warrior seemed fiercer than others, but he'd thought it was because of his lack of control. "I thought they obeyed me because Odin chose me as leader."

His *stallare* took a long swallow from the bottle. "They do as you say because they trust you. They know you have their backs."

"Good to know," Leif said. He would think about Harald's words later. He took a swig from his beer. "I'm having trouble controlling my warrior spirit."

Harald's face clouded over. "How bad is it?"

Leif faced his friend. "So far I can handle it."

"Through your evening walks to the nightclubs." Harald made it a statement.

Leif nodded.

"It's a dangerous gamble. A hard balance to maintain."

He appreciated his *stallare's* understanding, but a king who couldn't control his warrior was shameful. "There's more."

Harald waited quietly.

Leif picked up his bottle, but then put it back down. Damn.

He'd rather go through battle for days without sleep than talk about the new development with his berserker. He was close to his battle brother, they gave each other a hard time about the wenches, but an honorable man did not brag about his bedsport.

And true men didn't talk about feelings.

They weren't supposed to have them.

He swallowed loudly. "My berserker talks to me. It wants Naya."

His *stallare* opened his mouth. When no sound came out, he closed it again. Putting the pilsner bottle to his lips, he drank several deep gulps. Finally he pulled the bottle from his mouth. "Your berserker talks to you?"

Leif nodded.

"You mean it strengthens your anger, your battle fever."

Leif shook his head.

Harald blinked several times. "It converses? In actual words? About Naya?"

Leif nodded.

"Fuck."

"Exactly," Leif agreed.

His *stallare* sat still, staring at the half-eaten sandwich. "What does it say?"

Leif shifted in the chair. He picked at the label on his bottle. "So far only single words."

"Like what?"

"It has claimed Naya." Leif pulled up his sleeve.

Harald stared at the serpent tail, blinked a few times, and then looked back at Leif. "How could this happen? She's not a Valkyrie."

Leif sighed. "I don't know. At first I thought the mark was a side effect of the poison, but Irja insists it's real."

His friend was the first to break eye contact. "Our small warrior tribe would gain a true queen."

Leif cocked an eyebrow. "You don't mind having a queen who's not a Valkyrie."

His *stallare* paused. "I trust the bond. Torvald will have a problem, but the others will come around." Harald drank from his bottle. "It is truly a gift from the goddess to meet the one person who completes you. A queen would strengthen the king's berserker and all the warriors' bonds with their berserkers."

He'd expected Harald to be angry, but should have known his friend would believe in and obey an ancient magical tradition like the *själsfrände* bond. And maybe the bond could be used as a strategic advantage. "We would only grow stronger if the warriors accept Naya as their queen." He rubbed his face. "I don't even know if she'll accept me as her mate."

Harald cleared his throat. "Human women are known to be foolish, and most of them find you attractive." He grinned. "Shouldn't take you long before you have her in your bed and get her to the altar."

Leif's stomach clenched. "I'm in no hurry to get married." His duty was to prevent Ragnarök, to save the world. He didn't have time for romance or seduction. "I tried that once."

Harald's face softened. "Centuries have passed since you last took a wife."

"Back then I was only a warrior, and still, duty made me fail miserably as a husband." He'd sworn long ago to not let anyone close again. He was the king. His duty could only be to his gods and his warriors.

"You cannot blame yourself for Solveig's and the children's deaths. You didn't know—"

Leif held up his hand. "Let's not discuss this now. We have bigger things to worry about. Our first priority must be to thwart the wolverine threat."

Harald nodded. "But you can't ignore your *själsfrände*. You must complete the bond or you jeopardize your control of your berserker, and that will put all of us in danger."

Leif rose. "I know, but let's deal with one problem at a time." He stepped into the hallway. The throbbing between his temples resonated with his heavy footsteps as he walked down the hall.

Chapter 7

LEIF TURNED TO ADMINISTRATIVE WORK TO KEEP HIS mind off Naya while he waited for his warriors to track down the wolverines' poison grove.

He began an email to a particularly wordy chief's request to have Irja visit for a month. The Valkyrie had specifically requested to not go anywhere for the next year, and Leif would honor that, even if he had no idea why.

It would be a waste of breath asking her.

Harald and Sten came crashing through the door. Leif turned from the monitor to look up at his men.

"What's going on?"

"We found the van Per drove when he left this morning," Harald said.

"But not Per," Sten interjected, earning an impatient look from Harald. "I beg your pardon," the young Viking mumbled and bowed to Leif and then Harald.

The marshal acknowledged the gesture with a nod. "The van was abandoned in a lot down by River Park. No sign of our brother anywhere."

Leif rubbed the back of his neck. "Do we know if he picked up the weapons yet?"

The two men in front of him exchanged an uncomfortable look. "He had ten rifles and five handguns in the van when he left the supplier."

"Let me guess," Leif said. "They are as gone as Per?"

Both men nodded.

"Shit."

"What would you like us to do?" Harald asked.

"Our first priority must be to find Per," Leif said. "Hopefully we find the weapons with him, but he must be safe before we do anything else."

"I'll check with Ulf to see if we can get a lock on his cell phone," Harald said. "It wasn't in the van or anywhere around the vehicle." He left the room.

Sten stood in front of the desk, not looking at Leif.

"Is there something you want?"

"I'm worried, my king. Per would never have let anybody take those weapons without a fight."

"I know," Leif said. "But let's not plan for disaster until we have a clearer picture of what's going on."

"Yes, my king." Sten bowed again before walking toward the door.

"We'll find him," Leif promised his retreating back.

Leif found Naya in her bedroom, seated in one of the armchairs, typing away on a laptop. Strange how he already thought of it as *her* bedroom.

He'd been avoiding her. The emotions flooding his body whenever he was near her overwhelmed him, and he really didn't have the time to deal with something as crazy as the *själsfrände* bond. Not that there would ever be a good time, but right now he needed to concentrate on finding Per and keeping his people safe.

Mine, the berserker whispered, but stayed calm for a change.

Dressed in a flannel shirt three sizes too big, she

appeared completely absorbed in her work, muttering to herself as she stabbed the keyboard. The seventeen-inch screen obscured most of her upper body.

"Are you just going to stand there or did you need something?" she snapped.

He grinned, but lowered his chin before she looked up. She might have a tiny body, but it held a large spirit. As well as a big temper. "I came to see how you are." He reached out to check her forehead for a temperature, but pulled back when Naya flinched. "I would never hurt you."

"How do I know that?" She eyed him wearily.

Leif quieted the anxious berserker. "You don't. But I won't." He slowly reached out again and placed his palm against her forehead. "You are a little flushed, but I don't think you have a fever."

"I'm fine. I should be out of your hair soon. Irja says I'm recovering quickly."

Leif ignored the stab of anxiety in his chest and the pacing berserker. "There's no need to rush. You are welcome to stay as long as you'd like." Something of his frustration must have crept into his voice. Naya peeked up from the screen with a puzzled expression.

Leif hurried his words. "We still don't know who the man at the bus stop was." He might not want to deal with the bond, but he needed to keep her close until he figured out a solution.

She blinked a few times. "Thanks, but I have clients I need to attend to."

"What kind of clients?" He took a step closer, crowding her.

"Customers, for work." Her tone implied he was slow-witted.

He refused to rise to the bait. "What kind of work?"

"Security stuff."

So, she wasn't going to share. He'd find out eventually. He always managed to charm answers out of women. He crouched down to her level.

She directed her full gaze on him. "What are you doing in that lab?" Her voice wobbled a little.

"Irja uses it to prepare medicine and other treatments."

"What kind of treatments?"

He shrugged. "Whatever ailments my warriors bring her. It can be anything from an upset stomach to an open wound or a broken bone."

"Why do you need such an elaborate setup if you treat only minor injuries?"

He studied her for a few seconds before answering. "You are very observant. Are you familiar with labs?"

"Don't answer my question with a question. I know that game."

Leif smiled. She did indeed. She was playing it right now. "Then ask me what you really want to know."

"What makes you different from other humans?" Her dark-blue eyes remained steady.

The question took him by surprise. Both the directness of it and that she thought them human. "We are stronger and live longer, but are mainly the same as you." He tucked a wayward strand of her hair behind her ear, turning the motion into a caress of her cheek.

She held very still. "And the wolverines in the alley?" she asked.

Through the *själsfrände* bond he could feel her heightened anxiety, her increased heart rate. He lowered his hand and leaned back a little to create more space between them. "Also different, but not the same as us." The rapid pacing of her heart decreased. "At least that's what we think. They are new creatures we haven't seen before." He stared at her mouth. The thumping of her heart picked up.

"How did you become different?" She licked her lips.

"It's a very long story." Compelled to touch her skin again, he raised his hand.

She leaned out of reach. "That's what Irja said. She also said you would tell me the details."

He doubted very much those were the words Irja had used, but he'd have to share some of their secrets to get Naya to trust him. "All you need to know for right now is that I will protect you, and so will my people."

She quirked an eyebrow. "Your people?"

"I am the king of these Norse warriors." He focused on her lips and leaned in slowly.

"Warriors?" She was annoyed, but her lips parted and her gaze locked on to his lips.

At her heated gaze his cock rose, impatient behind the restriction of his jeans. "Will you tell me what makes you different?" he asked, leaning closer.

"I don't know," she whispered before he claimed her lips with his own.

Through their bond he felt the lie in her words. She may not know all the details, but she knew more than she was sharing. He forgot about the importance of truth when she returned the kiss and his berserker howled with pleasure.

Her lips parted farther and he thrust his tongue into her velvety mouth.

Odin's ravens, her lips fitted his perfectly. Heat rushed through his body. His cock stood at full attention.

The berserker egged him on. *Mine, mine, mine.*

She moaned in the back of her throat.

Sweat beaded on his forehead. He half rose, leaning over her.

The laptop slid slowly to the floor as he grabbed her ass to draw her closer. His hands fit perfectly around her surprisingly lush curves. A growl of pleasure from the berserker escaped through his mouth as she pushed up his shirt. He pulled her to the edge of the chair and pressed his cock against the sweet vee between her thighs.

It wasn't enough. He was about to lift her when Harald burst through the door.

Growling, he turned toward his friend. The words scolding Harald for invading Naya's bedroom died on his lips when he saw his *stallare*'s face.

Leif stood, pretending not to hear Naya's disappointed sigh. Shielding her with his body, he tugged down his shirt. "What have you found?"

Harald seemed too preoccupied to notice what he'd interrupted. "Ulf got an email sent from Per's phone. It's a ransom demand."

"A kidnapping?" This had never happened before.

Harald nodded. "We're tracing the message, but emails from phones are hard to pin down."

Naya snorted.

Leif and Harald turned toward her.

"It's not hard." She bent down to pick up her laptop. A frown marred her still-flushed face. "You just can't do it with computer IPs. You have to use the encoded cell matrix in the message and triangulate the towers it bounced off."

Her words made no sense to Leif. Judging from Harald's open, mouth, he too thought she spoke a foreign language.

"Do you know how to do this?"

She waved a hand in the air but didn't look up from the screen as she answered. "Sure."

Harald lasted all of five seconds before exploding. "Then get off your butt, *jänta*. Do the cell matriculate-whatever. Help us find Per."

Naya flipped the laptop closed. "Show me the email."

Crap. She'd almost had sex with Leif. One kiss lit her on fire and she let him do anything he wanted. She could still feel the imprint of his fingers on her ass from where he grabbed her and pulled her against his hardness. And what a hardness that had been, wide and long. She'd wanted to rub herself against him like a cat.

And it wasn't just her body that responded to his dangerous combination of hotness and confidence. Her emotions were all over the place when he was near. She wanted to please him while at the same time run away.

Shaking her head, she followed Leif and Harald into a room at the back of the game room. She'd figure out what he meant by being king later. Talk about delusions of grandeur.

Crew-cut from the night of the attack sat at a desk with two monitors. Typing away, he stared at lines of text scrolling on the screen in front of him. These dudes had a badass computer setup.

Naya peered over his shoulder at the message header logs. He had the right idea, but hadn't figured out that the trace code wasn't in the usual place when sent via phone. Instead of an IP address, he needed to locate the unique cell tower and phone identifiers.

"May I?" she asked the guy.

Startled, he flinched, glancing from Naya to Leif.

Leif only had to nod for the guy to give up his chair. "It's okay, Ulf. Naya knows how to trace the message."

Ulf bowed and stepped aside. Maybe Leif really was some kind of ruler. This guy obviously thought so.

Naya avoided looking at Leif. Her body trembled just from knowing he was near. She didn't want to think about her body's earlier wanton response. "Is this the ransom message?" She pointed at the screen.

Ulf leaned in and nodded.

Her fingers danced over the keyboard, decrypting each of the hidden marker strings, until she found the thread she wanted. "The public information shows it was definitely sent from the Pine Rapids area."

Ulf leaned in closer over her shoulder, staring at the screen. "What do you mean, 'public information'?" His body pushed against the chair. "Where did all that data come from?"

She turned and her nose was half an inch from his cheek. "Do you mind? I'm working here."

Leif grabbed the guy and jerked him back so fast Naya's hair fluttered.

Harald chuckled.

She looked up, trying to decipher what had just happened.

Harald beamed at her. "Please continue." He waved his hand.

Ulf looked pissed, and a little scared.

She smiled at him. "I'll show you later, promise." They obviously wanted to find this guy Per, but Ulf had just wanted to learn. No reason to be a jerk about it. She glared at Leif.

He calmly gazed back at her and raised an eyebrow. A slow grin revealed those lethal dimples.

Pretending she wasn't affected, she shrugged and turned back to the screen. "The message came from southeast of here. The cell phone tower identifiers are close to the ones used in Idaho."

"That's amazing." Ulf loomed up behind her again but kept his distance when Leif cleared his throat.

Man, the king was touchy.

"Can you give us more information?" Harald asked.

"It's going to take some time. I have to decrypt some of these data strings, and the government likes to make it cumbersome."

"You're breaking into government code?" Leif asked.

"Of course," Naya said. "Who do you think put this tracing in the header in the first place?" The government monitored all electronic communications through hidden tracers. She continued typing. "It would kind of help if you guys weren't breathing down my neck. Could you go away for twenty minutes?"

Harald muttered something about sandwiches, but Leif pushed him out the door and dragged the computer guy with him.

Naya relaxed a little. She was never comfortable with people standing where she couldn't see them. Especially one particular large Norse king standing so close her neck still hummed from the heat radiating off his body.

His very hard, muscular body.

Leif paced the length of the game room while Harald slumped on one of the oversize couches. Ulf leaned against the pool table in the middle of the room.

"She is one badass hacker," Ulf said. "Did you see how fast her fingers flew over those keys?"

The young warrior didn't notice his king's warning look.

Leif turned to Harald instead. "Find out everything you can about her. And I want to know about the man at the bus stop."

"Already on it," Harald said. When Leif quirked an eyebrow, he continued. "After you showed me"—he glanced briefly at Ulf—"your interest in Naya, I figured you'd eventually want more information."

"And?"

Ulf answered. "And there's nothing."

"What do you mean?"

The berserker, which had paced obsessively since they'd left Naya's bedroom, howled. Leif gritted his teeth and clenched his fists, forcing the warrior spirit to calm down. The gods were surely laughing. He needed information about Naya. He needed to know why his warrior spirit claimed her. "What about the man?"

"Ulf hacked into the traffic cams on that block. Some suits showed up to pick up the poor bleeding bastard. Ulf got a license number."

"I've run the number," Ulf said. "It's not in the usual

databases, but I have some contacts working on it. So far all signs point toward a government agency of some kind."

Shit. What was Naya involved in? "Why was she in the alley on the night of my attack?"

"We viewed footage from the security cameras on one of the warehouses. All we know is that she exited from the club. The cameras were at wrong angles to film the fight."

"Keep working on it, but make finding Per your priority," Leif said.

The door burst open and Naya stepped into the room. "Got it. The phone is on a farm southeast of here. Some of the farm's property is actually across the border in Idaho."

"How can you possibly know that?" Ulf asked, his eyes big as mead tankards.

"Google Earth," she answered with a satisfied smirk.

They followed her into the computer room. A satellite image of some buildings in the middle of a field was displayed on one of the monitors. Leif stared at the picture. It was so detailed, he could see a tractor plowing.

"Now, I can't tell you which building the phone is in. I can only narrow it down to within this cluster." She sounded apologetic.

"This is amazing." Ulf's voice was filled with awe.

Leif looked at Harald, but his friend just blinked and stared at the screen.

"Well?" Naya asked. "Go rescue the guy?" She waved a few printouts in the air.

"Right." Ulf jumped up, grabbed the maps she gave him, and headed out the door. "I'll get the others organized. We'll strike at nightfall."

"How did you know what to look for?" Harald asked Naya.

She shrugged. "It's what I do."

"What exactly is it that you do?" Leif asked, keeping his voice low.

"I'm a cybersecurity consultant."

"So you work for some kind of government agency?" Harald kept his voice light, almost bored.

Leif silently commended his *stallare* for slipping in the question so surreptitiously.

"I work for whoever can afford my fee," Naya said to Harald, squaring her shoulders, waiting for a confrontation. The two of them locked eyes for a few moments.

"Fair enough," Harald finally said, and the tension drained from the room. He turned to Leif. "We still have to find out how these fuckers knew where Per was going. It may have something to do with—"

"We'll discuss that later," Leif interrupted. He was not going to discuss the possible betrayal of one of his warriors in front of a stranger, *själsfrände* bond or not.

Harald looked like he wanted to protest but wisely dropped it. "Fine. I'll go help Ulf and the others prepare for Per's rescue."

Chapter 8

WITH EVERYONE GONE BUT NAYA, LEIF FELT HIS berserker hum and goad him to move closer to its mate. His mouth suddenly dry, Leif swallowed. Damn his restless warrior spirit and the way it whirled his body out of control.

Naya was still looking at the screen and the image of the farm. "What ransom did they demand?" she asked without turning.

"They wanted me." Leif took a step closer.

"That seems stupid." She still kept her eyes on the screen.

Leif smiled at her obvious attempt to avoid him and at the incredulity in her tone. "They think that by incapacitating me, my people will be weakened."

"Yeah, I get the whole role-playing game vibe, but why would you give yourself up?" Only a slight tensing of her shoulders hinted that she'd noticed him moving closer.

"It's what a king does." He leaned over her shoulder. His breath caressed her ear.

Take. He clamped down on the bond with the berserker.

She trembled. "You actually do rule these guys? Like some kind of gang leader?"

Leif's head started to ache. He pulled up a chair and sat down. How was he going to explain? "*Einherjar*," he muttered.

"Sorry?" She finally faced him, eyebrows raised.

He raised his head. "We're not a 'gang.' My warriors

are *einherjar*, elite Vikings and Valkyries. I truly am their king, their ruler." Her lips were very close to his. He watched her mouth intently.

"Like a religious cult?" Her breath caught and she nibbled her lower lip.

The ache in his head intensified and other parts of his body started to throb. "More like a sovereign nation."

"Like an Indian reservation?"

"Kind of. We weren't here from the beginning like the First Nations. We came from other countries." He wanted to taste her so bad he ached. The intensity of their attraction disturbed him.

"What countries?" She leaned away.

He smiled at her evasive tactic. Her brain might not admit it yet, but her body wanted him as much as his wanted hers. "Mostly Scandinavian." He put a hand on her shoulder. This time she didn't flinch at his touch. "Where did you pick up your computer skills? College?" His finger traced the side of her neck.

She shivered. "My education was of a different sort." Her brittle smile indicated an old pain.

He wanted to punch whoever or whatever had hurt her in the past. "Tell me about it." He lightly put both hands on her shoulders.

"Let's just say I had a knack that was honed over the years."

He leaned over, his breath caressing her ear. "Your help has been invaluable."

She shrugged. "We don't know if your guy is there. It could just be his phone." Pale pink colored her cheeks.

His hands had slipped off her shoulders when she

shrugged. "It's still a lot more progress than we could have made in such a short amount of time," he said.

He wanted to know why talking about her past bothered her. What was she hiding?

He needed to distract her into sharing more information. "Are you hungry?"

"Irja says it's too early for me to eat solid food."

"Better listen to her. We don't want to repeat the regurgitation of Harald's sandwich." He smiled to show he was only teasing, but her blush still deepened. "Let's go see if there's something in the kitchen."

"Don't you have a rescue mission to plan?"

"That's the bad part of being king. You never get to have any fun. I'll be manning the post here while my warriors are out enjoying themselves." His tone was more wistful than he'd intended. Shaking his head, he gestured for her to walk ahead out the door.

"That's a strange way of looking at combat." She continued through the game room and out into the hallway.

He enjoyed watching the gentle sway of her hips. "You don't enjoy fighting? You're very good at it." He didn't remember much from the night in the alley. But someone who could defeat four of Loki's creatures was not your average combatant.

"It's a necessary skill."

"In your line of work?" He kept his voice light as they entered the kitchen. Out of the corner of his eye he saw how she scrutinized him. *Keep it cool, don't scare her.* This was like trying to coax a wild doe to take food out of his hand. Any hasty movement might make her bolt.

"For anyone of my build or gender," she said casually, but he could hear an edge in her tone.

"We better see if we can build up those muscles, then."
He opened a cupboard and held out a can. "Split pea?"

She wrinkled her nose. "I've had nothing but soup for
the last four meals. Anything else available?"

He thought a moment. "What about oatmeal? Is that
too solid?"

"I'd love oatmeal." Her smile transformed her exqui-
site features into an ethereal beauty.

His breath caught. If that was all it took to make her
happy, he'd cook oatmeal every bloody day.

Shit. Where had that thought come from? He would
bed this woman without emotional entanglements—or
at least whatever would calm his restless berserker and
complete the bond. Once they'd rescued Per and had the
wolverine situation under control, he'd deal with how to
stop the *själsfrände* bond from messing with his mind
and his hormones.

Turning to fetch the canister, he braced himself on
the counter with one trembling hand. With his back
still toward her, he held up the prize. "Oats it is," he
said hoarsely.

"You cook oatmeal from scratch? That doesn't seem
very kingly," she mocked him.

"Whoever is not on patrol takes turns cooking. I do
my fair share."

"Vikings and Valkyries have mad skills in the kitchen
as well as on the battlefield?"

He chuckled. "Most of them. Not Torvald though.
He's only skilled in combat. When he's on cooking
duty, you want a contingency plan."

She laughed, a sweet, sunny sound.

Sweat broke out on his forehead. Curse the berserker

hormones. Burying himself in the pots and pans cabinet, he rested his cheek against a stainless steel pot. The coolness calmed his emotions, marginally. Pot in hand, he soon had the porridge simmering on the stove.

He risked a look back at the table.

Naya rested her cheek in her palm, watching. "I don't think I've ever seen a king cook."

"You don't believe I am really a king, do you?"

"I believe you think you are their ruler, and they do seem to obey you…"

"It's so generous of you to indulge me in my delusions."

She chuckled. "Which of the Nordic countries are you from?"

"Sweden."

"Where's Irja from? Her accent is different."

He was surprised she'd noticed. Spending centuries in the Americas had diluted much of their accents. "She's from Finland."

"Can you tell me what she does in the lab?" Her voice dropped when she asked a question important to her.

"She's our doctor and pharmacologist all wrapped up in one."

"Why do you need her?" Her voice remained low.

"Why is your biology different from other humans?"

"I asked you first."

"If I tell, will you?"

"I might, but first I want you to stop taking blood samples from me."

That was an easy request. "Okay."

She frowned. "And I want you to stop testing the samples you already have."

He grinned. She'd found the loophole. "Done."

He wondered if she ever shared secrets without striking a bargain. "Let's eat." He ladled generous portions into two bowls and carried them to the table.

"This looks great." Naya reached for the milk he'd put out.

"Hopefully it tastes good too. Let's take the bowls into my office so I can remain in contact with Harald and Ulf."

She must have said something to piss Leif off. Naya watched him from across his desk as he ate in silence.

She could do without the disturbing attraction she felt for this tall blond Viking. And yet, she missed the light mood that had been between them while he cooked. It bothered her how much she wanted this guy to like her. She wanted him to find her interesting, not just want her body. She set her spoon in her empty bowl and cleared her throat. "Thanks for the oatmeal, I really enjoyed it."

He studied her, eyes sky-blue and intense. "I'm glad."

The silence stretched. She fidgeted under his gaze. "You were going to explain why you have superior strength and need a full medical lab on-site." She smiled to take the sting out of the request.

A slight smile played at the corners of his mouth. "So I was. What will you give me if I tell you?"

Naya wasn't sure what game they were playing. "What do you mean?" Her voice sounded sharp.

Leif looked up. "You are very reluctant to tell me anything about yourself, but you want to know a lot about me, about my people. How are you going to make it worthwhile to tell you our secrets?"

"You want money?" She couldn't keep the disbelief out of her voice.

"Not money, I have plenty." He got up from behind his desk and moved to sit in the chair next to hers. "What else do you have to bargain with?"

Her mouth felt dry. "I could tell you something about myself." She hated how breathless she sounded.

Leif leaned closer. "Tell me why you were able to purge the poison so quickly from your body," he mumbled against her forehead, his lips searing hot.

She closed her eyes so he wouldn't see her lie, but also to savor the heat of his lips against her skin. She should pull away, but her body wouldn't heed the command. "I spent a lot of time in a lab…a medical facility when I was younger."

He pulled back. "Were you sick?"

Naya disliked how much she missed his touch. She opened her eyes.

His were a swirl of grays and blues. A storm moving in.

"Not that I remember," she said after a few beats. "Maybe I was and they cured me." She looked down. "I just remember a lot of injections and blood transfusions."

"I'm sorry." His look was sincere.

She almost felt bad for lying. "It was a long time ago."

"Didn't your parents explain why you were in the hospital?"

Naya didn't bother correcting the location. "My parents died when I was little."

"Who raised you?"

She shook her head. "Your turn."

Leif paused, but then nodded. "Fine. Ask me something."

"Why didn't the poison kill you?"

"I'm a very strong man." His finger traced circles on her thigh.

Heat rushed from where he touched her to the junction of her thighs. She couldn't think. She shifted in the chair. "How is your DNA different?"

"Who says it's different?"

"Irja does." The sensation of his touch overpowered her brain. "There's no way you are not enhanced in some way. You are freakishly strong."

He raised his hand and played with her hair and the sensitive spot at the nape of her neck. "We are stronger than most, but not through altered chemistry. We train."

"Nobody could train that much," she snapped. "Harald and Ulf threw the wolverines across the alley like their bodies were made of Styrofoam."

Leif chuckled. "Where were you hiding to see that?" His strong fingers loosened the kinks above her shoulder blades and then caressed her throat.

Clever Viking, clever hands. "I wanted to make sure they were your friends."

"You cared about me even then," he whispered, turning her face toward his.

"I don't know you." Her voice was breathless again.

"We could get to know each other better." Gently he pulled her closer.

The protest she meant to utter died when the heat of his breath caressed her skin. A groan slipped past her lips. She felt his smile as his mouth met hers.

His lips traced a featherlight outline of her mouth. Naya sighed.

Leif growled in the back of his throat. He nibbled her lower lip, sucking it between his lips.

She knew she should break contact before she got caught in the emotional whirlwind their touch created. Instead her traitorous body leaned into his.

He deepened the kiss, increasing the pressure until she opened her mouth.

Every nerve ending focused on her tongue mating with his.

Leif groaned again. Hooking his other hand below her knees, he slid her onto his lap, caressing her jaw with his lips.

His erection throbbed against her bottom. His mouth found the perfect spot between the nape of her neck and shoulder.

Her resistance crushed, Naya melted in his arms.

His hand moved down and caressed her breast through her shirt, lightly pinching her hardened nipple.

This was dangerous, but his hands made her feel too good.

Those clever fingers found their way under her top. Calloused palms rasped deliciously against the tender skin just below her breasts. One of them snuck behind her back. She heard someone panting loudly and realized it was her.

Leif tugged on her bra snap. The garment wasn't cooperating and he cursed.

Naya's enchantment broke. Swiftly, she scooted off his lap and braced her arms against the desk a safe distance away. When she'd caught her breath, she faced him. "We need to slow down."

"Didn't you like it?" His dimples deepened.

"That's not the point." She searched her overheated brain for why they needed to stop, but no good reason came forth.

"I'm attracted to you. You like me too. We're both consenting adults." He shrugged. "Why would we not indulge?" He stood and walked toward her.

She held up her hand.

He stopped.

"I don't know if I like you. I don't know you." The truth was she liked him too much. She wasn't equipped to deal with sex that also involved emotions.

"We *are* getting to know each other." Leif took another step.

She frowned. "You didn't answer any of my questions."

He laughed. "Is that what this is about?"

"Yes. No." Damn it. She couldn't think when he was close.

The mirth left his face and he closed the gap between them. His fingers traced the outside of her ear. "What else do you want to know?"

"Tell me about the monsters in the alley. Are they enhanced?" *And how did they know about me and my brother?*

He frowned. "I don't know."

"But you know what they are." She tried not to enjoy the closeness of him, the warmth of his body.

"I know who sent them." His hand played with her hair.

"Who?" Every fiber of her body wanted to lean into his touch.

"Someone who wants to destroy the world."

"I don't understand."

He traced her neck and shoulder with the tip of his finger. "If I tell you more, will you kiss me again?"

Electricity rushed downward, making her nipples pucker. "One kiss. No touching," she said, secretly thrilled to have an excuse to feel his lips again.

Leif smiled. "If that's all you offer, I'll take it." He leaned in.

Naya stepped back. "You have to tell me about the wolverines first."

He flashed his dimples. "I think you want me to kiss you first."

She shook her head, hoping they would both believe the lie. "Tell first," she croaked out.

With a smug smirk, he nodded. "I don't know how they are made, maybe through genetic enhancement. The one who sent them is an enemy of the ones who rule me."

"You said you are the king." What kind of weird power struggle had she walked into?

"That's true, but I'm an appointed king. I have to answer to the g—management above me."

"So, your job is to fight these creatures. Like some kind of military unit?"

"My warriors and I are a unit." He leaned toward her.

Her hormones rejoiced as his body heat engulfed her. "But not a branch of the actual armed forces." Naya made it into a statement.

His eyes were sky-blue again. "Not as you think of the military."

"Do you work for the government?"

"I've answered enough questions to claim my kiss now."

She swallowed loudly. A part of her couldn't wait to

taste his lips again. Another part, the part that handled self-preservation, told her to get out of the office. *Now*.

But she needed to know whose side Leif and his Nordic warriors were on. And she needed to taste those lips again. Wait, no. She shook her head to clear her mind.

That self-satisfied smirk played on Leif's lips again, as if he sensed her internal struggle.

She kept her promises. And she never backed down from a challenge. "Okay. One kiss, but your hands stay where I can see them."

He lifted his hand.

She stepped back. "I said no touching."

"You said I should keep them where you can see them. You can see the front of your body."

Her nipples tingled as he made a point of looking at her chest. "No hands anywhere on my body."

He sighed, but lowered his arm.

He hoisted her up on the desk. She squeaked in protest.

"I can reach you better here." Leif leaned in, placing his hands on either side of her.

Clever king.

Slowly, he lowered his head. Pressing his lips against her mouth, he pushed her back until she was lying flat on the desk. Bracing himself above her, he assaulted her mouth.

The kiss before had been gentle compared to this. His mouth devoured hers, offering no reprieve, almost punishing her.

She couldn't catch her breath. She didn't want to. She wanted him, more of him. Naya moaned. Her skin was on fire. She arched. Wanting to feel him. Needing him closer.

Leif raised his body out of reach. His biceps bulged but he kept kissing her effortlessly, licking her lips, nipping them with his teeth. He sucked her tongue into his mouth.

Pressing his hardness against her, Leif set a fierce pace with his hips and his mouth. Her hips moved on their own accord, matching the rhythm he set as he sucked and plunged. The seam of her denim shorts hit the right spot between her legs, rubbing her sensitive nub through the underwear. She moaned again, needing his touch. All of his touch.

He tore his lips from hers. She whimpered in protest, but he shushed her, whispering her name as he trailed kisses down her neck.

He sucked her nipples through her shirt, first one and then the other.

Craving the heat of his lips on her naked skin, she grabbed the material and ripped it apart. Buttons clattered on the desktop.

He murmured his approval before he nuzzled her bra out of the way and lavished his attention on her bare skin. Hot moisture from his mouth shot sparks of electricity straight to her clit. An animalistic growl echoed through the office. She realized it came from her. Arching off the desk, she slapped her hands down to keep from hitting the floor. Leif's hands grabbed her hips, steadying her.

His mouth traveled downward, tracing a trail of heat along her sternum. His tongue circled her navel while his hand made quick work of unbuttoning her shorts. Together with her underwear, he pulled them down her legs. The cloth bundle hit the floor with a dull thud.

His hands grabbed the outside of her hips and then

slid inward between her thighs. She forgot how to breathe when his thumbs stroked her clit. His mouth took the place of his fingers. Heat shot from that small nub to her core. White stars flickered in her vision.

She arched her back, her hands desperately gripping the surface of the table. His teeth grazed her skin and she cried out. He bit down lightly and then licked her clit to soothe the nip before biting again.

Her eyes rolled back in her head. She buried her hands in his silken hair.

The pressure built inside her body until it reached the boiling point. She tried to hold back, but the pressure was uncontainable. Her body trembled violently as wave after wave of orgasm traveled through her.

He slowed down the pace, changing from sucking and biting to gently nipping the sensitive spot between her legs. When she stilled after what felt like an eternity, he stopped altogether.

Burying his hands in her hair, he touched his forehead to hers. "You okay?" he whispered against her mouth.

She could taste herself on his lips. She'd never fallen apart like that before. Never become so undone she felt like she'd never make the pieces of herself fit together again. "I'm fine." Her voice was hoarse.

Leif stood and, grabbing her hand, he pulled her into a sitting position.

She'd growled like an animal. Embarrassed, she avoided his gaze. She needed to get out of here so she could think again. Leif's pull was too dangerous. She could drown in him. He had too much power over her responses, sexual and emotional.

"Are you sure?"

She nodded. "Yeah." Naya straightened her shirt. Most of the buttons were gone. She overlapped the panels of cloth and jumped off the desk, wincing at the sensitivity and wetness she felt between her legs. "I have to go." She dipped down and pulled on her shorts, stuffing the underwear in her pocket.

He moved as if to touch her again, but she ducked under his arm. She struggled briefly with opening the door but finally fled from the room. He called out her name, but she ignored him.

Chapter 9

Hours later, Leif paced his office, agitated and pissed off. He'd tried to talk to Naya, but she'd barred her bedroom door to him. When he'd heard the shower come on, he'd left her alone to try later. Before he had a chance to see her again, she'd left the fortress. Somehow she'd caught a ride with Irja when she went into town for supplies.

A nagging voice in the back of his mind told him he'd moved too fast. He'd rushed into being intimate with her. He squelched the voice. Naya had enjoyed their time together as much as he had. He shook his head and sighed loudly. Women were hard to understand under normal circumstances. Naya had too many secrets. And she didn't seem to understand that he knew best how to handle things. He was the king for gods' sake. She should listen to what needed to be done to keep her safe. According to Irja, for the bond to work, there had to be trust and mutual respect between them. He respected Naya, but how could he trust someone who wouldn't confide in him? He was so fucked. But he still needed to keep track of her. Ulf was working on tracking her cell phone.

Rubbing the back of his neck, he steered his mind to yet another problem. Someone had given information to their enemies. Someone who lived in this house. Leif still couldn't believe one of his warriors had betrayed him. They were handpicked by Odin and Freya. A traitor among them went against every law of the universe. As he stepped out of the office to get a drink from the kitchen, the massive front doors slammed open and his warriors burst into the entryway. Harald led the way for Sten and Ulf carrying Per between them, his body battered and bruised. Torvald limped behind them, holding his shoulder. Astrid brought up the rear, loaded down with bags of guns and other weapons.

Carrying her medical bag, Irja came running from the passage that led to the lab. She cradled Per's head in her hands. The young Viking gave her a weak smile.

"Upstairs," Irja commanded.

Sten hoisted Per over his shoulder and ascended the stairs, nodding to Leif as he passed.

Irja examined Torvald. "It's just a flesh wound," the older warrior insisted.

"I'll tell you what kind of wound it is," Irja snapped. She prodded his arm. "I want you upstairs too."

"What can I do to help?" Astrid asked.

"Get more sterile pads and bandages," Irja said over her shoulder as she kept a firm grip on Torvald, almost dragging him up the stairs.

Harald grinned at Leif before he lowered his head in a more formal bow. "*Min kung*, the wolverines didn't know what hit them. Astrid disposed of the only two guards with her throwing blades."

"Was Per injected with anything?"

"Irja will know better. But he's been worked over good. I'd bet at least a few broken ribs and a bruised jaw."

Leif allowed himself a slight smile. "Probably from mouthing off too much."

Harald's grin spread. "Four wolverines guarded the stash of weapons. We had a bit of trouble with those fellows. One of their bullets grazed Torvald, but that was our only injury." He wiped his forehead, tracing grime and dirt across the skin. "Also, we were able to bring back a sample of the wolverine blood for Irja."

Leif sent a silent thank-you to Freya for the success of the mission. Maybe this would rein in Loki for a while. He nodded to his marshal. "Great job as always. Please email me an official report."

Harald's grin crumbled. "Yes, *min kung*." He ambled down the hall to the computer room and the hated administrative work.

Leif went to Per's bedroom and looked down on the Viking as he slumbered. Irja washed his injuries. "I've given him a mild sedative. All we can do now is wait," she said and left the room with her head bowed.

Leif nodded, hating how defeated the medical officer looked.

Per's bruises and cuts showed how the wolverines had used him as a punching bag, but at least they hadn't drugged him. Leif shuddered as he remembered his own body purging the poison.

The door opened and Harald entered the room. "My king, Per is going to be fine. He'll have a few battle scars, making him even more popular with the girls."

Leif ignored the attempt at cheering him up. "How can I protect my people if one of them is a traitor?"

Harald sobered. "We will find who is to blame for this and for the attack on you. And he or she will be punished."

They stood in silence for a while.

"My king," Harald said, "we should also discuss... that is, I wonder if we might talk about—"

"Naya," Leif interrupted.

Harald exhaled a long breath. "Yes, your *själsfrände*. What are your plans?"

"I have none."

His friend frowned. "Have you explained the situation to her?"

Leif laughed bitterly. "Not exactly. I managed to seduce her, but then she took off like a spooked horse."

Harald scratched his beard. "She's not like other humans. Maybe that would make it easier for her to understand."

"Or harder."

The ceiling was suddenly of great interest to his *stallare*. "So you...er...bedded her?"

"No," Leif ground out.

Harald muttered something and continued to study the ceiling. "Strange. You've always had great success with human women."

Leif leveled a look at his *stallare*, but Harald still watched the ceiling and the silence stretched between them again.

This time Leif broke it. "Let's work on things we have a chance of changing. A woman's mind not being one of them. How do we find our traitor?"

"I'll gather everyone in your office and we'll share what we know."

"Is that wise? If there is a traitor, he or she will be in the room."

"This way we can watch everybody's reaction."

Leif gave his *stallare* a curt nod.

Harald left.

After one more long look at Per and his injuries, Leif did the same. The gods would do what the gods would do. Worrying about what would happen didn't change this.

Frustrated, Leif shook his head. He wanted action, preferably in the form of a good fight.

Or a good fuck.

Naya surveyed her client's office as she waited for him to arrive. Luke Holden had taste.

Rich burgundy drapes covered the windows and matched the plush sofas. A massive dark cherry desk sat in one corner, so well polished she could see her reflection in its surface. A low bass vibrated through the floor from the dance club below. She checked her cell phone clock. Holden had asked for a late evening meeting, but was fifteen minutes late. She sighed.

He was the client, and therefore got some leeway, but she still didn't like her time being wasted.

And she didn't like having time to think about what had happened with Leif in his office. Instead of pulling answers out of the Viking king, he'd seduced her and now her mind buzzed with even more questions. About the wolverines, about her attraction to Leif.

She pulled her laptop from her bag and plugged in the USB flash drive she'd packed full of data from the Vikings' computer. She didn't for a minute believe Leif's story about being the king of some kind of sovereign nation. That was just nuts. She knew he was holding out on her, but she had her own important secret to guard.

She scanned the data scrolling on her screen. While in the mansion's computer room, she'd not only pinpointed Per's location, she'd also copied a crap-load of files and mirrored the hard drive to an untraceable server. She was now able to read all computer traffic. So far, she'd found out they were investigating her. They were also running a license plate number. She made a note of finding out who the owner was.

Holden stepped through the door. "I'm so sorry to have kept you waiting."

Naya closed her laptop and pulled out the memory stick. "No problem at all," she said while slipping the small device into her pocket. She'd stopped by her apartment to get dressed for the meeting. Her black jeans, black silk shirt, and black ankle boots had looked professional when she headed to Desire, but compared to Holden, she felt shoddy.

A charcoal suit jacket covered broad shoulders. The garment looked expensive and obviously tailor-made. The color highlighted Holden's silver-blond hair and gunmetal eyes. He moved with catlike grace. Naya swallowed. His body language screamed predator. The man was over six feet, but still a little shorter than Leif.

Why she had to make that observation, she didn't know. She clamped down on any more thoughts of the Viking. She needed to focus on business.

Holden took a seat behind his desk.

Naya heard the door click closed and the lock turn. She turned.

An African American man, skin so dark it had a blue tint, blocked the exit. He assumed the standard bodyguard pose. Wide stance of the legs, arms in front of his body, one hand gripping the other wrist, eyes straight ahead. Not looking at anything, but seeing everything.

She recognized him as the same man that had guarded the door last time. "Hello, Rex," she said and hid a chuckle when she saw the black man's eyebrows rise. She turned back around.

Holden watched her with hooded eyes. "You remember my bodyguard's name?"

"You hired me to look over your security. It's my job to know your team."

Something like respect flickered in his eyes.

She pulled a binder from her bag. "Here are the schematics and plans for the club's proposed security upgrade. I also recommend that you hire me, or someone like me, to integrate your home into the plan."

"Why do you think I need extensive security at my house?"

"Anybody who wants to protect his property to the extent that you do has enemies. They don't always attack during business hours."

Holden leaned back, placing one ankle over the other knee, and smoothed out an invisible wrinkle on his pant leg. His black Italian loafers gleamed. "And you want me to name them so you can safeguard me."

"Not at all. I don't need to know who they are. My job is to design a system that protects you from all your enemies." She flashed a smile. "Old and new."

Holden watched her for a moment. "I see." He reached for the binder and then leaned back again, turning the pages. "You could have couriered these plans over."

"You would have had to contact me with questions."

"Who else is on my team, Ms. Driscoll?"

Naya had given him the name on her driver's license. She recited the names of his other three bodyguards and considered mentioning the Glock he carried in a side holster under that impeccable suit, but refrained. Sometimes clients spooked when they found out exactly how much Naya learned about them.

"Why are your cameras three times as expensive as my other quotes?"

It didn't worry her that he had contacted other consultants. She was the best, and he could afford to pay for quality.

"The cameras I suggest have no indicator diodes and take high-resolution images under extremely low light conditions," she answered.

"They will be almost invisible," Holden said.

She nodded. "If you want to cut corners, you can always switch to regular cameras in the public areas."

"But you don't recommend that."

"I don't," she confirmed. "In my experience, the people you want filmed know how to avoid cameras."

"Impressive." Holden threw the binder on the desk. "Draw up plans for my house as well. When would you like to see it?"

"Email me the blueprints and we'll only have to meet there once, maybe twice, before my final estimate."

She stood.

Holden did as well. He reached out his hand. "Good to do business with you, Ms. Driscoll."

She shook his hand and walked toward the door. Rex slid out of her way. She grinned at him and was rewarded by a quick wink as he held the door open.

Naya took a taxi to the storefront she rented under another assumed name. She unlocked the door to the fake comic shop that never opened and walked through the dusty room until she reached the back. Walking down a set of stairs, she continued through an enormous basement, tunneling under three city blocks. At the end, she popped out in an apartment building.

She slipped out the back of the building and walked four more blocks, then through an alley and up a pair of back stairs. Once inside her apartment, she flipped all the locks and took a look at the footage her own security cameras had recorded while she was gone. There was nothing to see but the empty hallway outside her door.

Satisfied, she went into her bedroom and changed into yoga pants and a tank top. Irja had given her some tablets to counteract any reoccurrence of fever spikes. Like a malaria virus, the poison could lay dormant then attack again. Naya hoped it wouldn't. Sick didn't fit in with her lifestyle. Just thinking of how weak she'd been scared her.

She'd caught a ride with Irja, who had pressed hard for Naya to stay at the mansion. Or, at least tell Leif she was leaving. Technically, she could have worked on Holden's plans in the mansion, but she'd had to get out of there. Leif made her forget herself, and intimacy, physical or otherwise, was not something she could afford. She always disappointed people when they wanted to get closer.

Trust was the one thing Naya couldn't afford. It gave people too much power, and the Viking king already proved too strong of a lure.

When she first broke out of the lab, she'd worried

about her brother. Alone and anxious, she'd met Zack, a friend of a client. A few years older than her, successful and confident, he'd seduced her, and she'd been inexperienced enough to think sex meant love and that she could trust him.

One night, she forgot to be careful and had lifted his full entertainment system with an eighty-inch screen on top, one-handed, because she needed the other hand to fish out an earring. Zack had freaked. She didn't want to think about the ugly things he'd said.

Leif knew about her strength, but when he found out about her cognitive abilities, he'd also label her a freak.

Better to go back to quick and anonymous hookups.

Never mind that her encounter with the blond Viking had blown the lid off anything she'd experienced before. Her nipples tingled and a heaviness settled at the junction of her legs. She quickly ordered her hormones to stand down—not that they listened.

She sank cross-legged into the computer chair. She searched through the files she'd copied from the Vikings again and entered the license plate into her own search. Columns of numbers scrolled down the screen. After ten minutes and still no match, she yawned and stretched.

A muffled sound from the bedroom had her hyper alert. She looked for her gun and swore quietly when she realized she'd left it in her bedroom.

The hardwood floor felt cool against her feet as she crept to the bedroom. She stopped abruptly, one foot inside the doorway, and stared at the gun barrel aimed straight at her.

"Ms. Brisbane, I was starting to wonder if you would ever grace me with your presence." The handler's smile belied the hard glint in his eyes. "I figured you heard me breaking the window lock awhile ago." Dark purple bruises covered the skin just below his eyes and bled down over his nose where the color ended under a butterfly bandage.

Her elbow had done some serious damage to his face.

While that pleased her, she berated herself for being careless and not resetting the alarm and leaving her weapon in the bedroom. She stared at the man seated on her bed.

"No witty comeback for me today? I'm disappointed," he said.

Naya cocked her head. "Nice nose job."

His eyes narrowed and he stood. "The pain you caused is nothing compared to what will happen to you."

She needed to think. Even when she wasn't purging poison from her body, her reaction times were slower than a bullet. "I bet you say that to all the girls." She flipped her hair back and gave him a cocky grin.

His jaw clenched. "We don't have time for games, Ms. Brisbane. It is in your best interest to cooperate." He took a step forward.

Forget cooperation. She was going to make it as hard as possible for him to remove her from the apartment. She needed to disarm him first, and then she'd elbow him in the face again. "What is it you want?"

"What we've always wanted, you and your brother to return to the lab."

She laughed bitterly. "That's never going to happen."

The handler smiled coldly. "If I were you, I'd listen to the alternatives. How old are you now?"

"What the hell does that have to do with anything?"

He kept smiling.

She cursed inwardly and forced her heart rate to return to normal.

"According to our records, you'll be twenty-three in ten months."

"Then why the fuck did you ask?"

He tsked. "Your tendency of cursing when upset is most unbecoming." He sat down again.

She made a quick move to the right, but he immediately adjusted his aim.

"I'd be very happy to shoot you, Ms. Brisbane. My orders are only to bring you back alive." His eyes roamed from her feet up her body. "And my tastes are eclectic; they don't require your consciousness."

She struggled not to shudder. "Your threats are disgusting and unoriginal."

He laughed again. "I like your spirit. It will be a pleasure to break it." He jerked the gun in the direction of the armchair by her window. "Have a seat, please."

Gritting her teeth, she sidled over to the chair and sat down.

"Good girl. As I was saying, you are getting close to your twenty-third birthday. The day when all hell breaks loose in your delectable little body."

"What are you talking about?" She forced herself not to include any curse words. It was hard.

"The chemicals in your bloodstream are tiny ticking time bombs." He wagged his finger back and forth. "Tick, tock, tick, tock."

She wanted to rip that finger off and shove it up his broken nose. "And why would this make me want to go with you?"

"We have the antidote that will shut off the clock. Without it, you'll turn into a raging monster in just about ten months."

"And why should I believe you?" She studied her nails. "You could be making up this entire thing."

"You can't really afford not to. Without the antidote, you'll most likely go on a murdering spree before the fever will literally cook you from the inside out."

"Injecting your designer soldiers with something deadly is counterproductive."

He looked away and brushed some invisible lint off his pants. "Let's just call it a design flaw in your generation." He looked at her. "The new soldiers do not have these...side effects."

New ones.

They were still making people like her. She'd been naive to think she'd prevented that with one explosion. She swallowed hard. "How many of us are there?"

"You'll find out when we get back to headquarters."

"Are the new generation those black-eyed monsters?" She forced her tone to remain light as she pretended deeper interest in her cuticles. When he didn't answer, she looked up.

Eerie green eyes studied her coldly. "When did you see the wolverines?"

"None of your business." Ice spread through her veins. If he knew what they were, they must be linked to the lab.

His smile was pure predator, shiny teeth and dead eyes. "Oh, but it is my business. They have orders to bring you back."

He stood abruptly, the gun still aimed at her. "My

superiors will be very interested to hear about your run-in with our new creations."

So there it was. The program now experimented on nonhuman creatures. Bile rose in her throat, but she forced it down. "I'm still not going with you."

He pretended surprise, widening his eyes. "I thought the gun made a strong argument. As I said, I don't really care which condition you are in when I drag you back."

She laughed bitterly. "I don't really care if I live or die."

His eyes glittered. "Do you care if your brother lives or dies?"

She clenched her hands. "You will never get to Scott."

"You'll lead us to him if you want him to stay alive." The handler sighed. "We both know the outcome of this situation."

"Do we?" she said, forcing calm into her voice.

"Get your ass out of the chair. We're going—now."

So, Mr. Nice Guy was gone. Shit. She was running out of options. "Can I at least put on shoes?" Maybe she could strike when she stood up after tying them.

"You won't need those."

She studied him for a moment. If they went outside, she'd have more room to maneuver. She'd kick the gun out of his hand then.

As they stepped on the hot asphalt, she made a point of flinching when her bare feet touched the pavement.

The agent gave her a hard push. He had taken off his jacket to cover the gun and had a loose grip on her arm.

She pulled her arm back, positioning her feet to pivot and kick. Before she had a chance to execute, a dark sedan pulled up. A gun barrel glittered in the open passenger window.

She couldn't get into that car, but she also needed to stay alive for Scotty.

Concentrating on the new threat, she prepared to get her one hit, and then she needed to make a run for it.

The pinprick in her shoulder took her by surprise. She saw the satisfied grin on the agent's face before her vision blurred. She snarled and lunged for him, but her legs and arms flopped like overcooked noodles.

The handler looped her arm around his neck and half carried her to the car as the other man got out and held the door open.

She slid down onto the floor in the backseat. She tried to speak, but her lips wouldn't form words.

In the front seat, the man from her apartment turned to look at her. "Just relax now, Ms. Brisbane. We have a couple of hours before it's time for your next injection. I want you calm but conscious when we stop for the night."

Naya silently vowed he'd never get her calm enough for what he had in mind.

Inertia propelled her backward as the car sped up. Her hand fell against the shape of her cell phone in her jeans pocket.

Sweat broke out on her forehead as she forced muscles to cooperate. Finally, she slid the phone out. Mustering all her willpower, she turned to shield the phone from the handlers' view.

Squinting at the display, she scrolled down the numbers and pushed the dial button.

Chapter 10

LEIF PINCHED THE BRIDGE OF HIS NOSE AS THE CHAOS of his warriors arguing engulfed him. They had been discussing things fairly peacefully until Harald threw out, "Someone in here is passing information to the wolverine freaks. And I'm going to kill the bastard." He'd then looked straight at Irja, who'd stared back, chin raised, while everyone else shouted at the top of their lungs.

Irja stood in the farthest corner of the room, hugging herself tightly.

Sten and Torvald took turns yelling at Harald.

Leif bellowed, "Silence!" Quiet spread through the room as his troop one by one turned toward him. "We're getting nowhere with baseless accusations. Rein in the tempers before your berserkers respond to the adrenaline rush."

"Can you blame us, *min kung*?" Astrid's cheeks flamed red. "Your *stallare* just accused us of being traitors." She threw Harald a dark look.

"We're all chosen by Odin and Freya," Sten interjected. "The gods wouldn't send a traitor to Midgard." He looked around the room for support.

"Maybe they can't recognize a traitor," Harald said, looking first at Astrid before addressing Sten. "They still allow Loki among the gods. That bastard's evil schemes go unchecked. What makes you think they'd be able to spot dishonesty among our warriors?"

"You would get away with a lot too, if you saved Odin's wife," Torvald spat at Harald.

"Silence!" Leif shouted. "For once in your life, use what's inside your thick skulls instead of just bashing them together."

After some scattered muttering, his warriors quieted down.

He glanced at Irja. If possible she'd shrunk further into herself, staring at the floor.

"Somehow, Loki's creatures knew exactly where I would be when they attacked in the alley. They also knew exactly where Per would be when he went to collect the weapons."

"They could only know those locations if someone revealed the details," Harald insisted, face flushed.

"I was the only one at the house when Leif went out," Irja said quietly.

Everyone turned to look at her. She didn't meet anyone's eyes.

Leif sighed. He knew she hadn't betrayed him, but how he would prove her innocence he didn't know.

"So?" Astrid finally said. "That doesn't mean it had to be you who told the wolverines. Any of us could have been watching the house and told them when Leif left."

Irja looked up, surprise clearly visible in her eyes.

Astrid smiled encouragingly at Irja, and then threw Harald a dirty look.

The big Viking's face was red, but he kept quiet.

"But that was one of the few nights we actually paired up for patrol," Sten said.

"Doesn't mean you couldn't have hired someone to

watch the house," Torvald countered. "Or maybe there are two traitors, working together."

"Anyone not a Norse warrior would have triggered the enchantments," Irja interjected.

Leif winced. Why would she make things worse for herself?

"Not if they were watching the end of the road," Torvald said stubbornly. "Someone devious enough to betray our king would be smart enough to delegate the dirty work."

Harald squared his shoulders. "Fine. But how would they find the road?"

"You're right. They wouldn't." Torvald frowned. "Even if they were outside the reach of the enchantments, we would still notice someone watching the road. The area is too isolated for anyone to set up a surveillance spot without calling attention to themselves."

And they were back to square one, unless there were two traitors. Leif didn't want to contemplate the possibility.

The warriors mumbled among each other again.

Before he had a chance to add anything to the discussion, his cell phone rang. Puzzled, he pulled it out of his pocket. Unknown number.

"Yes."

"Help… Please…"

He strained his ears to make out the voice. "Naya? Where are you?" He tried to tap into the emotional connection he'd felt when she passed out in the lab. Nothing. *Shit.*

He listened closely for any sound that hinted where she might be. All he heard was humming. Engine noise? Voices spoke in the background. Male.

The berserker's fury rose in his chest. Someone had taken his woman. He met Harald's worried gaze. "We need to find her," Leif said.

His *stallare* gave a short nod and turned to the others. "You heard the king. Find Naya."

Ulf stepped forward. "If you keep the line open, I can trace her."

Phone in hand, Leif quickly followed Ulf to the tech room.

Ulf threw himself in front of the monitor and started typing. "Naya showed me how to trace cell phones using both GPS signals and cell phone tower connections before she left."

"Just do it," Leif said.

The younger warrior nodded and continued hitting the keyboard as window after window flitted on the screen. A few minutes later, Ulf stopped. A blinking red circle moved along the highway map, heading east out of town. "That's her," he said. "As long as the phone stays on, I'll be able to trace the signal."

"Find Harald," Leif said. "I'm going to go get her."

"My king," Ulf interjected, "you should remain safe by using your warriors for this mission." Heat flushed his cheeks. "You could keep an eye on the signal for us."

Leif silenced him with one look. *His* woman. *His* fight. His berserker howled.

Without looking at Ulf again, Leif strode out the door. In the hallway, Harald held out a Glock. Leif holstered the weapon and nodded at his friend. Walking side by side, they left the fortress through the main door.

Dressed in black leather, helmets in hand, Sten and

Astrid waited beside two black Kawasaki ZX-14Rs and a silver Porsche Boxster-S.

Leif stopped by the motorcycles, but Harald nudged him on.

"I understand you want in on the action, but the front line is too dangerous." He glared at Leif.

Leif refrained from arguing only because it would take up time. Nodding to the other two warriors, he slid into the passenger seat of the silver sports car.

As Harald took the driver seat, Astrid and Sten mounted their motorcycles, and then shot down the driveway at full speed.

"I've linked the car's cell communications and the motorcyclists' helmets with me on this four-way call," Ulf's voice said through the car speakers.

Harald started the car and they accelerated out the gates behind the two Kawasakis.

"Not so tough now, are you, kitten?" The man with the broken nose laughed at Naya from the passenger seat. "The boss isn't going to believe how easy you were to capture."

On the floor, Naya ignored him and concentrated on staying conscious. She really couldn't move. Every attempt to crawl up on the backseat ended in a painful slide back down. But she'd get the bastard when he tried to inject her again. Eventually they would have to stop for something. Gas or food, she didn't care, but she'd get away then.

"The boss won't like that she met the wolverines and managed to get away," the driver said.

"Shut up," the first handler barked. "We'll talk about that later."

"I'm just saying that Dr. Trousil's client is going to be pissed. We promised him the wolverines would capture her. He's paid a lot of money for them."

The man in the passenger seat slapped the driver in the back of the head. "Shut your mouth, or I will shut it for you."

Naya lost track of their argument. She tried to lift her head and keep her attention on the men, but her eyes refused to focus. The seat bulged in and out, as if reflected in a fun-house mirror.

"We'll have some fun with you tonight." Broken Nose leered at her.

She shut out the man's voice. Had to stay focused. The phone she'd shoved under the backseat glinted in a beam of sunlight streaming through the back window. Leif. She'd called Leif. She'd never asked for help before.

Naya smiled bitterly. She could use a warrior king right now, even a delusional one.

Leif stared straight ahead as Harald weaved the Porsche in and out of the traffic on the interstate.

In a synchronized dance, Astrid and Sten streaked well ahead of the sports car, switching lanes back and forth as they zipped past the cars and followed Ulf's directions.

It sucked not being in the lead.

"You should be close now," Ulf said through the car's speakerphone. "Your signal is almost on top of hers."

"Car's in sight," Astrid's voice crackled over the line. "I see a dark sedan with government plates up ahead." She read them the license plate number.

Ulf's voice transmitted clearly across the line. "That's the same car that picked up the guy at the bus stop after Naya broke his nose."

"Moving in for a closer look," Astrid said as one of the motorcycles peeled ahead, gaining on the sedan.

——∿∿∿——

Angry voices argued in the front seat. Naya tuned in to see what had changed.

"Just outrun them for God's sake."

"I'm flooring this car as fast as it will go. Those bike engines can outrun this car."

"They're on two crotch-rockets, just run them off the road."

"Shut up."

The whining of motorcycle engines approaching reached Naya's ears. *Cops?*

She craned her neck to look through the window. An alien with a disproportionately big head peered back at her. She shook her head to clear her vision.

The alien raised a hand in greeting.

She tried to wave back, but managed only a weak flop.

——∿∿∿——

Leif willed the sports car to go faster.

"She's in the back!" Astrid shouted. "On the floor and looks to be okay. She just waved."

Leif let out a breath he didn't know he'd been holding. He turned to Harald. "I want these bastards."

Harald responded by pressing down on the gas pedal. The car shot forward, engine thrusting harder.

"They're exiting," Sten said. "They're trying to shake us."

Astrid's war cry echoed through the car's speakers. She was always the first to catch battle fever.

Leif's berserker needed to see Naya alive and he needed to fight—to kill—those who had taken her.

"What exit?" Harald shouted. "Never mind, I see you." He switched lanes and followed the two motorcycles down the exit ramp.

They bounced down a barely paved country road. Astrid and Sten zigzagged behind the car, each switch bringing them closer to their prey. Finally, they both shot up on opposite sides of the car.

The sedan swerved, but before long, the bikes forced the car to the shoulder. The back wheels lost traction in the gravel and the sedan fishtailed.

Astrid and Sten whizzed back and forth like maniacal bees.

Astrid's laughter crackled over the line.

Sten whooped a happy war cry.

"Careful!" Leif shouted. "Naya is in the back." He watched in horror as the car swerved again, and then careened off the road.

It skipped through a bumpy field before hitting a large boulder. Metal groaned as the hood scrunched up like an accordion. Astrid and Sten pulled up just behind the crashed car and dismounted their bikes.

Leif threw himself out the door before Harald had completely stopped the Porsche. He ran across the field, reaching the driver's side first.

The door opened. A man staggered out. Leif didn't bother asking any questions. With a quick twist, he broke the man's neck and shoved the lifeless body out of the way without a second look.

Blind to anything but reaching Naya, Leif tore open the backseat door. She lay on the floor, her eyes closed. He reached for her. Before his hands touched her sweet skin, her limp body was pulled through to the front seat.

A man with bruises under his eyes held her in a choke hold, a gun pressed to her temple. "Slow down, big guy. The lady and I haven't finished our conversation."

Leif cursed his berserker for reacting on instinct and not noticing the second person in the car. He forced his body still, focusing on the arm around Naya's neck. Battle fever surged like hot lava through his veins.

"Stay the fuck away from me." The man kept the gun pressed to Naya's head while he reached behind and opened the door. Repositioning his grip, he slid out of the car, dragging Naya with him. "Call off the others or I blow her brains out."

Leif slid across the mangled hood. "Why do you want her?" He held up his hands as the other Vikings advanced.

They stopped but bounced on the balls of their feet, arms hanging loosely by their sides. A dagger glinted in Astrid's hand.

The man smirked. "She belongs to us. We made her." He shook her.

Astrid took a step forward, raising her weapon.

The man twisted around and shouted, "Stay back or I terminate this bitch permanently." He edged toward the Porsche. "Who has the keys?"

Nobody answered him.

"Give me the fucking keys!" he shouted, hysteria creeping into his voice.

Harald held up his key ring. "These what you want?" He threw them on the ground, away from Naya and the man.

"That was stupid." His finger tightened on the trigger.

"No!" Leif shouted. "I'll give you the keys." Holding up his hands, he walked over and carefully picked up the keys. "See, here they are."

"Nice and steady, walk them over to me," the man said.

Leif kept his eyes on Naya as he approached. She opened her eyes, looked straight at him, and closed them again. He kept the surprise from his expression as he held out the keys. "Don't hurt her."

The man frowned. To grab the keys, he would have to let go of Naya or the gun. "Start the car," he finally said.

Against every instinct, Leif did as he was told. His body shook with the effort of controlling the berserker.

"Get out."

Leif exited the car, breathing deeply to hold back the battle fever. His inner warrior wanted to tear the enemy into pieces. Tiny, tiny, bloody pieces.

The man dragged Naya to the car and stuffed her in the front seat. "Nobody move." Training the gun on Leif, he walked around to the driver's side.

Out of the corner of his eye, Leif saw Naya slowly twist in the seat. The man would hear her if he didn't do something. "Let her go and we'll leave you alone." He banged his fist on the hood.

The man laughed. "If I return without her, I might as well be dead."

Naya slowly raised her legs.

The man turned around to sit down in the driver seat.

Swiftly, Naya kicked him in the head with both feet. As bones crunched, his body slumped to the ground.

With a battle cry, Astrid ran up and kicked him in the stomach, then the head.

The man wasn't moving. He never would again.

The Valkyrie still ran her dagger through his heart.

Sten pulled Astrid off the mangled body and then leaned down to retrieve the gun. "What do we do with the bodies?" he asked.

Leif didn't care. He ran around the car and opened the passenger side. Crouching down, he peered in at Naya. "You okay?" he asked in a low voice.

"I've been better," she said, her eyes unfocused. An indented ring decorated her temple where the muzzle had pressed against her skin.

He felt like walking over to the bastard on the ground and kicking him one more time just for good measure. Instead he lifted a hand and gently caressed her temple.

She flinched, but held still as he touched her skin, brushing a few strands of hair away and tucking them behind her ear.

"I'm sorry it took me so long to find you," he said.

"Your timing was perfect." She smiled, and then leaned back into the leather seat, sighing contentedly. "Bitchin' bikes," she mumbled. Her body relaxed and her breathing deepened.

Naya stretched in the chair in front of her beloved desk. After the kidnapping, Leif had informed her she was moving in with him and the rest of the crew.

On principle, she'd protested—for about a minute. When the Vikings moved her furniture from her apartment into this room, she knew protest was pointless.

Living in the mansion meant she didn't have to find a new place to live. Irja's research on the wolverines might also shed some light on Scott's condition. Naya just had to make sure she kept her connection with the wolverines a secret for as long as she could. Plus, the house was basically a freaking fortress out in the middle of nowhere. The security systems could use some upgrades, but overall she felt safer than she had in years. She'd be able to finish Holden's contract with relative ease before she moved on to a new city. She'd already ordered the hardware she needed for the club. Another day or two and she'd visit his house to finalize those plans as well.

Her irritating internal voice whispered that the close proximity to one blond Viking king had other perks, but she squelched it. As much as feeling like she belonged filled her with joy and ease, her main priority was her brother. Nothing else could matter.

Naya rose and stretched some more. She'd been at the computer for five hours straight. Time to find something to eat.

She made her way downstairs and stopped in the kitchen doorway, watching Leif as he munched on a sandwich at the table. His gray long-sleeved T-shirt stretched across broad shoulders and outlined his pecs through the cotton. A scrap of leather tied back his blond hair.

He swallowed, raised a glass of milk, took a big gulp, and then grinned at her.

Her breath caught. Those dimples and milk mustache should come with a warning. He was hot and cute all at the same time. She tried to ignore the heat rushing through her body and the way her nipples tightened.

His smile widened, as if he knew how her body reacted to him. "I just made a huge roast beef sandwich. Want half?"

"Sure." She sat down across from him, reaching for the offered plate without meeting his gaze. Heat trailed along her nerves as his eyes assessed her. When the silence stretched to the point of awkwardness, she looked up. "What?"

"Are you ready to talk about those men?" His eyes were solemn.

She'd put him off all day, explaining that she was tired or busy or couldn't remember much. But she owed him an explanation.

He reached across the table and rested his hand over hers. "Look, you don't have to tell me if you don't want to. But I do want to reassure you that you're safe here."

She was afraid of them coming after her again, but even more scared of Leif looking at her differently. Right now his gaze said she was someone he liked. Compassion reflected in his clear light-blue eyes. Naya didn't want that to change.

What would happen when Leif figured out she and the wolverines shared a creator? When he realized she might be a threat and he couldn't trust her around his people?

She took a deep breath. "I didn't grow up like most people."

He quirked an eyebrow. "How do most people grow up?"

"You know, staying long enough in one place to go to school and maybe make some friends." She slowly drew her hand out from under his and traced a crack in the table with a finger. "We moved around a lot. We'd just pack up in the middle of the night and go somewhere new. Dad used to call it 'going on an adventure.'" She dared a quick glance.

He was watching with calm eyes.

"What I didn't know was that we weren't just moving, we were escaping. When I was twelve, we didn't escape quickly enough." A chill rippled down her spine. She pulled her arms closer, hugging herself.

He got up and sat down on the chair next to hers. He didn't touch her. She leaned into him.

"Men came to our house. They had guns. They made a huge mess, rifling through our things. I hid under the stairs. They found me and dragged me into the living room. My parents were on the sofa. Mom was crying." Naya had to stop and breathe. Furiously she blinked to clear the moisture in her eyes. Her brother had been under the stairs with her, but there was no need to tell Leif about him.

Keep it simple. Keep Scott safe.

Leif slipped his arm around her shoulders without moving any closer. Just a comforting gesture that still gave her space.

"Dad looked at me with such sadness in his eyes. He kept saying he was sorry. I didn't understand what for. Then the men dragged me away. Mom screamed. Dad shouted 'no' over and over again." She stopped.

Leif squeezed her shoulder and pulled her closer. "Take your time." His voice vibrated deep in his chest as she leaned against him.

"Mom ran after me and grabbed the man holding me. He hit her face so hard, her nose started bleeding." Tears trickled down Naya's cheeks. Impatiently she wiped them away with the back of her hand. "Another man shot her between her eyes." She swallowed.

"It's all right," Leif said. "I got you. You don't have to say any more." He tightened his hold.

"No, I want to." Naya snuggled closer. "Dad came running out of the house. He looked right at me, screaming my name. They shot him in the back of the head." She closed her eyes against the memory, the shot and Scott's screams ringing loudly in her ears.

Leif hooked his arms under her knees and pulled her into his lap.

The steady heartbeat against her cheek gave her courage. She needed it to get through this part. "I spent the next ten years in captivity at some sort of pseudo military camp. They injected me with enhancement drugs and trained me on weapons and computers."

Leif said nothing, but tightened his arms around her.

He smelled of fresh air, clean, and something uniquely him, something male and vaguely spicy. "The reason I am stronger and faster than most humans is because I'm filled with weird chemicals. A killing machine. A super-soldier." She waited for him to say something. Anything.

She couldn't look at him. The disgust in his eyes would kill her.

His strong hand cradled her chin, forcing her to look into his eyes. "I'm so sorry about your parents."

She searched for horror in his gaze, but found only sorrow and compassion.

"Those men who abducted you today, they were from this camp?"

Swallowing to get rid of the lump in her throat, she nodded. "They've been hunting me since I escaped."

"How have you avoided them until now?"

"I keep a low profile."

"Naya"—he made her look at him again—"how long have you been on the run?"

"A little over a year."

Leif cursed under his breath. It wasn't in English. His lips brushed against hers. "You are safe now. I will protect you."

She wished the kiss had been longer. When she was in this man's arms, she wanted dangerous things, impossible things. "Thank you. But I will only need to impose on you for a week, two at the most. Then I'll be able to free up funds and move on." Far enough to where he couldn't find her once he figured out that she and the wolverines were spawned by the same devils.

A muscle on the side of his jaw twitched. "There's no need for you to leave." Leif growled fiercely. "You'll stay with us."

"I'll stay for a while, but then I will have to go," she said slowly. Even if it took Leif a while to figure out the connection between her and the wolverines, there was still the ticking time bomb that the handler told her about. She might be a threat to Leif and his people.

Leif's eyes bored into hers. "You have to stay here."

She bristled. "Nobody tells me what to do. Not even a king."

He breathed deeply and unclenched his fist. Slowly. "Of course. I wouldn't force you to do anything you don't want to do." He slid her off his lap, stood up, and walked out of the kitchen without looking at her. "I need to talk to Harald about this."

She stared after his retreating back. That was so not the reaction she had expected.

Chapter 11

NAYA SEARCHED THE FORTRESS FOR IRJA. SHE IGNORED the guilt eating her for not coming clean with Leif about the connection between the wolverines and the lab. If Irja could find something medical that Dr. Rosen had missed, she'd gladly tell the Norse warriors everything she knew. And then hightail it out of there before the Vikings killed her. Until then, she had to keep anything that might alienate her from them a secret.

She found the dark-haired Valkyrie in the medical lab, elbows deep in test tubes and pipettes.

Irja turned and smiled when she saw Naya. "Are you settling in okay?"

"I'm only staying for a little while." After Leif's freak-out, Naya thought it best to mention a time limit.

Irja looked disappointed. "Oh, you're not happy?"

"It's not a matter of being happy. I just need my own place."

"Why?"

"I can't really mooch off you guys for the rest of my life."

"That's not how it would be." Irja frowned.

How had the conversation gotten off track so quickly? Naya rotated her shoulders. They were still stiff after her kidnapping adventure. "I think maybe we should drop this topic."

"I don't want to drop it." Irja's face was stubborn.

"Is that how you see the rest of us? 'Mooching' off Leif, our king?"

Great, now she'd managed to offend the one person who felt like a friend. Well, what she imagined friendship felt like. "No of course not. You guys are like family to him."

"You are now family too." Irja's dark eyes were solemn.

Naya had to swallow past the lump that unexpectedly filled her throat. "You hardly know me." It had been so long since there had been anyone to care for other than Scott.

"That's not important. What's important is that you are one of us." Irja took a step closer.

"When did I become one of you?" This was happening a little too fast. Why did both Irja and Leif insist that she stay? What was their agenda?

Irja opened her mouth and then closed it. "Never mind. Our king has accepted you and that means we accept you."

She ignored the happy flutters in her stomach caused by those words. "Leif decides what all of you should do?"

Irja looked surprised. "Of course. He's our leader, approved by Odin."

"Odin?"

"The ruler of Valhalla."

"Ah." It was as if she'd landed in an episode of a game show where everyone but her knew the rules. And the answers.

"Didn't Leif explain all of this to you?"

"Not exactly," Naya said.

Irja loaded some test tubes into a centrifuge. "What can I help you with? Or did you come to keep me company?"

Naya felt guilty for wanting something other than a visit. "A little of both," she said, sitting on a stool. "Did you find out anything else about my blood?"

Irja frowned. "Leif said you didn't want me to run any more tests."

"You stopped investigating the blood because I asked you to?"

"Of course."

Naya didn't know what to say. She'd assumed Irja would continue doing the research. "Thank you for that."

The other woman nodded. "Do you want me to look for something specific?"

Naya smiled, appreciating Irja's way of cutting to the chase. "My blood is contaminated with chemicals. I would like to know what they are and how they function."

"What effects have you noticed so far?" Irja reached for a pen and pad of paper, then calmly looked at Naya as if they were discussing where to go to lunch.

Naya hesitated. If Irja could help Scott, it was worth the risk. But how far could she trust her? What would happen when the Valkyrie got around to investigating the wolverine blood?

"I am much stronger and faster than a normal human. I also heal abnormally fast."

Irja nodded. "I knew this already. Your body purged the poison as well as Leif's. A regular human would have died from the dose you received."

"Leif didn't die."

Her hand stilled mid-sentence. "Leif is not a regular human."

"Do all of you heal as quickly as Leif?" Naya watched

Irja's face closely to detect any facial twitches indicating a lie.

"We do." Irja's face gave nothing away. "But we are not like you. Nothing was added to our blood." Irja sighed. "It is not my place to tell you this."

"I know, Leif is supposed to discuss this with me." Naya jumped off her stool. "But he seems a little agitated at the moment. Why don't you tell me who you people are?"

Irja held up a hand. "I've already said too much. Let's get back to your blood enhancements."

Naya opened her mouth to protest.

The other woman shook her head, and then looked down at the pad. "I don't think what you have described could be caused by just one drug." She looked pensive.

"I don't know how many different kinds of drugs there are in my system."

Irja nodded. "Your blood definitely does not function like regular human blood. At first I thought it was a by-product of the poison you'd received."

"I don't know very much about the poison." How much had Irja found out about Naya's weird abilities?

"It's derived from plants and shuts down the circulatory system. You should have died, but your body fought the effects. Maybe because of these added chemicals."

"Is there any way you can find out exactly what's in my blood and how to remove it?"

Irja thought for a moment. "I'm not sure. Why would you want to eliminate it if it is to your advantage?"

Naya wouldn't meet her gaze. "I don't know what the long-term effects are."

Irja nodded. "One day, I hope you trust me enough to tell me how you received this anomaly."

Naya paused and then decided it was worth the risk to share a little about Scott. "My brother grew up in the lab too. His blood is probably also filled with nanoparticles."

Irja's hands stilled. "You have a brother." She kept her head down. "Are you close?"

"After my parents died, I took care of him. Scott is two years younger." She hesitated; she hadn't meant for his name to slip out. Irja's quietness, her stillness, made you want to share things. "He's not well."

Irja looked up. Sadness flickered in her eyes. "What's wrong with him?"

"The super-freak injections fried his central nervous system." She had to be careful not to give too much away. "He's not coherent and doesn't respond to anyone, or anything."

Irja touched her arm. "I'm so sorry." She pulled back, studying Naya intently. "This is why you want me to test your blood. You want to diagnose your brother's illness."

There was no need to deny it now. She nodded.

"Where is he?"

Naya gazed into Irja's eyes a little longer before answering. Understanding and compassion flickered in their dark depth, and something else. Despair?

She looked away. "I can't tell you. The people who kidnapped me are hunting him too."

Disappointment pulled Irja's lips into a frown. "One day you will trust me, but I understand. I had a brother."

"Had?" Strangely, this surprising revelation eased a hardness in Naya's chest.

Irja avoided her eyes. "He went out to battle and didn't come back." She gave Naya a sad smile. "You're one of us now, but I don't speak about my brother to anyone."

"What do you mean I'm one of you? Because my blood cells have been altered?"

The Valkyrie frowned. "No, because you are bonded to Leif."

Naya snorted. "I barely know him." *But you do have feelings for him.* She blushed when she thought about what had happened in his office.

"You will both get to know each other, which will bring love. And peace and contentment." A secret smile pulled at Irja's lips.

Naya decided not to comment. Let Irja believe in fairy tales if she wanted to. "When do you think you'll know more about the contamination of my blood?"

"I wouldn't call being stronger and more likely to survive a contamination." Irja stood. "I'll get to work right away. I might need some more blood from you later."

Naya nodded and left the lab. Strange how comfortable she felt around Irja. She had never had a girlfriend, or any real friend for that matter. The only person she'd ever been close to was Scott. Her family had never stayed long enough in one place for her to make friends.

Back in the main house, she poked her head through various doors, trying to find Leif. In the game room, Ulf and Sten played some kind of car racing game on the big-screen TV while Astrid watched.

When she saw Naya, she sprung up from her lounging position on the couch. "Why don't you join us?"

"I'm looking for Leif." The tall blond Valkyrie made Naya nervous. She was too full of energy.

"He and Harald are yelling at each other in his office. Give them some time to simmer down." She held up a bottle. "Beer?"

Naya hesitated. They all seemed nice, and they had saved her life. But she lacked the chatting gene. Things got awkward when she tried to be social.

"Come on." Astrid gestured toward the two men. "Don't leave me alone with these bozos."

Right then, Sten let out a howl when Ulf's racer forced his car off the road. "That's not fair."

"Didn't your mother teach you life isn't fair?" Ulf countered.

"She was too busy consoling your mother over having delivered a bastard," Sten countered.

Astrid turned to Naya. "See what I mean?"

"I'll join you for a drink." It couldn't hurt to stall a little longer. She preferred a calm version of Leif when she saw him next.

"Excellent." The tall blond strode over to a mini-fridge. Pulling out a bottle, she popped the cap in a bottle opener attached to the wall. "*Skål*," she said as she handed Naya the beer.

"What language is that?"

"Swedish. It means cheers."

"You and Leif speak the same language?"

"Pretty much," Astrid said. "All of the Nordic languages are close. Icelandic is a little different, but I can usually understand people from there."

"But you mostly speak English when you are together?"

Astrid hesitated. "It's quicker that way. No room for misunderstandings."

"I don't understand," Naya said.

Astrid took a sip of her beer before answering. "The word *rolig*, for example. In Swedish it means funny. In Danish it means easy or calm."

That would complicate things if you were fighting together or trying to pass on information quickly. Naya studied the woman beside her—the long, straight blond hair and high cheekbones. Astrid could be any age between twenty and forty. Her face was wrinkle free with a smattering of freckles across her nose. She held herself with a dignity most women didn't acquire until well into their forties.

Naya curled her legs underneath her on the couch, enviously checking out Astrid's long jeans-clad legs stretched out in front of her. Even dressed casually in a plain T-shirt, her curves showed how much of a woman she was.

Compared to Astrid's womanly shape, Naya had the body of a girl. She cleared her throat when Astrid gave her a funny look. "How long have you and Leif known each other?" Naya didn't know why the thought of Leif with this tall, gorgeous blond bothered her, but it did. They made a striking couple with the same icy Scandinavian features and matching heights.

"Quite some time now," Astrid answered. "Why?"

Naya avoided her gaze. "I was just wondering why he doesn't have a girlfriend."

"A girlfriend?" Astrid's tone was sarcastic. "When would he have time to find a girlfriend? He's the king."

"Doesn't the king need a queen?" An alien zombie queen.

Astrid gave her a funny look. "Maybe, but that's a big decision."

"He had a wife," Ulf interjected.

Astrid swore loudly.

Ulf turned away from the game, throwing Astrid a perplexed look.

"What happened?" Naya asked, ignoring Astrid and Ulf grimacing at each other.

"She was killed," Ulf said.

"Together with their five-year-old twins," Sten volunteered.

"That's awful." Naya's heart ached for Leif. "How did it happen?"

"There was a raid on his village while he was... traveling overseas," Sten said without looking up from the screen.

"That was all a very long time ago," said Astrid. "Besides, he wasn't king then."

"Sure," Ulf said, "but he's not likely to get married again. He takes his duties too seriously. A wife would get in the way."

The words depressed Naya more than she wanted to admit. She told herself it was because of the tragedy of Leif losing his wife and children at the same time. Not because she wanted her relationship with Leif to develop into something more than just sex.

Liar.

She ignored her annoying inner voice.

Astrid interrupted her thoughts. "You two are blabbering on like idiots. Show your king some respect."

"We're not saying anything everyone doesn't already know," Sten said, but reddened a little when he looked at Naya. "Well, at least they would find out soon."

A scowl darkened Astrid's face.

"He's not getting married again," Ulf said, turning back to the TV screen.

Astrid stood, lobbing her bottle at him. Ulf yelped when it bounced off his shoulder.

"Nice shot," Sten said.

"I was aiming for his head." Astrid walked out of the room, clenching her fists.

Naya watched the tall woman leave. Was Astrid holding out for Leif? She didn't blame her. He was protective, incredibly hot, as well as charming, when he wanted to be. She frowned at the bottle in her hand. With Astrid as the competition, she might as well give up.

Whoa, where did that thought come from? She didn't want Leif.

Liar, liar—

She was only here to finish her contract, and then she'd be on her way to Colorado. Hopefully with results from Irja that would help Dr. Rosen treat Scott.

Besides, Leif had been married. He'd had kids. She finished her beer and threw the bottle in a recycling bin next to the fridge. Enough mooning over the sexy Viking king. She should get back to reality and finish Holden's plans and prepare for their meeting.

Pushing aside thoughts of Leif and how he made her body tingle, she mentally reviewed the security blueprints as she walked back to her room. The details blurred as her thoughts circled back to what she'd learned about Leif.

How could he not tell her he'd been married? Even if she hadn't shared everything with him, she had told him about her parents. She'd opened up, and yet he had shared nothing.

She quickened her pace as she passed his office. Now was so not the time to run in to him. Her feelings were too raw.

Loud voices erupted from the slightly ajar door. Leif's low rumbling voice argued with Harald's booming timbre. She heard her name and slowed.

"Be reasonable," Harald said. "You have only known Naya for a short time."

Anger rose in her body, heating her skin. Leif better not share any of her personal details with Harald. She pushed on the office door a little harder than she'd intended. It hit the wall with a bang.

The men turned in unison.

"If you have anything to ask me, do so in person instead of gossiping behind my back."

Leif couldn't help the smile tugging at his lips. Naya stood in the doorway, fists on hips, glowering. She might be small, but Naya was magnificent. She reminded him of a Valkyrie. Not in stature, but in spirit. She possessed the same temper and the same courage.

His berserker had chosen well.

His marshal stuttered as he tried to deny they'd just been talking about the angry dark beauty. "*Nej*, we were discussing security logistics."

"What kind of logistics?" Naya tilted her head, a suspicious frown on her brow.

Harald looked at Leif, a panicked plea for help in his eyes.

Leif shrugged and covered a cough with his hand to hide a grin.

His friend cleared his throat several times. "We have a leak in the team."

"How do you know?" Naya walked farther into the room, closing the door behind her. She strode confidently across the room and sat down in one of the chairs.

Leif took pity on his *stallare* when Harald gave him another desperate look. "The only way the wolverine creatures could know exactly where Per and I would be on the nights we were attacked is if someone told them about our plans." He sat on the edge of the desk.

Naya leaned forward as if he'd pulled on an invisible string. "Maybe they have you under surveillance."

Harald jerked. "What do you mean?"

Naya shrugged slim shoulders. "Did you have any repairmen in the house lately? Any deliverymen skulking around? They could easily have planted a bug."

"We don't get deliveries and we do our own repairs," Leif said. "There's no way anybody could plant a bug in this place. No strangers are ever allowed in the house."

Harald cringed.

"What?" Leif asked.

His friend looked away. "There was a problem with the network access that neither Ulf nor I could fix. We had to bring in a serviceman from the Internet provider."

Naya snorted.

Both men turned toward her. Leif raised his eyebrows.

She waved her hand. "That's the oldest trick in the book. Jam the network signal to get the target to call for service. Then intercept the van before it arrives at the house. Used to be done with phone lines before the web." She shrugged her shoulders. "The guy who came didn't repair anything. He just unblocked the signal when he was done." She jumped out of the chair. "I'll go get some scanners."

Harald turned to Leif as Naya rushed out of the room, anguish in his eyes. "I've failed you, my king."

Leif stood and put a hand on his friend's shoulder. "Let's see if Naya finds anything before we assign blame."

"No." Harald took a step back so Leif's hand fell off his shoulder. "I've resisted technology and have become a liability. Security is my responsibility."

Leif slipped his hands into the pockets of his jeans. "The security of our people is my responsibility."

Harald shook his head. "No, my king. I should have known better—"

The door opened. "Could the two of you do that later?" Naya interrupted. "Your listeners are having a grand ol' time laughing their heads off right now." She handed a small black device to Harald. It looked like an old-school cell phone with a short thick antenna attached. "Help me with this."

The red-bearded Viking looked lost. "What is this?"

"A frequency scanner," Naya said, assembling another one. "The listening devices are most likely wireless. These scanners detect both digital and analog signals." She turned on her device, nodding at Harald to do the same. Several of the scanner's diodes started blinking.

Naya slowly walked around the room, sweeping the detector over bookcases and other furniture. Harald followed, mimicking her movements.

Leif watched, fascinated. The determination on Naya's face showed she was fully in her element. He loved how fierce she looked. *Wait, wrong word.* Any strong feelings he had were caused by his berserker being drawn to her. It had nothing to do with love.

He concentrated on Naya and Harald. They had reached his desk, both devices vibrating with an insistent buzz.

"Check everything on top," Naya told Harald and crawled under the desk.

Her backside caught Leif's interest. His groin tightened and he forced himself to look away.

Harald caught his gaze with a knowing smirk. Leif pointed at the desk, adjusting himself when his *stallare* looked away.

"Got it," Naya's muffled voice said from under the desk. She crawled out holding a silver box about the size of a credit card, but thicker. Fishing out a tiny screwdriver from her front pocket, she quickly loosened the casing. "It's a beauty. Pretty much state of the art." She pulled out one of the wires with a quick jerk of the wrist. "That one's disabled. Let's see if we can find more."

"Can you tell who planted it?" Leif asked.

Her nose wrinkled as she studied the device. "No, these can be bought online by pretty much anyone." Scratching her chin, she traced a smear of dust across her face.

He wanted to kiss her. "We should continue searching."

Half an hour later, they'd uncovered another bug by the fireplace and one under a small corner table. Naya showed Harald which wire to pull.

Leif hid a grin as the tiny woman showed the large warrior how to stuff his fat fingers into the small box. Although angry to know their plans had been overheard, Leif was also relieved. His warriors were as loyal as he'd thought.

"What other rooms did the network guy visit?" Naya asked.

Harald led them to the computer room where the frequency scanners revealed two more bugs.

"Is there any chance they're monitoring our computers?" Leif asked.

Harald flinched.

Naya shook her head. "I scanned your hard drive when I traced Per's email. Your firewall could use some work, but you're clean."

Harald groaned.

"What's with you?" Naya asked him. "Are you ill?"

"I don't know how to do any of that."

"Okay," Naya said slowly. "Does Ulf?"

"If he did, he would have already," Leif said. He watched Naya's face, hoping she would come to the right conclusion. He could always tell her, but he'd rather it was her idea. She hadn't responded well to being told what to do earlier.

She paused. "I could upgrade your system and then teach Ulf and Harald how to maintain the processes."

Leif had a hard time keeping the triumph off his face. "We'll pay you," he said.

Naya shrugged. "Consider it payment for room and board."

"There must be something we could do to compensate you."

She watched him, her eyes swirling with emotion. "You could tell me the truth about who you are and why the wolverines are trying to kill you." She cocked her head to the side.

Leif swallowed. He knew he'd eventually have to

tell her, but he'd hoped for more time. "Right now I need you to sweep the rest of the house. I'll explain after dinner, when we are alone." Hopefully he'd know what to say by then.

She watched him a moment longer, then nodded and left the room.

Leif now had a few hours to figure out how to explain who he was and that she was bound to him for life.

All without making his *själsfrände* bolt.

He sank into a chair. *Shit.*

Harald shot him a look of sympathy, clearing his throat. "You haven't told her yet?" His hand stroked his jaw. "The bond only works if you make her fall in love with you."

"I know that," Leif snapped. He glared at his *stallare* and knew they were both thinking the same thing. The bond also only worked if Leif fell in love with Naya. He was so fucked.

His friend was the first to break eye contact.

Leif owed it to his people to complete the bond so he could stay in the mortal realm as their king. The trick was how to be involved enough to get Naya to fall in love with him and still be able to keep his distance. Although he did look forward to her sharing his bed on a permanent basis.

Chapter 12

Naya waited in the bedroom she'd started thinking of as hers, expecting Leif any minute.

She'd spent the evening with Ulf, sweeping for bugs. The only other place they'd found one was in the game room. She'd wanted to keep it in place so they could send misinformation to whomever listened, but Ulf had quickly disconnected its wires and crushed the device with his fist, a grim expression on his face.

As she waited, she fiddled with the objects on the dresser. Her mom had given her the hairbrush. She'd never before felt safe enough to leave it out. Its regular place was an outside pocket on her bag with other essentials, an always ready to-go bag.

A soft knock on the door made her turn. "Come in," she called.

Leif stepped through the doorway. A black long-sleeved T-shirt strained over his shoulders and broad chest. A pair of black jeans hung low on his hips. All that darkness highlighted the radiance of his ice-blue eyes and the angled planes of his face.

Naya swallowed.

Leif strode toward her, stopping a few paces away, concern on his face. "Are you okay?"

"Yeah," she croaked. The air between them crackled, making the hairs on her arms stand up. Was she the only one feeling this?

He took a step closer and cupped her cheek in his palm. "Are you sure? You look a little pale."

She resisted the urge to rest her head in his hand. "No, I'm fine." She took a step back.

He frowned.

"We found one more bug in the game room." Her voice sounded rough.

"Ulf told me." He stepped toward her, eyes blazing.

"We're working on the computers tomorrow," she whispered, taking another step back. He crowded her. His body heat confused her, making her want impossible things. She cleared her throat. "It shouldn't take us long to improve your firewall and install a few security checks."

Leif watched her silently.

"You want to sit down?" She gestured toward the arm chairs.

"Sure," he said, but didn't move.

Naya had to step around him. Her skin sizzled when her arm accidently brushed against his. Relieved, she sank down in one of the blue chairs. A small table created a barrier between her and Leif. "So," she said. "You were going to explain what makes you different from regular humans."

He sat down in the empty chair, elbows on knees, studying his clasped hands. After a few moments he tilted his head and looked at her. "I'll try to answer all of your questions, but some of this may sound a little crazy."

"I'll keep an open mind."

Leif's eyes met hers. Whatever he saw in them seemed to satisfy him. "I died in 1050." He paused, watching her reaction.

Naya kept her gasp from escaping and instead nodded encouragingly.

"In the Norse culture, warriors who die in battle or die a heroic violent death are sent to live with the gods in Asgard. The men spend their time training in Valhalla with Odin. The women are schooled by Freya."

Naya's mind reeled. What he described didn't seem possible, but he was so sincere. Obviously he believed his story to be true. "I thought there were only male warriors in the Nordic tradition."

"Most stories are based on the old Icelandic sagas. They describe Valkyries as leading the men to Valhalla."

"And that's not the way it is?"

Leif smiled. "The sagas were all written by men long after the Viking age ended. They didn't know what happened in Freya's meadow and took some poetic license."

"So, typically male, instead of just saying 'I don't know,' you make up shit instead."

He smiled, his dimples stealing her breath. Again.

She looked away. "So, this place where the gods live, this is the Nordic heaven?"

"Not exactly. It's the warriors' reward for dying an honorable death. They are allowed to live on, to fight again." He studied his hands. "I don't remember much of Valhalla. Time flows differently there. All my memories run together as if they happened the same week."

She looked up to find him watching her. "I'm sorry, I'm trying to follow what you're saying. But—"

"It is a little crazy?" He smiled.

"A little." *A lot.*

"Is it any crazier than being abducted and kept in a camp? Any crazier than enhancement injections?"

"Touché."

So maybe her history was a little nutty, but living with gods? Seriously, way crazier. "So, why are you not in Valhalla?"

Leif sighed. "If you thought I was delusional before…" He smirked. "In addition to the Icelandic sagas, there are ancient rune stones that speak of a Viking king defeating Loki and preventing the final battle, *Ragnarök*."

I've fallen down the rabbit hole. Her forehead furrowed.

"Loki is also a god, well, half god, half giant. He likes to stir up trouble. The old stories depict him as a 'trickster.' But that is too benevolent for what he is. He can't leave the gods' dwelling, so instead he sends his minions to earth to instigate the final battle—minions like the wolverines."

"Sending monsters to kill you does seem more serious than a practical joke." How did this Loki tie in with the wolverines being created in the lab? She shook her head. "What about the battle you mentioned?"

"The Icelandic sagas foretell a battle between the gods and their enemies. According to legend, Ragnarök destroys the world and all of civilization."

"Why does Loki want to destroy the world?"

"He thinks he'll be the only surviving deity and thereby rule the universe."

"But there's a king who can stop this?" Naya scooted closer to the edge of the seat.

His blue eyes bore into hers. "That's how some interpret the ancient rune stones."

"And you are that king?"

"That's what Odin and Freya think."

Naya couldn't process what he'd told her while he watched her so intently. She stood, the heat of his gaze tracking her, prickling her skin. "So you are over a thousand years old."

"Not exactly. I was twenty-eight when I died, fairly old for a Viking. We start raiding and fighting in our early teens."

Naya stopped and turned to look at him. "You look younger. Do you age backward, like Merlin?"

Leif laughed out loud. "No, I'm not a wizard. I didn't age in Valhalla, and I have aged very slowly, maybe not at all, since I returned to Midgard."

Naya stared at him. "I'm sorry, what?"

He shrugged. "Midgard, it's where the humans live," he said, as if it was something everyone knew. "Earth."

She shook her head. "When did you return to… the humans?"

"A century ago."

Naya just watched him for a moment. He seemed sane, but what came out of his mouth was not. "This is a lot to take in." Like a hundred years' worth of cray-cray to process.

Leif stood and walked toward her.

She forced herself to stand still although her body screamed to meet him halfway.

He stopped a few inches from her. "I don't expect you to understand or even believe us right away. Just know that none of my warriors will hurt you."

The crazy thing was that she did believe she was safe in this house. But she still had to ask. "Why are your people so protective of me?"

Leif avoided her eyes. His hand encircled her

wrist and he pulled her toward him. "Because you saved me."

"And you are their king." Him stroking her arm made it hard to concentrate.

He nodded. "And they are grateful to you."

Naya wanted to resist, but her legs had a will of their own and didn't listen to her brain. "But they have already repaid me by saving me from the handlers."

Leif captured her other hand. "And then you helped us again by finding the listening devices." He buried his face in her hair.

The heat between them scorched her brain. She couldn't breathe. "Anyone with a similar security background could have found those bugs."

Leif nodded against her head, then held her a little farther away by her shoulders and looked into her eyes. "But it would have taken us much longer. Now we don't have to worry about a traitor. My people are much relieved." His voice lowered to a whisper. "Most grateful." He leaned in and brushed her forehead with his lips. His hands moved lower, stopping on her hips. Slowly, he moved her backward.

The bed hit the back of her knees. "I just did what anybody would have done."

"Not anybody." He cupped her ass.

Her body leaned toward him. Traitorous body.

"Why didn't you tell me you were married?"

His body stilled. He leaned back and nudged her chin up until her eyes met his. "That was a long time ago."

"Still seems like something you could have mentioned."

Leif sighed. "My wife and children died long before I did."

"Why didn't they go to live with the gods?"

"They were murdered," he answered. "And dying in your sleep isn't an honorable death."

She wanted to ask him if he missed his wife, if he still loved her, but wasn't sure she'd like the answer. And didn't like that she wanted to ask. "I'm sorry," she said instead.

Leif's hand traced her jaw, and then pushed an errant strand of hair behind her ear. "It happened long ago. It has nothing to do with us."

She couldn't afford to think about an "us," and yet the word sent tendrils of warm longing through her body. Her heart swelled. "What makes a death honorable? I don't understand the rules for who gets to live on."

A smile quirked his lips. "I'm not sure I do either, but I don't want to talk about death and dying anymore."

She was standing close enough to feel his voice vibrating in his chest. "What do you want to talk about?" She closed her eyes and leaned into his caress.

This was so dangerous. So good.

"I don't want to talk at all." His whisper heated her skin.

She sighed. She didn't want to resist anymore. But this wouldn't be casual. Sex with Leif would mean something. She didn't want to think about the hurt that would come later.

His lips caressed hers and she automatically parted her lips, a satisfied sigh escaping.

He groaned and deepened the kiss. His tongue plundered her mouth, claiming it as his territory. Leif's hand moved to the back of her neck. He tilted her head for better access.

Her knees buckled. They tumbled into bed together, Leif bracing himself above her, hands on either side of her body.

Naya arched against him. She needed his heat, his strength. Impatient, she reached for his belt and undid the buckle. Tearing the button open, she reached for the zipper.

He reached down, capturing her hand in his. "Patience." He chuckled. "I want to take my time."

Naya shook her head, looking straight into his eyes. "We can go slow later. I want you now."

His pupils dilated. Something flickered deep within but disappeared before she could identify the emotion.

"Are you sure?" he asked, his voice hoarse.

She ignored his question and continued to unzip his jeans. This time he didn't stop her. "Yes," she hissed as she stroked his hardness.

He pressed into her, growling deep in his chest. Grabbing both her hands, he raised her arms over her head. "Slow down, little one, or I won't last." He nuzzled her neck.

A sigh escaped her lips as heat rippled through her body. Her nipples tingled. She arched her back, moaning with pleasure as the hard buds rubbed against his chest through her shirt.

Leif claimed her mouth again, moving his tongue in and out.

She matched his motion, the pace driving her crazy. When he pulled his mouth away, she whimpered in protest. The sound turned into another moan as his lips found her nipple through her shirt. She arched again, wanting increased contact.

He held both of her wrists with one hand and used the other to pull her shirt up and over her head. The snaps on her bra provided little challenge, and the garment quickly followed the shirt. His lips caressed her naked breasts, one after the other, before settling on one nipple. Using his teeth, he gently tugged.

"Please," Naya whispered. She tugged her wrists, trying to get free. "I need, I want…"

"Shh, I know, *älskling*." He kissed her and released her hands. She buried them in his hair as he unbuttoned her pants, swiftly pulling them, and her panties, down her thighs. His fingers tangled in the curls between her legs, finding her wetness, pressing in until one, then two, fingers entered her.

She pressed against his palm, grinding her hips, matching the pace he set.

Leif's clever hot mouth found a nipple again, then the other. He spoiled them both.

Licking. Sucking. Biting.

Heat rushed straight to her core. Pressure built deep in her womb, radiating out until it exploded. Her body shook as she orgasmed. Screaming out her pleasure, she relaxed in a puddle on the bed.

She tried to catch her breath.

He captured her mouth with his and quickly swept her garments off the bed. He raised his head and torso, kneeling on the bed as he pulled his shirt over his head. It followed her clothes, landing in a heap on the floor.

Moonlight from the uncovered windows cast silver shadows on his broad chest as he freed his legs from his jeans. They caught on his boots. He tumbled off the bed with a thud, cursing as he tore at the tangle around his ankles.

Naya laughed and rolled to the side of the bed. She peered down. "Are you okay?"

"I will be in a minute." Leif kicked off his boots and captured her face in both his hands. He kissed her deeply, pushing her back on the bed, stretching out above her. "Wait just a little longer," he said, slipping off the bed. She heard the rip of a wrapper, a quick snap as he put the condom in place, and then he was back beside her. He moved one hand to cup her bottom, pressing her groin against his.

She opened her legs to give him access.

Leif stopped for a moment, his face hovering above hers. Pupils dilated, myriad emotions swirled in the deep pools of his eyes.

Her breath caught as the same turmoil echoed deep within her. But then the head of his shaft found her entrance and she closed her eyes, forgetting everything but how good it felt to have him slide into her.

She raised her hips, forcing him deeper.

With a guttural groan, he thrust all the way.

Naya gasped as he filled her, widening her, stretching her, the friction between them delicious.

Leif plunge into her again and again, setting a fast pace.

Angling her legs, pushing against the mattress with her heels, she matched him stroke for stroke.

Her body burned, every nerve ending on fire. She couldn't breathe. She tightened around him as she came, the orgasm crashing through her body.

One final thrust and Leif joined her, shouting her name.

Panting, Naya felt a strange sensation of soaring up out of her body toward millions of tiny lights. The pinpricks danced and melted together into a white flashing circle. Passing through them, she reached a complete darkness.

Complete silence.

Complete stillness.

She floated in balmy darkness until a rush of sound approached, building like a waterfall, rushing faster and louder.

She was swept away with it, crashing down back into her body. She jerked violently, opening her eyes wide. Breathing hard, she turned her head.

Leif was watching her, his eyes serious. He stroked the hair off her forehead and face. "You okay?"

She couldn't form any words, but nodded.

A grin filled with male satisfaction spread across his face. He gathered her in his arms.

She melted into the comfort and warmth of his body. Her heart slowed to match the rhythm of his, her breathing calming as her chest rose and fell with his. Contentment spread through her limbs, flooding her heart.

It felt like coming home.

Naya closed her eyes and drifted off, her limbs heavy as sleep claimed her.

—⁓—

Leif covered them both with the down duvet.

Naya sighed softly in his arms.

Had she experienced the same thing he had while they completed the bond? The rushing white light and the beckoning darkness beyond had been incredibly beautiful, overwhelming.

And scary as hell.

What would this mean for both of them?

The skin on his left hand tingled and he raised his arm. Illuminated by the moonlight streaming through the window, the tail of the serpent tattoo spiraled up his forearm, past his elbow, joining the head on the upper part of his bicep.

A cold spike of fear pierced his heart for a fraction of a second as the snake glowed white hot on his arm. He watched as the two parts joined into one and an immense peace spread through his body. His heart rate and breathing calmed.

For a moment, he felt a slight twinge of unease as he thought about Naya not knowing the full story of the *själsfrände* bond. But he had already told her so much tonight. He'd tell her the rest when she'd processed that information. Still, *he* didn't know the full story. His berserker had chosen her. They'd consummated that choice, but was the tattoo the end or just the beginning of the *själsfrände* bond? He had strong feelings for her, but was it love? Did this mean she loved him?

Exhaustion claimed him before he found the answers. He snuggled closer to his mate, closed his eyes, and relaxed his body.

Chapter 13

NAYA PERCHED PRECARIOUSLY ON A STOOL IN THE LAB while Irja collected blood from her arm. Irja gave Naya a cotton swab to press against the pinprick. Naya wiped the small wound but didn't bother applying pressure. She healed fast.

"Are you any closer to figuring out what the chemicals in my blood do?" she asked.

Irja labeled the test tubes while she answered. "There is still much to learn, but the particles seem to be related to production and levels of epinephrine, commonly known as adrenaline."

Naya prodded the skin of her arm to see if the bleeding had stopped. "That explains increased speed and tolerance of pain, but what about—" She stopped herself. She hadn't told Irja about her cognitive abilities.

"I hope you will one day trust me enough to share more of your secrets," Irja said. "Until then, I'll tell you a little about how adrenaline works and then maybe you can share enough information to help me in my tests."

Naya nodded for her to continue.

"Adrenaline regulates your heart rate and breathing." She finished putting away the equipment and sat down on a stool, facing Naya. "It also rules the body's metabolic shifts and the human fight-or-flight response. Your cardiovascular system has extreme control over your adrenaline release and can channel larger-than-usual quantities to the organs in your body, instantly." She waited for a beat. "I've never seen anybody synthesize epinephrine that quickly."

"Does the hormone affect cognitive abilities?" Naya kept her voice level, almost bored.

"Not exactly. Some neurons of the central nervous system produce adrenaline, but the hormone is more involved in maintaining organ functions like heart rate, dilation of pupils, muscle contractions. It controls things like your pH levels and temperature."

Excitement welled in Naya's chest. Could adrenaline synthesis be why her brother could no longer control his muscles? She struggled to keep an even tone of voice. "Could you find out if I produce the same adrenaline as normal humans?"

"Sure." Irja leaned forward. "Tell me more about why you need to know these things. It could speed up the process."

Naya hesitated. "I'm sorry. I just can't."

Disappointment flared in Irja's eyes. She looked away.

"Not yet," Naya added. "I will try to share as much as I can later."

The taller woman nodded. "I understand."

Naya doubted she did, but was thankful for the respite. She didn't expect it would last long.

Feeling strangely guilty for not telling Irja the whole story, Naya returned to her bedroom—her *empty* bedroom. She ignored the slight hitch in her chest that absolutely was not disappointment. What did she expect? Naya had woken up with her head resting on Leif's chest, his arms providing a cocoon of warmth and contentment. She'd felt safe and protected.

Scared out of her mind, she'd bolted into the bathroom, grabbing some clothes on the way. After showering and getting dressed, she'd escaped to the computer room.

Leif had still been asleep when she left.

She'd worked on updating the mansion's cybersecurity walls until she'd gone stir-crazy and decided to search for Irja.

She stared at the spot where she had left him. Leif had made the bed.

The smooth bedspread was the exact opposite of how the bed looked that morning. She remembered pillows thrown on the floor, rumpled sheets, and one very sexy Viking slumbering in the middle of it all. She frowned. There had been something different about him. Closing her eyes, she accessed the memories of that morning.

Leif sleeping. In her bed.

He'd been on his back with one arm flung over his head, those impressive pectorals highlighted by the morning sun slanting through the window. A trail of dark hair started just below his ribs and narrowed as it grew closer to his navel and the regions hidden under the sheet.

She swallowed. *Concentrate.*

She zoomed back up. Tussled blond hair framed his face. Dark stubble graced a strong chin.

The arm had been different.

The tattoo no longer ended by his bicep. Instead the runes spiraled down along a snake's long body to a pointed tail just below the wrist. The ink had glistened in the morning sun. He must have retouched the body art recently. When had he found the time?

Her stomach rumbled, reminding her it was well after lunchtime.

She didn't want to risk running into Leif in the kitchen. Until she had a handle on these new emotions, she'd avoid one-on-one time with the king. She turned her back on the bed and wiped her mind of the images she'd just reviewed. She dug out a few granola bars from her computer bag. They would have to last until dinner. At least the other warriors would distract her from Leif—and distract him from her.

She turned one of the plush blue armchairs to face the door and sat down with her laptop. Maybe she'd be able to concentrate with the bed out of sight.

———

At the dining room table Leif tried to concentrate on what Harald was jabbering on about, but his mind kept drifting to Naya. He'd faked sleep that morning when she'd jumped out of the bed like a spring lamb let out to pasture for the first time. Her reaction shouldn't irk him.

He checked the doorway again, forcing his jaw to relax. It was ten minutes past dinner start time. Where was she?

"*Min kung.*" Harald raised his voice.

Leif glared at him.

His *stallare* returned the look and lowered his voice. "You need to concentrate and stop thinking about your woman."

Leif sighed. He'd hoped to keep the completion of the bond a secret a little longer. His warriors' reaction to a non-Valkyrie queen were bound to be, if not volatile, then at least spirited. They needed to concentrate on the threat of the wolverines. And he didn't know how Naya would react to her new role.

Since he hadn't explained the details of the bond, she'd probably freak out.

Harald had caught him leaving her bedroom. Leif had asked for his silence, but it was just a matter of time before everyone would notice him bedding her. He rubbed his arm, covered by a long-sleeved T-shirt. The tattoo tingled and itched. "I'm listening," he snapped.

"You haven't heard a word I said," Harald shot back.

Leif dragged his thoughts away from his *själsfrände* and gave his second-in-command his full attention. The two of them sat on either side of a corner of the large rectangular table, keeping their voices low to allow some privacy despite the regular ruckus from his warriors seated at the table. "I'm sorry." Leif rubbed his temples. "This bond messes with my mind."

"What do you propose we do next?"

At first Leif thought Harald meant about the bond, but quickly adjusted his mind back to war. "Call everyone to a briefing after dinner. We'll escalate the timetable for finding where the poison is grown."

"Per and Sten are due for patrol tonight."

Their standard night shift had two warriors out patrolling alone. They'd considered increasing the number of people on duty, but, so far, two warriors were plenty to take care of the wolverines roving the streets while the other Norse warriors searched for the poison. "Do we need more people on duty?"

Harald scratched his beard. "We're watching the

fortress walls and the property boundaries extra carefully, but I don't want to alert the creatures that roam around in the population center that we're up to something."

Leif nodded. "That's fine. Send Per and Sten out. Everyone else will meet."

"Including your queen?" Harald raised his eyebrows.

Leif paused for a moment. "Including Naya."

As if she'd heard them talking about her, his *själs-fründe* appeared in the doorway. She wore jeans, faded and hanging on her hip bones. Her plain white T-shirt draped loosely from her shoulders, covering the delectable curves hiding behind the cotton. She wore no makeup and her usually smooth hair was mussed like she'd rubbed her hands through it too many times.

Sexy as hell, she stole his breath.

Mine, the berserker growled.

Leif agreed.

Tentatively she took a step into the room, looking around.

Astrid stood up and hollered for Naya to sit next to her. "Grab a plate."

Naya flashed her a tentative smile before serving herself from the side buffet. She threw a quick glance Leif's way.

He tried to concentrate on Harald's description of the search grid, but the details ran together. Instead Leif watched Naya join Astrid at the table.

He couldn't look away from her lush lips scraping spaghetti off the fork. Shit, he had it bad.

"Irja, any progress on finding an antidote for the poison?" His voice was too loud. All discussion around the table ceased and the healer startled.

Usually he didn't discuss business at the dinner

table, except for with Harald. He wanted his warriors to relax from duty at least once a day. Raising his eyebrows, he encouraged his medical officer to answer the question.

She put down her fork and cleared her throat. "No, my king. The potions I've developed have not been successful."

"Keep trying." He regretted the terse tone.

Irja nodded and picked up her utensil again.

Leif glanced at Naya. Through the whole interchange, she'd kept on eating as if the words had nothing to do with her. He sighed inwardly.

Explaining her new duties as his *själsfrände* would be harder than hunting winter fox in snow.

An hour after dinner, Leif watched from across his desk as his warriors assembled in front of him in their usual configuration. When Naya entered, Harald hesitated and almost rose out of his chair, which earned him a strange glance from Ulf.

Tradition dictated that the king's woman sit closest to the king.

His *stallare* looked to him for guidance, and Leif briefly shook his head.

Naya took a seat next to Torvald on the sofa at the back of the room without so much as a glance Leif's way. Irja perched on the armrest next to her, both of them deep in conversation.

He bit back a sigh. Figured that the two most secretive and troublesome women he knew would connect.

Right then, Astrid bounced into the room and flung her body into the middle seat of the sofa, pushing

Torvald farther to the edge. She said something that had all three females laughing out loud.

Leif's sigh escaped. Make that *three* of the most troublesome women he knew.

As they settled in, he made eye contact with each of his warriors and Naya before speaking. "Let's begin. Ulf, report."

The short-haired Viking sat up straighter. "Naya's been teaching me more about firewalls and cybersecurity."

Leif glanced at his mate, but she was concentrating on Ulf, a small smile playing in the corners of her mouth. A stab of jealousy pierced Leif's chest.

His berserker growled, impatient with the other male stealing Naya's attention.

Ridiculous.

There was nothing between Naya and Ulf. Although they did spend a lot of time together in the computer room. He shook his head. "No."

Startled, Ulf paused in his report.

Leif cleared his throat. His warriors and Naya stared at him.

"I'm sorry, carry on." He waved his hand.

Ulf nodded. "We've beefed up all security measures, and anyone attempting a cyber-attack will be tracked through our software."

An appreciative mumble spread through the room. Several of the Vikings turned toward Naya.

His *själsfrände*'s face turned a pretty pink.

Leif turned toward his *stallare*. "Harald?"

"We swept the lab and sheds for listening devices. None were found, so at least we know only the main house was breached."

Ulf stood again. "I cleaned up the images you took with your phone that night in the alley." He pointed a remote to the screen on the wall behind Leif. "I think you meant to take pictures of the wolverines." He scrolled through a couple of images. "Then there's this."

Leif stared at the image of a wolverine with a long tube in his hands. A hazy memory of thinking the monster wanted to engage in staff combat rose to the surface. "What is that?"

"A blowgun," Irja said. "That's how they managed to poison you while keeping their distance."

"A blow-what?" Harald blinked, baffled.

Irja stood, pointing at the screen. "They're used by indigenous people of the Americas. You force a projectile through the tube using your breath. It shoots out as if through a gun."

"Fuck me." Harald scratched his beard.

Leif scratched the spot behind his ear where he'd felt a bee sting. "I want everyone to be extra careful when you encounter wolverines. Neutralize this weapon first before engaging in combat."

"Just shoot every one of the fuckers," Harald exclaimed.

An excited mumble spread through his troops. Leif held up his hand. "Our priority is to find out where they grow the poison, so we need one or two of them alive for interrogation. Continue working on Harald's search grid."

His *stallare* stood. "Meet me in the game room in ten. I'll have your weekly patrol schedule ready."

The warriors filed out of his office.

"Naya, could you stay a moment?" He had to project his voice across the room as the slight woman was about to slip out the door.

She turned reluctantly, but walked to the desk and sat on the edge of the seat Harald had vacated.

Leif pinched the bridge of his nose, trying to relieve a headache. During the last half hour, the pain had gone from a dull throb to shards of ice penetrating his brain.

The berserker paced, angry over the male attention Naya had received during the meeting. His warrior spirit also protested the emotional walls she erected between them.

He felt her pulling away. The mental connection he'd shared with her through the bond weakened each hour. After last night, it should be getting stronger. Something was wrong.

She was doing something wrong.

"I want you to move into my room," he said without looking up.

A sharp intake of breath announced her protest. He held up a hand to stop her words, but the gesture didn't work.

"Not going to happen." Naya leaned back in the chair, deceptively calm.

He held his breath, counting to ten. "Look"—he smiled at her and leaned forward—"I want you. You want me. Why not make it easier on both of us and share a bed?"

"Of all the arrogant asshole-ish statements in this world—I'm not moving in with you."

"Why not?" Her physical response last night showed how much she wanted him. Why did she have to make things so difficult?

"I like my privacy." She stared straight at him, her eyes turning dark and stormy.

"You can have privacy in my room."

She tossed her head, flicking her hair. "My clients expect me to keep the details of their accounts confidential."

"I'm offended you think I'd spy on you. Besides, you don't need to work now. I can take care of you."

She shot off the chair faster than a crossbow's bolt. "*Take care* of me?" Hands on hips, she glared at him. One tight bundle of fury.

Uh-oh. He had never treated Irja or Astrid as anything but equal battle partners, so why was this so difficult for him? Why did he want Naya to obey without questioning him?

The tattoo on his arm throbbed. "What I meant to say is that we need you full-time here in the fortress. You won't have time for outside clients."

She glared at him. "You can't afford my full price."

He rubbed his arm and tried again. "Fine. Keep your work, but I need to know where you are at all times for your safety and protection. It's just easier if we share a room."

Naya took a deep breath. "Last night was good."

He quirked an eyebrow.

She rolled her eyes. "Okay, fine. It was great." She waved a hand in the air. "But just because I slept with you does not mean we are in a relationship or that you can tell me what to do. I can take care of myself." She raised her chin, daring him to defy her statement.

"Which I don't doubt." He stood and stepped around his desk. He needed to touch her. "I'm not explaining this very well. There are reasons why I need to sleep beside you each night."

Suspicion flared in her eyes. "What reasons?"

Leif sighed. "This is the reason," he said, pulling up his sleeve to show the completed tattoo. "After last night, we are fully committed. It's called a *själsfrände* bond. It's an ancient Norse tradition. A sign that we are handfasted."

Naya quirked an eyebrow. "I see you completed your tattoo, but I'm not getting a matching one and calling myself engaged."

This was going to be harder than he thought. "The tattoo completed on its own." He pulled down his sleeve. "Did you notice anything strange last night?"

"What do you mean by strange?" From the way she glanced away, he could tell she had experienced the balmy darkness, or at least something like it.

"After we completed our…joining, I left my body and floated in a peaceful darkness." He paused to watch her reaction.

Naya just shrugged, still avoiding his eyes.

"When I came back to my body, the tattoo completed on its own."

"I don't see what this has to do with me." She finally looked up. "You can't just decide that we're in some sort of relationship without discussing it with me."

Leif frowned. "I didn't decide. It was decided for me—for us. We are destined to be together, whether we want to or not."

She opened her mouth to reply, but before she had a chance, Harald sprinted into the room. "Sten has been poisoned."

Leif dropped his sleeve down. "Where is he?"

"Per is bringing him in now. Irja is meeting them downstairs." He ran out the door again, his boots pounding the stairs as he went to join Irja at the front door.

Leif turned to Naya. "We'll finish this later."

She raised her chin, still defiant, but gestured for him to leave.

He chased after Harald to see to his youngest warrior.

Naya walked quietly past Sten's room on the way to her own. The young Viking had been unconscious when they'd brought him in. His partner, Per, had been battered and bruised but managed to avoid the blowgun the wolverines used to shoot Sten.

She was a few paces past the door when Irja slipped out, a medical bag in her hand.

"How is he?"

Deep lines creased the tall Valkyrie's forehead and her skin was pale. "Only time can tell. I don't know enough about this poison to say more."

Naya took a step forward and grabbed the other woman's hand. "I'm sure he will be fine. Leif purged the poison."

Irja returned her squeeze. "He's the king." She dropped Naya's hand. "Sten is much younger and received a much larger dose."

"But aren't all the Vikings similar?" She tucked her hands in her pockets. "I mean, don't their bodies work similarly?"

Irja shook her head. "Sten has only been in the human realm for a short while. His body is not as well adapted as Leif's."

Naya didn't know what to say. "I'll check on him." She opened the door and slipped inside, not sure if she meant to check on Sten or Leif.

The blinds were drawn and only one lamp illuminated the room. Sten lay on the bed, a sheen of perspiration covering his face.

Leif sat in a chair next to him, one hand holding his warrior's, the other bridging across his forehead, shielding his eyes. He didn't react until Naya reached the bed.

Startled, he looked up. "I thought you were Irja."

Naya's heart skipped a beat at the pain in his gaze. She pulled another chair over and sat down next to him.

"We don't know if he's going to make it."

Naya took his hand in both of hers and rested them in her lap. "He's strong."

"But young." Leif shook his head. "I can't lose him. I've not lost a warrior yet."

"I'm sure he'll appreciate you being here for him."

He let out a bitter laugh. "I'm sitting here because I don't want any of the others to see what a mess I am. They rely on me to be strong." He rubbed his eyes. "I should have put more people on night patrol. This shouldn't have happened."

Naya hadn't thought about the burdens of being the king. Always a loner, she'd never belonged to a group. In the camp, each soldier had to be self-sufficient, a one-person killing machine. She couldn't fathom being responsible for a whole group of warriors, no matter how skilled. "I'm envious of how close you are to your warriors. How close they are to each other. You are a family."

Leif's piercing blue eyes bored into hers. Something shifted between them. Breathing became harder, the air too dense. She wanted to run but forced herself to remain in the chair. She let go of his hand.

He quickly grabbed her hand again. "Don't."

She squirmed. "It's not my place. I don't really know Sten."

"I need you here." His eyes darkened. "And I've explained about our *själsfrände* bond. You *are* one of us."

His words warmed distant places in her heart. She leaned back in the chair. "We still have a lot to discuss. I'm not ready for what you're suggesting."

"Don't talk about leaving. Please."

She opened her mouth to tell him that she didn't do long-term relationships.

He shook his head. "I know there are still things we have to figure out. For now, just let me know where you are so I won't…worry." His eyes pleaded with her.

"Okay," she said. For now, she'd just sit with him, savoring this brief moment of connection.

Leif had seduced her body into his bed, and her mind and heart followed because of his strength, his loyalty, and how much he cared for his people.

She swallowed the lump of sadness lodged in her throat.

Once he learned the whole truth of her origins, he'd make her leave. And then she'd be alone again, just like before.

But now she'd know what she was missing.

Chapter 14

Naya stood and stretched her arms out behind her back before rolling her shoulders. Her bones creaked. She sighed contentedly as tension left her body.

Luke Holden looked up from the blueprints spread out on the bar. "You're too young for your body to make sounds like that."

"Too many hours in front of the computer." More like too many old injuries and bruises. Naya returned Holden's smile with one of her own. She took a peep around the nightclub. They were on the first floor of Desire. "You spent some money on the decorating." She swept her arm along the long bar where they'd spread out their papers. Made entirely of glass, it was actually a huge aquarium. Rainbow-colored Japanese koi swam around sunken treasures and a model pirate ship.

"The bar was Rex's idea." Holden extended his thumb in the direction of the door, where the large man stood in his usual bodyguard stance.

Rex shrugged. "I like fish."

Naya smiled and stifled a yawn. Irja had eventually taken over watching Sten. Naya had snuck off to her own room while Leif talked with the medical researcher. The intensity of her feelings overwhelmed and scared her. Why could she not stop thinking about him?

"Ms. Driscoll?"

It took her a moment to react to her fake name, but

finally she turned. Holden was staring at her. "Sorry." She shook her head. "I was thinking about the plans for your home."

Concern reflected in his gray eyes. "Me too, that's why I was asking you if you are still going with me on Thursday to implement your suggested home security measures."

"Absolutely." Two more days and she'd be far away from Leif for at least a night. Maybe that would calm her feelings, or at least her libido.

Holden picked up the list of new equipment again. Before he could move on to the next item, a loud banging rattled the back door.

Rex swiveled around and had a Beretta in his hand in less than half a second. He placed his hand on the door handle and glanced back at Holden.

Holden slipped a Glock under the blueprints.

She wished she had her own gun, but Rex didn't allow guests to carry weapons.

At least she still had the switchblade tucked in her boot. A girl should always carry at least one weapon, the most essential accessory.

Someone should tell *Vogue*.

Holden nodded at Rex who opened the door.

"About freaking time." Astrid strode through the door, giving Rex a slow once-over, mumbling something appreciative before surveying the room. She stopped when she saw Holden but then quickly directed her attention to Naya. "Sorry to come barging in, but I need to speak with my friend."

Naya hopped off the bar stool. "Is Sten all right?"

"No change." Her voice faltered and she cleared

her throat. "But that's not why I'm here." Astrid took another step into the room.

"Hold on." Rex put a hand on her shoulder. "No weapons allowed inside the club."

Astrid aimed a brilliant smile at him. "I don't have any weapons."

The tall black man didn't even raise an eyebrow as he looked pointedly at the broadsword strapped to Astrid's back.

"Oh, this little ol' thing," the Valkyrie chirped, touching the straps crisscrossing her chest. "It's practically an antique, for accessory purposes only. It matches my boots."

Rex stared unblinkingly at her. "Please remove all weapons, ma'am."

Astrid made a big point of sighing. "Oh, fine. Just don't call me ma'am." She unstrapped the sword and handed it to Rex.

"Can I go now?" Astrid put a hand on her hip and pouted.

Rex glanced over at Holden again, who nodded.

"Taking orders makes you less sexy," she threw over her shoulder to the bodyguard as she approached Naya. "We have big trouble, Miss Hacker."

Naya frowned at the nickname Astrid had started using a few days ago.

"What are you talking about?"

The Valkyrie sighed. "Leif found out you borrowed my bike and is having a hissy fit about you leaving without telling him."

"Shit." Naya glanced at Holden. The nightclub owner followed their conversation with obvious interest on his face, but didn't say anything. "How did you find me?"

"All vehicles have GPS." Astrid tried to turn the security plans so she could read them.

Naya slapped her hand away, earning a pretend-hurt look from the Valkyrie. "How far behind is he?"

"Not much." She held up a bundle of car keys. "Although this will detain him for a while."

Naya started rolling up the drawings of the club. "I'm really sorry," she said to Holden, "I'm going to have to cut this short."

"Are you in trouble?" he asked.

Rex took a step forward, the gun still in his hand.

Testosterone apparently made all men overprotective. "I'm fine. It's just a misunderstanding."

Astrid snorted.

Holden watched the Valkyrie, heat flaring in his eyes for an instant.

"Just a case of not telling her boyfriend where she went. He's a little worried." The Valkyrie traced an invisible pattern on the bar, pointedly not looking at Holden.

Interesting.

Holden came around the bar. "Ms. Driscoll, you know you can come to me for help." He put a hand on her shoulder.

Naya shrugged it off. "If I need help, I'll ask for it." Being small and female did not make her helpless.

"Of course." Holden took a step back.

Shit. Now he'd think her rude. "Thanks for the offer, but I'm really okay." She smiled. He was, after all, a client.

"It's an open offer." Holden nodded at Rex. "Since we're finished here, I need to leave for an appointment across town."

Rex walked to the front door. "I'll pull the car up at the front."

"We better get going too." Astrid flung her hair over a shoulder and walked toward the back door. Her stride was hard, angry.

"I'll see you on Thursday," Naya said before nodding at Rex and following Astrid out the back door. Why was Astrid peeved all of a sudden?

Behind the building, an identical motorbike was parked next to the one she'd borrowed from the Valkyrie. In the late afternoon sunlight, the black paint glistened as if wet.

"You took Sten's bike."

"It's not like I could ask him, so yeah." Her voice laced with worry, Astrid straddled the bike.

"He's going to be okay." Naya put her hand on the Valkyrie's shoulder. "Irja will find a cure." Naya hoped that outcome was as certain as she made her voice sound.

"I hope so." Astrid raised the kickstand with her boot. "You're a good friend." Starting the bike, she put on her helmet and shouted over the engine noise. "Hop on your bike so we can get your butt back to the house."

A little dizzy over the warmth spreading in her body at the word "friend," Naya nodded. Before she had a chance to straddle the other bike, a silver Porsche pulled up next to them. Leif stared at them through the windshield.

"I'm out of here!" Astrid shouted before shooting off on the Kawasaki.

Some friend she turned out to be.

The driver-side door of the car opened.

Naya squared her shoulders and lifted her chin, ready to take on another male thinking her small and helpless.

A brown motorcycle boot hit the ground and a jean-clad leg appeared. The tall Viking took his time easing out of the sports car. He closed the door behind him and leaned back against it.

He exuded dangerously sexy, but nobody told her what to do. Not even the Viking king who'd somehow taken a piece of her heart. *Shit, where did that thought come from?* Her heart needed to remain whole. She couldn't afford sharing it with anyone else, not even a small part of it. She fiddled with her gloves while she waited for Leif to say something.

He crossed his arms, stretching his shirt across his chest and shoulders. A frown marred his face as he continued staring at her.

Naya glared back for a minute before getting tired of the game. She straddled the bike.

Leif was in front of her in three quick strides, grabbing the handlebars. "Don't you dare," he growled.

"I'm going back to the mansion. Thought that's what you wanted." She retrieved the helmet from the back of the bike.

He gazed up at the sky, sighing heavily. "What I want is for you to tell me when you leave the fortress and where you are going. What part of keeping me informed do you not understand?"

Bullshit. "You mean you want to be able to stop me from going."

He looked her in the eye. "I need to know where you are at all times."

"Why?"

He averted his eyes. "So I can protect you."

"We've been over this. I don't need your protection." She put on the helmet but left the visor up.

"I disagree. Last time you were on your own, you were kidnapped."

Of course he had to bring that up. "Last time you were on your own, you were poisoned and got your ass kicked."

A tic appeared at the side of his jaw. "Fine. We both need to tell each other where we are."

"Not going to happen. I don't really care where you are or what you do." She popped the visor shut.

"Naya," he growled.

She shook her head and leaned forward to raise the kickstand with the back of her heel. She could protect herself. The sooner Leif understood that, the better.

Before her heel made contact with the metal of the stand, a blur behind Leif's back made her turn. Three wolverines grinned back at her. One of them raised a blowgun to his lips. "Look out!" she shouted and shoved Leif out of the way.

The dart grazed her helmet. She leaped off the bike, widening her stance and bouncing slightly on the balls of her feet. She was totally up for a fight. Maybe that would get rid of the restlessness that had plagued her for the last couple of days.

Leif brushed off the seat of his pants as he stood up. His slip of a *själsfrände* had brushed him to the side as if he weighed no more than an empty flour sack. Even now, she stood in front of him, shielding him from the wolverines, exposing herself to danger.

He grabbed her arm. "Get behind me." He swept her behind his back.

She struggled, of course. Why couldn't anything be easy with this woman?

"Get the fuck out of the way," she growled, whipping off her helmet. A bird's nest of black hair surrounded her flushed face.

One of the wolverines had moved closer while they argued. Leif pivoted and struck the monster's head with a roundhouse kick. The bastard went down and the blowgun skidded across the asphalt.

Naya tried to slip around him, but he pushed her back as one of the other monsters advanced. "Get on the bike. When you're far enough away, call Harald for backup."

"Get over yourself. If you want backup, you call it in." She leaned to the side and threw the helmet at an advancing wolverine.

The creature ducked and grinned as the black dome bounced across the ground and hit the building. "What do we have here? A lovers' tiff?" His nails elongated.

Naya shot out from behind Leif, aiming a side-kick toward the creature's head. Watching Naya run toward the other two wolverines, Leif's berserker roared and he struggled to maintain control.

She delivered a flying punch to the chin of the one to the right.

The creature went down, but kept scrambling on the ground, his claws scratching at gravel as he tried to get up.

The one on the left growled. "I know you killed three of my kin," he said as he threw a jab at her head. "Consider this payback."

But Naya ducked and bobbed. The blow scraped

the side of her head without doing much damage. She quickly recovered and grinned. "I killed four, not three." She cross-countered and then slammed his jaw with an uppercut.

The wolverine's head snapped back, making hard contact with the brick wall of the building. A sickening crack of crushed bone vibrated through the air before the creature slid to the ground.

A scraping behind him made Leif turn around. The blowgun wolverine had recovered and was trying to stand up.

In two strides, he reached the monster, kicked him over, and then crushed his windpipe with his boot heel.

He turned around and inhaled sharply as the remaining wolverine back-fisted Naya's cheek before landing a cross in her stomach. Strangely, the monster's claws were retracted. She hunched over and sank to the ground, but turned her body to the side and swept her leg out to hook the wolverine's legs.

Her movements were off. The blow to the head must have dazed her.

The berserker inside Leif howled in anger, taking control over his body.

Throwing his head back, he bellowed a war cry as he embraced his warrior spirit. His vision blurred and he now viewed the world through a crimson filter.

He focused on the wolverine threatening his queen. Fists clenched in anticipation of encircling the animal's neck. It would be a slow death.

Car tires squealed. A black nondescript sedan pulled up behind the Porsche. The wolverine swiveled his head toward the car. The passenger-side door opened with a pop. The monster took one last look at Naya before sprinting to the car.

Leif's berserker screamed in frustration as its prey escaped.

Naya was up on her feet and shot past him quick as a rabbit. She reached the car just as the sedan drove off.

He caught up with her and cradled her face in his hands. As soon as his palms made contact with her skin, the berserker calmed, sighing contentedly and retreating to the back of his mind. "Are you okay?"

His *själsfrände* shook her head free. "What the fuck were you doing back there?" A bruise flashed angry red on her cheek.

The berserker stirred. "Protecting you."

"Protecting me?" she yelled. "You almost got me killed."

"If you would have gotten on the bike like I told you, you'd be safe." He lifted his hand to touch the mark, and then clenched a fist in frustration when she flinched. "I only want you safe."

"I know how to fight." She stalked past him, picking up the discarded helmet.

He followed. "Did you not hear what the wolverine said?" He towered over her, using his body size for intimidation. "They know you killed their brothers."

"I've had a price tag on my scalp for a long time. Another group of monsters out to get me doesn't make much of a difference." She glared up at him, her dark-blue eyes glittering.

Damn, she was beautiful.

"It makes a difference to me."

"It has nothing to do with you." She bit her lip.

He focused on her mouth and closed the distance

between them. "You are in this mess because you saved me. It has everything to do with me."

Naya squared her shoulders. "I can take care of myself."

"The point is you no longer have to." He cradled her neck and leaned forward. "You're mine now," he whispered against her lips before claiming them with his own.

Her body tensed and she resisted the kiss.

He loosened the grip on her neck, turning it into a caress, lingering on the spot below her earlobe before sliding a finger along her jawline. He coaxed her lips with his.

She leaned into his kiss, dropping the helmet.

Her surrender stoked the fire within him. He groaned, deepening the kiss and grabbing her hips, pressing her body to his. Teeth knocked against teeth as he devoured her mouth, wanting to make her understand what he couldn't get across with words. She belonged with him—to him. There wasn't anything he wouldn't do to protect his *själsfrände*.

She moaned into his mouth. Grabbing her ass with one of his hands, he pressed her against him. The other hand slipped under her jacket, cupping her breast. His thumb flicked the nipple, which instantly hardened. He did too. His damn jeans zipper was about to leave a permanent imprint.

He pushed her back against the motorcycle, pressing his throbbing cock into the heat between her legs.

She half sighed, half moaned in the back of her throat.

He almost expired on the spot.

A car horn blared in the distance.

Naya stiffened and pushed against his chest.

He sighed reluctantly and kissed her once more before lowering her to the ground. Smiling, he watched his tousled queen try to straighten her clothes, her face bright red. She picked up the helmet and then winced as she straddled the bike. He dipped his chin to hide a satisfied grin. At least he wasn't the only one who was uncomfortable.

He dug out the keys to the Porsche from his front jeans pocket, whistling as he walked to the car.

Naya's bike shot past him, spraying his boots with gravel.

Two wolverine bodies were halfway decayed by the sunlight already and blended in with the ground. Another half an hour and they'd be gone completely. Loki's creatures always disintegrated in sunlight, once the life magic he'd granted them was gone. Leif climbed into the Porsche and followed his *själsfrände* back to the fortress. They still had much to clear up. He still needed to convince her mind to surrender to him as easily as her body did.

Chapter 15

THE PULSING SHOWER BEAT NAYA'S SKIN LIKE pebbles of hot hail. Her bruises hurt, but she welcomed the pain. It distracted her from thinking about what had happened in the parking lot after the fight. She concentrated on the sensation of the water massaging her skin and emptied her head of all thoughts of a sexy Viking. Unfortunately, her body still remembered. Her skin tingled, recalling what his calloused hands felt like scraping against the tender surface of her breasts.

She sighed and turned off the water and then swathed her body in an oversize white towel.

Things would never work out between her and Leif. Even if he didn't find out about her connection to the wolverines—which he would—the way he blocked her fighting proved that, although he may have lived among humans for a few centuries, his attitude toward women had obviously stayed in the dark ages. She shouldn't be upset about this.

She tightened the towel around her chest and padded out into the bedroom, stopping at the sight of Leif on her bed, leaning back on his elbows. He'd tied his wet hair back in a ponytail and wore a navy long-sleeved T-shirt tucked into black jeans. He wasn't wearing any shoes.

Strangely fascinated, she stared at his strong bare feet. Why was every part of his body sexy?

He cleared his throat. His ice-blue gaze traveled

from her bare feet up to her damp hair, lingering on her breasts where the damn towel was coming loose again. Her nipples tightened.

A seductive smile played on his lips. "I like what you are wearing."

She glanced away to hide the blush covering her cheeks. "What do you want?"

"To continue our…conversation, of course." His smile turned smoldering.

Heat pooled low in her belly and between her legs. Her mind might be angry with the Viking, but her body certainly was not. "There's nothing else to talk about." She walked to the dresser and picked up her mother's brush.

She heard the sheets rustle as he left the bed and then felt the heat of his body against hers as his hands covered her shoulders.

"Then let's not talk." His breath caressed her ear, moving down her neck where he peppered her skin with kisses.

She couldn't stop a small sigh escaping her lips. "We need to stop this," she whispered.

"Why?" His hand traveled down the length of her arms, crossing over her chest and covering the hand holding up the towel. "You like it." He punctuated the short sentence by lightly kissing below the shell of her ear. "And I like it."

Her knees weakened and she dropped the brush. It clattered on the dresser, waking her from the sensual trance. She stepped away from him, keeping a tight grip on the towel. "This complicates things."

He laughed. The low, sexy sound vibrated through

her body as he embraced her again. "This is the only thing between us that is not complicated," he whispered against her hair.

He smelled like soap and, underneath that, a scent uniquely his, a mixture of pine and spice. She leaned into his chest. He smelled like home.

She tensed. She had no home.

Leif loosened his hold, but leaned down to nibble her ear. "Stop thinking. Trust your instincts."

"I can't," she muttered. "My brain won't stop thinking about you almost getting us killed today." She forced herself to break his hold, no matter how good his hands felt on her body.

He used his knuckle to tilt up her chin. The pupils of his eyes were large, making them darker blue than usual. "I'm sorry about holding you back in the fight. I was trying to protect you."

She laughed. "You're just saying that to get me into bed."

Anger flared in his eyes for a brief second. He turned his back to her and raked a hand through his hair, messing up the ponytail. "I have never told you untruths." He faced her again. "And I never will. It is not my way."

She believed him. The last few days she'd seen how much he cared about his people. And how much they respected him. He might not share everything with her, but lies were not part of Leif's nature. "I'm sorry," she said.

He acknowledged her statement with a small nod before grabbing her hand. "I need you. Not only in my bed, but in my life."

Naya's breath hitched. "I can't make any long-term promises."

"Why not? You've made friends. My people like you." He tugged her hand back when she tried to pull away.

She swallowed. He was making this very difficult. "There's stuff I need to do, responsibilities to take care of." *And secrets I need to keep.*

"Take care of those from here. I will help you with your responsibilities."

A lump formed in her throat. She swallowed it down and blinked back the tears threatening to spill. What would it be like to have someone to trust? Someone to share her burdens with? She shook her head, chasing away the temptation.

Scott was her responsibility and the only person she needed in her life. She couldn't endanger him any more than she already had by telling Irja about him. "I prefer to work alone. I'm not good with teamwork."

He fingered a strand of her hair and tucked it behind her ear, turning the gesture into a caress by tracing the outside of her ear.

She couldn't resist the temptation of tilting her head into his palm.

He leaned down, his breath hot against her lips. "Stop overthinking what we have," he whispered before claiming her lips.

Liquid fire traveled from her lips to her nipples. They pebbled against the towel. She leaned into the kiss. Her body didn't care about logic or obligations. It cared only about getting the Viking naked.

His hot body pressed against her.

She tried to think of all the reasons why this was a bad idea, but her brain fogged over.

Just feel, the traitorous voice in the back of her mind whispered.

She was tired of telling it to shush, or maybe she was just tired of fighting what she wanted.

Leif's hands claimed hers. He lifted them to clasp behind his head. The towel unraveled, but stayed up when he pressed against her body, the heat transferring from his chest to hers, smoldering. She moaned his name.

"I know," he growled against her mouth and then grabbed the towel, throwing it across the room. He stepped back.

Her hands fell from his neck. She traced his chest through his cotton T-shirt. Nipples hardened beneath her fingers.

Reaching behind him, he grabbed the collar and pulled the shirt over his head. It followed the towel.

She grabbed his belt buckle, groaning in frustration when she couldn't get it undone.

He chuckled, stilled her hands, and loosened the belt. He undid the buttons and zipper before stepping out of his jeans. He wasn't wearing any underwear.

She caught a glimpse of his impressive erection before he crushed her to his body. Finally they were skin against skin.

Hers was on fire. She needed all of him right now.

With her hip, she pushed him backward toward the bed and pushed on his chest when the edge hit the back of his knees. He fell backward, grabbing her hands and pulling her on top of him.

She straddled him, but stayed high on her knees, teasing herself, and him, by keeping her wetness away from his hardness. "I'm clean and on birth control," she breathed. "We don't need any additional protection unless you want to use it."

He growled and grabbed her hips.

She clasped his hands and pushed them over his head. Securing them both with one hand, she used the other to cradle his face and leaned in for a kiss.

He struggled against her hold, but not seriously enough to break free. Maybe he didn't think she was strong enough to hold him.

He'd learn.

Heat flushed her body as she anticipated not having to hold back, of participating fully without a part of her always monitoring her strength. "I'm in charge this time," she said against his mouth before nipping his lower lip.

A lazy smile spread over Leif's lips. "Sounds good to me." He bucked his hips.

She quickly moved her hand from his face to press his hips down. "Not until I say so."

His grin grew broader. With a wicked gleam in his eyes, he lifted his head and captured one of her nipples in his mouth. He grazed it with his teeth before biting down lightly.

Sparks shot from where his mouth touched straight to her core. She lowered herself slowly, allowing only the tip of his shaft to enter.

He inhaled sharply. "Naya," he hissed and closed his eyes.

She smiled down at him. "I told you we were playing by my rules."

"Your rules," he repeated, his back arching as she lowered herself another inch.

His width created a slow burn and her breath caught as she felt herself adjusting to the thickness. A guttural moan escaped her throat. She'd never made a sound like it before.

Leif struggled against her grip on his wrists, but she held on tight.

He opened his eyes. "I don't like your rules anymore."

"Too bad." She flexed her muscles around his length inside her.

A mischievous glint entered his gaze. His body relaxed before he twisted his hips, trying to flip her over.

She slipped one leg between his, anchoring her knee against the bed and pressing down on his chest with her torso.

The expression on his face when her strength matched his was priceless.

Naya laughed.

"You've been holding out on me," Leif growled. "Why didn't you tell me how strong you are?"

"You never asked." She flicked her tongue against his nipple. His sharp intake of breath made her do it again. "Now, where were we?" She grinned.

He smiled back. "Your rules."

"My rules," Naya whispered, her voice hoarse. This time she took his whole length inside her and moaned when he was fully sheathed.

Leif bucked his hips.

She let go of his wrists and sat up, taking him even deeper into herself. She rode him, setting a fast pace.

He grabbed her hips, slowing her motion. One hand slid forward, his fingers tangling in her wet curls. He slid his thumb between her swollen lips, finding her tight nub, pressing against it.

Ripples of pleasure radiated through her body. Tilting her head down, she watched his hand working her. The runes of the tattoo on his arm glowed, and she joined him as they both found their release.

White light exploded on the inside of her eyelids. She soared out of her body again, through the pinpricks of light and the circle they formed. She floated in the dense darkness, her skin warming in the balmy air pressing against her. Then the edges of the universe brightened, light rushing toward her.

From far away, a woman with silver hair in a white dress smiled at her.

Naya blinked, and the image disappeared. With a rush, she returned to her body, the sensation of Leif's presence solid beneath her.

He mumbled a protest when she rolled away. Turning on his side, he pulled her backside closer, spooning against her.

She pulled on the sheets until they untangled and then covered them both. His hot breath tickled her neck.

Cocooned in the warmth of his body, she drifted off to sleep, the image of the silver-haired woman still glimmering in her mind.

—◦◦◦—

Leif walked through the empty game room to the computer room door. He'd woken up by himself in Naya's bed, but this time he hadn't heard her leave. The time they had slept together before, he thought their union the most powerful he'd experienced.

He'd been wrong.

Last night he'd been visited by Odin in the beckoning

darkness as he climaxed. The Wise One hadn't spoken to him, but touched his shoulder. He was honored and humbled by Odin's blessing. With the head of the Norse gods approving his berserker's choice of mate, Leif felt certain their union would somehow work out.

He found his *själsfrände* sitting in front of the computers with Ulf. Both of them were staring at a screen filled with numbers.

Naya wore her standard plain T-shirt and jeans, her hair still moist from her morning shower. She turned when he entered. "Hi." She blushed a pretty pink. "Did you sleep okay?"

He leaned over and brushed her forehead with his lips. "I did. You should have woken me when you left the bed."

She glanced quickly at Ulf and cleared her throat. "I…um…you looked like you needed some sleep."

"Good call. He works too hard," Ulf said without glancing up from the screen.

Naya squirmed in the chair and coughed.

"What?" Ulf turned toward her. "There are no secrets in this house. Everyone knows the king spent the night with you."

She put her fingers on the keyboard. "Let's just find these license plate registrations. They may lead us to the wolverines."

Ulf nudged her with his elbow. "And everyone knows it was the second time."

She squawked. Actually squawked.

If Leif hadn't known how much it would hurt her pride, he would have laughed. "I think Naya would like to keep our sleeping arrangement private," he said to Ulf, putting some authority in his tone.

The Viking straightened in his chair. "Yes, *min kung*. I was only teasing. No disrespect intended."

"None taken," Leif assured him, putting his hand on Ulf's shoulder.

"Can I say just one more thing?" Ulf asked.

"No," Naya said at the same time Leif nodded.

The short-haired warrior frowned, but met Naya's gaze. "I'm happy you and the king have found each other."

Her eyes widened and she glanced at Leif. "Okay, fine. Can we get back to work now?"

"What are you working on?" Leif asked.

Naya pointed at the screen. "We're running the license plates from the car that kidnapped me and the car the wolverine escaped in yesterday."

"You wrote down the numbers?" He didn't remember her writing anything down.

"Something like that." She continued typing on the keyboard.

Leif couldn't help himself, he had to touch her. He ran his fingers through her dark hair.

"There's nothing in the DMV records, but Naya's hacked into some other registries," Ulf said with pride in his voice.

Leif sighed. How many federal and state laws was Naya breaking now? Hopefully she knew how to cover her tracks. One of the ways he kept his warriors' battles from being noticed by the police was to stay within the boundaries of the law as much as possible.

Naya mumbled something while tapping away on the keys. She shook her head, freeing the strands from his fingers.

Smiling, he stopped playing with her hair. He got the message. Don't disturb her while she was working.

Ulf peered over her shoulder. "They are both registered to the same place."

Leif froze. The wolverines and her kidnappers were connected. They had common enemies. He moved closer to the screen. Surely Naya would understand how important it was for her to stay in the fortress now. To stay out of danger.

"Who owns the cars?" he asked.

"Some company called Consultant Management, most likely a dummy corporation," Naya answered.

"Run by your kidnappers." Ice filled his veins. If the lab that had kept Naya captive was connected to the government as she suspected, and Loki was associated with them, then this made the threat to his people—the threat to the world—enormous.

Naya turned around. "We'll do some more digging. Maybe we'll find something that can help Sten." She avoided his gaze.

His youngest warrior had still not woken up. Although stable, his heart rate was too fast and his temperature soared too high. "I want everyone to remain in the fortress until we figure out what the connection is."

Ulf opened a new window on his screen. "I'll text everyone."

Leif turned toward Naya. "This means you too. Don't leave this house." When he saw her grimace, he added, "Without telling me first."

She scrunched up her nose. "Fine."

The door opened behind him. Irja stepped inside. She paused when she saw him.

"My king, I need to speak with Naya."

His *själsfrände* swiveled her chair around. "What do you need, Irja?"

The healer's skin was gray and she had dark circles under her eyes. "A favor." She looked at Ulf. "We should have this conversation in private."

Ulf snorted. "Don't mind me."

Naya stood up. "Will you keep looking for information on Consultant Management?" she asked Ulf.

The Viking squared his shoulders. "You bet. Now that you got us into these supersecret databases, I'd love to dig through them."

Leif sighed and stood. "How do we know they can't trace the security breach to us?"

Naya walked toward the door. "Because I'm doing the breaching and nobody's caught me yet."

Irja led them to the medical lab. She pointed at some stools. "If you sit, I'll show you what I'm working on."

Naya shuddered before jumping up on the chair.

"Cold?" Leif asked, putting his arm around her shoulders.

She shrugged. "Just not a fan of labs."

"This won't take long," Irja said.

Leif sat down next to Naya. "What is it you want to show us?"

"Sten's body is not purging the poison fast enough." She turned to Naya. "Our white blood cells can purge foreign substances from our bodies—substances that interact directly with cells."

"Like the wolverine poison," Naya said.

The Valkyrie nodded. "But Sten has only been in Midgard for half a century. His blood cells have not adapted enough."

"What do you need from me?"

"I have been testing your blood, trying to isolate the chemicals you were injected with."

Leif stood. "Why was I not notified about these tests?" The policy was to inform him of everything that went on in the fortress, his warriors knew this.

Both women gave him an impatient not-now look.

He held up his hands in surrender. "Fine. Proceed."

Irja turned toward Naya. "I tested both the blood I took when you first arrived here and the blood we drew a few days ago…"

Naya nodded encouragingly.

"They are different." Irja sat down on a stool. "In this early sample, your white blood cells are human, but the plasma, the liquid surrounding blood cells, contains free-floating nanoparticles. Also, some of your red blood cells have merged with the nanoparticles in your blood."

"Wait, what do you mean 'merged'? What are nanoparticles made of?" Naya frowned.

"They're usually made of metal and almost undetectable. Nanoparticles of titanium dioxide are what give plastics, papers, medicine, even toothpaste their bright white color."

Naya appeared stunned. "And I have these in my blood?"

The other woman nodded. "They were probably in the injections you received. I don't know exactly what type they are."

"And you found a difference in the newer sample?" Leif asked.

Irja glanced at him briefly before turning back to Naya. "In the later sample, the nanoparticles and the red blood cells look the same as before, but your white blood cells are more like ours."

Naya jumped off her stool. "How can my blood be altered? Did you give me any injections while I was sick?"

Irja shook her head. "I think your blood altered because of the bonding."

His *själsfrände* laughed bitterly. "I'm more of a freak than I thought. Apparently great sex doesn't just give me an orgasm, it alters my biochemistry."

Although he already knew she'd liked their time in bed, it pleased Leif that she thought they'd had "great" sex.

He cleared his throat. "I've tried to explain to you about the *själsfrände* bond, but it appears not even I know all the secrets of how it works. The gods know what they're doing, even if we don't yet see their purpose. For now we just have to accept that we are bonded."

Naya shook her head. "This is too much. I don't understand what's happening."

Leif put his hands on her shoulders. "I know. Just trust me for now, and we will figure everything out. Right now, let's see what we can do to save Sten."

Naya studied him for a moment, and turned to Irja. "What do you need from me?"

"I want to try to give Sten a transfusion, using your blood. You're O negative, the universal donor blood type."

"What if the nanoparticles are dangerous to him?"

"That's a chance I'll take. Right now, all I can do is watch him waste away." Irja's voice broke.

"You don't understand." Naya glanced at Leif and then flicked her gaze away. "The injections don't work on everyone." She swallowed. "Some people in the camp ended up...damaged."

Irja nodded. "I understand, but I will only give Sten a small amount of your blood and monitor his progress." She paused. "I wouldn't ask if I wasn't desperate."

"You don't have to do this if you feel uncomfortable." Leif caressed Naya's cheek.

Her midnight-blue eyes turned darker as she studied him. "I'll do it," she said. "Just know that the nanoparticles may turn out to be worse than the poison."

Chapter 16

AFTER IRJA HAD PULLED ALL THE BLOOD SHE NEEDED, Naya found Leif in Sten's room. The Viking's head was bowed as he held his warrior's hand. It looked like he was praying. He looked up when the door closed behind her, his blue eyes bleak.

"How is he?" she whispered.

"No change." His voice sounded gravelly.

"Irja is preparing the injection right now." She hated seeing Leif so defeated. "It will take a while because she's isolating my white blood cells and will give them to Sten as boosters." She pulled up a chair and sat down beside him.

He turned and caught her hand in his. "Thank you for doing this."

"I just hope it works." She couldn't bear it if someone else were to end up in the same state as Scott.

He nodded and turned back to look at Sten. "This is my fault. I should have made the warriors patrol in larger groups." He shook his head. "I should have gone on the offensive, attacked instead of searching for the grove."

"You couldn't have known this would happen."

He turned to her, anguish in his eyes. "I'm supposed to know. I am their king. It is my duty to protect my warriors."

He cared so much about these men and women. She had to tell him about the risks of using her blood. "When

I was kidnapped, the handler told me my blood contains a self-destructive agent." She had to look away. "I don't know how this will affect Sten."

"What do you mean, self-destructive?" Something flashed in his eyes. Anger?

"I don't know if it's true, but he said I will self-destruct on my twenty-third birthday." She'd keep the part about turning into a mindless killing machine under wraps for now. She'd make sure she was far away from Leif and his people before that happened.

Leif's jaw clenched. "When is your birthday?"

"In ten months."

His shoulders tensed, but he took a deep breath as if forcing himself to relax. "That is still ten months for Irja to find a cure, for both you and Sten." He released her hand and raked his fingers through his hair. "If we're lucky, the *själsfrände* bond will help you defeat this self-destructive agent. And this gives us an even bigger reason to complete the handfasting."

Naya tensed. "I can't enter into any kind of commitment with you." Irja had to delay testing the wolverine blood since Sten got sick, but eventually the Norse warriors would figure out Naya had been spawned in the same lab as the wolverines. A sharp pain pinched her heart when she imagined Leif's reaction.

His eyes turned a darker shade of blue. "The handfasting is just a way to formalize what's already happened and to strengthen our bond."

"But—"

Leif shook his head. "No!" he roared, and then shot a quick look at Sten before lowering his voice. "There is nothing to argue about. This bond is blessed by the gods and unbreakable. If you do not help me deepen our connection, you endanger me and my people."

It sounded like an arranged marriage, something he didn't have a choice in either. Did he resent this bond that he believed so strongly in? He'd said nothing about feeling anything for her beyond the obvious sexual attraction. "I can't stay." Even if she didn't have to leave, basing a relationship on nothing but spectacular sex was a bad idea.

"You have to." His eyes searched hers. "It is your duty now. You belong to me and therefore to my people."

Naya forced down the panic rising in her chest. "I have other duties."

He shook his head. "Your work is not as important as taking your role as my queen. This bond between us requires that of you. And I demand it."

Queen? She wasn't fit to rule anything. She could barely take care of her little brother. A manic laughter rose in her throat. She swallowed hard before it could escape. "I have a younger brother. He is not well, and I need to be with him."

Leif's eyes narrowed. "Why have you not told me about this brother before?"

The crazy laugh escaped as a short bark. "It's not like we've done much talking."

A flush spread across his cheeks. "What's wrong with your brother?"

"He was a prisoner in the lab with me, but the injections made him weaker, not stronger." She grabbed his hand. "I have to help him. He's my only family."

Leif shook his head. "I am your family now. My warriors are too. Irja will help you find a cure for your brother. Where is he? We should have him moved to the fortress."

"I can't tell you. The handlers from the camp are hunting him too." His loyalty would always be to his warriors first. And when he found out about her connection with the wolverines, he'd protect his tribe, not Scott.

Disappointment pulled Leif's lips into a frown. "One day you will trust me automatically, but for now I will demand it." He released her hand. "We are going into battle against the wolverines, but after, we will move your brother here so that I can keep both you and him safe."

Naya worried her lip. She'd lost complete control over the conversation. Leif was in full alpha king mode and there would be no negotiations. She shook her head in protest, but before she could say anything, the king continued. "We will have a handfasting ceremony. It works like an engagement. After one year and one month, you will be my bride."

Naya stood. She had never planned on getting married, but she knew what a proposal should look like. And this wasn't it. Where was the declaration of, if not love, at least some deeper feeling? Some sort of respect? Leif demanded her loyalty, her undivided devotion, but didn't reciprocate. "I can't be your fiancée or your wife."

"With the bond, you don't have a choice. Neither of us does. But I will be a good husband and I will take care of your brother." Still only talk of duty. She'd obviously fooled herself into thinking they could ever share any kind of emotional connection. She felt a chasm growing between them and a painful emptiness filled her heart. She too had duty to consider, and it would always be to her brother before everything else, no matter how it would hurt her to leave Leif.

She couldn't risk moving Scott. He wasn't well enough. Besides, the fortress would not be a safe place for either of them once the warriors figured out they shared a creator with the wolverines. Even if Leif would spare her life because of this bond, would he spare Scott's? And even if he did, one of the other warriors might kill them. Torvald thought everything associated with Loki needed to be eliminated.

"Let's talk about it after your battle." That would buy her some time.

Leif watched her for a moment. "There isn't anything to discuss, but I will give you some time to adjust to how things will be."

As if she could ever get used to living with someone who dictated her life. Someone who didn't respect her enough to let her make her own decisions. It would be as if she were back in the lab.

The door opened and Irja and Per entered the room together. Naya quickly schooled her face to not show the panic still storming inside her. "Everything set?" she asked in an overly cheerful tone.

Irja placed her medical kit on the nightstand and removed a syringe. "Just about." She swabbed Sten's arm and pushed the syringe into his arm.

The plunger went in all the way. Per clenched and unclenched his hands. "How long before we know if it works?"

Irja straightened her back. "We have to wait and see."

"I'll sit with him." Per took Naya's abandoned seat. "It's the least I can do."

"This is not your fault," Naya said softly.

"You should not blame yourself," Leif agreed.

The Viking shook his head, anguish reflected in his eyes. "I failed Sten. I should have been covering his back. Instead I chased some wolverines down an alley. After I killed them and returned to Sten, he was lying on the ground unconscious."

Leif placed his hand on Per's shoulder. "You did what I would have done."

"*Nej, min kung.* You would not have left Harald to fight on his own." Per hung his head. "I will take the punishment I deserve."

"I would and I have," Leif insisted. "In the heat of battle, we don't have time to deliberate. You made a decision that felt right at the time. Second-guessing is unproductive."

"*Tack, min kung.*" Per bowed his head.

Irja had been wiping the sweat off Sten's forehead. All of a sudden she jerked upright. "He's reacting to the injection."

Sten thrashed on the bed, pulling his arm out of Irja's hand. Turning his head from side to side, he mumbled.

"What's he saying?" Per asked.

Naya leaned forward, concentrating on the sick man in the bed, rather than on her brother who was always at the back of her mind. "It sounds like numbers and letters."

"Truck," Sten groaned. "Plants on truck…" He repeated the numbers and letters.

Naya jerked back. "He's giving us the license plate of a truck where wolverines are growing poisonous plants."

Per's eyes widened. "You got all of this from his mumbles?"

Naya straightened. "We can't find their grove because it is mobile."

"*Ja.*" Sten sighed and settled back into his pillow, his breathing easier.

"His heart rate is settling down," Irja said, holding Sten's wrist. She put the back of her hand against his cheek. "His fever is down too."

Leif stood. "How do we find this truck?"

"Ulf can access the traffic camera system and search for it." Naya was already halfway to the door.

"How did you make out the registration from Sten's mumbles?" Leif asked.

"Enhanced hearing," Naya said and strode toward the door, revealing yet another secret. She would have to figure out a way to make him understand that, bond or no bond, her duties required her to leave.

"Gather the others," Leif said to Per and Irja. "We'll hunt for the truck as soon as Ulf and Naya have a location, but first we'll do the *blót* oath." He followed Naya. "The threat has escalated. We will renew our warrior bonds so we can fight stronger. This is war now."

Outside the room, he turned to Naya. "I know you still need some time to adjust, but for the sake of my warriors, please take your place at my side during the *blót* ceremony."

She started to protest, but he interrupted her. "Please, let's not argue about this. My people are about to risk their lives."

As much as she didn't want to, she did owe these men

and women for rescuing her. Silently she nodded. How bad could it be?

———~~~———

Naya walked beside Leif as the Norse warriors marched solemnly through the tall pines behind the mansion. They wore sleeveless, charcoal-gray tunics with a Nordic design of a bear on the back over plain white shirts. Their legs were covered in slim black trousers tucked into knee-high boots.

"Why a bear?" she asked Leif in a low voice.

"It symbolizes our warrior spirit," he whispered back without looking at her.

Naya glanced up at him. His blond hair glimmered in the sun as he walked with purpose, looking straight ahead. This side of Leif—his "kingly" side—intimidated her. There were no signs of his dimples or the laughing, playful man she'd shared a bed with. On this forest track, there was no mistaking his role among this group of warriors. He was their leader. Their ruler. And if she wasn't careful, he would fully rule her too. After leaving the lab, she'd sworn never to be shackled by anything or anyone again.

A few minutes from the Viking house, they arrived at a clearing. At the far end, a large throne made of stone sat on top of a flat rock. Behind the rock stood a giant ash tree, its branches reaching high above the canopy of evergreens. Even if it hadn't dwarfed its neighbors, it would still have stood out because of the gray bark and lighter green leaves glittering in the sunshine against the darker pine needles.

With a nod to Harald, Leif took Naya's hand.

Together, they strode across the grass and stepped up on the rock to stand in front of the majestic chair. He pulled her close beside him.

She gazed out at the warriors facing them. Astrid, Irja, Harald, and Ulf seemed unsurprised, while the rest of the warriors looked at her with mild curiosity. Only Torvald frowned back at her, hostility evident in his expression and tense shoulders.

The king raised the hand not holding hers. "My brothers and sisters, we are about to go to war. We will fight a cunning but cowardly enemy. They have kidnapped one of our own and tried to kill me." He turned toward Naya. "If it weren't for this brave woman, I wouldn't be here."

Harald and Astrid both nodded.

Naya swallowed nervously. She thought participating in this ceremony would involve a more passive role. Definitely should have thought this through before accepting.

Leif pulled up his shirtsleeve, revealing the serpent twisting up and around his left arm.

A collective gasp spread through the warriors.

Leif held up a hand, silencing the group before him. "My berserker has chosen. Naya is my *själsfrände*." He grabbed her hand again.

Harald cheered, the others slowly joining him. Torvald spit on the ground and earned a sharp elbow from Astrid.

Heat flushed through Naya's cheeks. She tugged on the hand trapped by Leif's, but he held on. "This bond has made me stronger, made *us* stronger. As your king, I can no longer stay at home while you fight our enemies. It is my duty to take my place among my warriors." He raised his voice. "Will you stand with me in battle?"

"*Ja*." In a united voice, the warriors' answer rumbled across the clearing.

Leif sat down on the throne, guiding Naya to perch on one of the enormous armrests. The warriors in front of them bowed down on one knee.

"Will you take the *blót* oath with me?" the king asked.

"*Ja*," the warriors shouted.

Harald rose and faced the others. He held a silver bowl in his hand. "Will you swear fealty to Leif Skarsganger, our king chosen by Odin, the father of war and wisdom?"

"*Ja*." Their answer echoed among the trees.

The hairs on the back of Naya's neck rose and the air seemed denser. She took a deep breath, trying to ease the pressure in her chest.

Harald placed the bowl on the flat rock and drew his dagger. With a swift stroke, he slashed his palm and held it over the bowl. Blood dripped into the vessel, a tinny sound escaping as it hit the metal bottom.

Harald held the bowl in front of Torvald and the older warrior stood and repeated the gesture, adding his blood to the bowl. Harald then proceeded down the line as each of the Vikings and Valkyries cut their palms and bled into the silver vessel. By the time he reached Per at the end, the drops splashed instead of pinged.

Holding the bowl above his head, Harald stepped up on the flat rock and kneeled in front of Leif. The rest of the warriors took a knee again as the king stood, pulling a dagger with a jewel-encrusted hilt from his belt.

A wind whispered through the pines and playfully rustled Naya's hair.

Leif cut his palm and added his blood to the bowl. "I accept your fealty, brothers and sisters of blood." He returned the dagger to his belt and dipped his index and middle fingers into the bowl. Red drops splattered against the flat stone as he held up his hand and smeared a circle on his bicep around the head of his snake tattoo. His nostrils flared. "My serpent is bound to your warrior spirits." He wiped his fingers on a piece of cloth Harald handed him.

The red-haired Viking stood and dipped two fingers into the bowl. Tracing a circle around the head of his own tattoo, he repeated, "My serpent is bound to your warrior spirits."

The wind gusted, whipping the warriors' tunics around their legs and Astrid's and Irja's hair into their faces. Naya wondered if she was supposed to add her blood to the bowl, but it seemed her main duty was to sit next to Leif. She was fine with that.

Harald walked down the line and each warrior repeated the smeared circle and the words about the serpent and the warrior spirit.

The leaves of the ash tree rustled and whooshed violently. Harald walked over to the base of the tree, bowed three times, and then poured the blood from the bowl over the roots. The wind died at once.

When the branches stilled and dipped down to their original position, it looked as if the giant tree bowed to the Vikings and the Valkyries. Without meaning to, Naya too bent down with the Norse warriors as they returned the tree's gesture.

Leif sat back down on the throne. He looked up at Naya. She met his gaze and something passed between them, something significant. Before she could identify what it was, Leif looked away and placed his cut hand palm down on the armrest Naya wasn't sitting on. He smeared the stone and then turned his hand palm up.

One by one, the warriors approached the throne and covered Leif's injured hand with their own before bowing down, touching their forehead to the entwined hands. Each of them said the same phrase, "*Min kung*, I give you my sword, my honor, my life," while Leif briefly touched his uninjured palm to the back of their heads.

Naya felt like she was intruding on an intimate moment. She didn't believe she could ever truly be his wife, or his people's queen, but there was so much power in this ceremony. It unsettled her.

Once each warrior had paid respect to the king, the whole troop marched back to the house. Naya rushed ahead of Leif, needing a few moments to collect herself.

Half an hour later, she found Leif in his office, putting on battle gear. His back was turned to the door, and she paused to admire his body. Snug black leather pants hugged his lean hips and muscular thighs. On his feet, he wore black combat boots. The defined muscles of his back flexed through his shirt as he fiddled with something on the desk in front of him.

"I hate Velcro. What's wrong with laces and hooks?" he muttered.

She crossed the room and grabbed the Kevlar vest he was trying to sort out. She'd come to continue their discussion from before and to get clarification on what had happened in the clearing, but now was not the time. She understood the importance of mentally preparing for a fight. Had done so many times herself. "Let me help."

The front of him was even more impressive. She glanced at the six-pack abs visible under the cotton material and had to swallow to relieve her suddenly dry throat.

She switched her gaze to the vest in her hands. The bulletproof garment was state of the art, superthin, and flexible. Quickly loosening the straps on the sides, she held it by the shoulders. She eyed his bandaged hand. "How's your palm?"

"My palm is going to be fine. The ceremony only requires a shallow cut." He bent at the waist, waiting for her to put the vest on him. "Thank you for untangling the vest," he said grudgingly.

Naya slipped the Kevlar over his head, allowing her hands to touch his silken hair for a minute. "Do you ever think about cutting it?" What she really wanted to ask was what that look across the clearing had meant, but she felt too raw to discuss it now. He was getting ready for a fight, and emotions didn't belong in battle.

Leif straightened and held out his arms so she could reach the straps on the side. "Why? A Viking's hair is a sign of strength."

She stepped to his side. "Ulf must be very weak then." Ignoring the tantalizing smell of his skin, she tightened one of the straps. Why did her body ache for him when her mind shouted to run away?

He grunted as the vest tightened around his chest. "My technical genius is enamored with everything of this time. Not only the gadgets, but the clothes and the hairstyles too."

"Long hair can be a disadvantage in a fight." Her scalp tingled with the memory of the wolverine grabbing her hair the night she'd saved Leif in the alley.

"True, but long hair on a Viking is a tradition. I like traditions." He gave her a meaningful look as another puff of breath escaped through his lips when she tugged on the strap again.

She secured the Velcro and Leif lowered his arms. His tattoo ink glimmered, remains of the blood smear still encircling the snake's head, and, for one moment, she thought a rune glowed as she brushed his arm by accident. "The others have the head and partial body around their bicep. Will they too find a soul mate?"

Impatiently, he checked that his vest was secure. "The *själsfrände* bond is a blessing from the goddess Freya, but very rare. We are honored that she has bestowed her gift on us."

She bristled. He still only talked of the bond in terms of honor and duty. "I still can't accept that we are bonded." The unease she'd felt at the clearing tightened her chest again.

Leif stilled and cradled her face in both his palms. "It doesn't matter what we think. The gods have spoken and we are now bonded for life. If you were a Valkyrie, your serpent would be whole as well."

Naya took a step back, forcing him to release her. She didn't mean to distract him from his battle preparations, but he had brought it up. "I'm not okay with this."

"Neither of us had a choice, the connection triggered the day you saved me in the alley."

"I don't want this." Her voice sounded shrill.

Shit, shit, shit.

What happened to a soul mate who turned out to be a monster? Would she just get kicked out or worse— imprisoned and studied?

"We'll discuss this further when I get back," he said. "Right now, I need information about the truck."

She swallowed the angry words threatening to spill out of her mouth. He was right. The truck should be their first priority. Plenty of time to set him straight about their relationship later. Or at least she wouldn't be around and he could deal with it all on his own. She unfolded a piece of paper from her back pocket and thrust it at him. "We traced the truck's path through closed-circuit security and traffic cameras. It's at the farm where Per was held captive."

Leif studied the satellite image she'd printed out. "This is a sharper focus than last time."

She shrugged. "Google Earth doesn't update often enough. I hacked into a satellite to get real-time footage."

He studied her. "How many laws did you break?"

"I'm sure the gods won't mind." Her sassy tone earned a small smile from him. Embarrassed over how much that pleased her, she averted her eyes.

Studying the image, Leif put his finger on a spot in the middle. "Astrid and Torvald searched this place again a few days ago. They found nothing and this truck was not there."

"It's ingenious to have a mobile growing grove. I'm surprised more potheads don't use trucks."

"Probably because they'd drive too slow." Leif grinned at her.

His attempt at lightening the mood and the modern reference took her by surprise and she found herself grinning back. "The truck is registered to Consultant Management, like the other two cars."

His head jerked up. "We'll have to study this

connection between the wolverines and your kidnappers further." He studied her closely.

She avoided his gaze. "The others are waiting for you. Ulf has updated them."

Leif crossed his arms across his chest. "Naya, you need to share everything."

"I have. I told you about the license plate number."

He shifted impatiently. "I've waited for you to tell me about your connection with the wolverines."

Her heart sank. How had he found out? "They're somehow connected through the company that owns the vehicles."

"You must think me stupid," he growled. "There's more of a connection than that. What did you kidnapper mean when he said 'we made her,' and why do the wolverines always find you?"

"How do you know they're not finding you?" She swallowed the panic rising in her throat. "I'd never seen them before the night they attacked you in the alley."

He just watched her, one eyebrow raised.

She relented. "I don't know the whole connection, but somehow the wolverines know who I am and they know about my brother."

"You must have some theories."

She looked up at him watching him intently to gage his reaction. "I think they were made in the lab where I was imprisoned."

Except for his jaw clenching, his face gave nothing away. "You could have shared this information with me."

"I was afraid you'd consider me your enemy."

His face turned cold. "I have done nothing for you to think I would hurt you." He looked away. "I need my weapons." He grabbed a leather jacket from the back of the chair and strode toward the door. "I can't be distracted by you joining the fight. Stay at the fortress. We have much to discuss when I get back."

Naya swallowed nervously. "That depends on how long you'll be gone."

He paused mid-stride, slowly turning. "What do you mean?"

She shrugged. "I have business out of town."

Taking a step toward her, he lowered his voice. "You will stay here until I return."

"I heard you the first time." Earlier, she'd suggested joining the fight, but Harald and Leif had both protested vehemently. Even Astrid had objected, probably because the Valkyrie would also be left out of the mission. Leif had insisted on going on the mission, and with the king gone, a warrior had to stay and guard the house. Naya suspected it really meant someone had to stay and babysit her, guard her. Astrid had pulled the short straw.

"Consider it a request." His eyes turned dangerously dark and his nostrils flared. "From your king. Whom you are bonded to." He stepped closer, bending down. "For this to work, you have to trust me and do as I tell… as I *ask* you."

She stilled. He was too close. "I'm not comfortable with all of these rules."

His lips hovered over hers. "Some rules are good," he whispered, his breath caressing her lips.

She wanted his kiss so bad, she ached. Forcing herself to take a step back, her body tingled with disappointment. "I have my own rules." She put her hands in her pockets to keep them from grabbing on to him.

"They include not having to ask anyone for permission. I leave town tomorrow."

"Why?" His hand reached out to touch her face, but she ducked out of the way.

"A client needs me to assess his security needs."

"You're leaving town with a man?" His hand dropped and clenched into a fist.

"A client." Was Leif jealous?

You wouldn't like it if he went out of town with another woman. She pushed the thought out of her head.

"The wolverines are connected to those hunting you. Traveling by yourself is not safe," he ground out through clenched teeth.

She stared him in the eyes. "I am not going by myself. The client and his bodyguards will protect me."

"*I* will protect you." He waved his hand in the air. "It is my duty to do so."

Again with "duty." She should never have slept with him. If she had resisted, whatever this bond thing he insisted had formed would not be an issue.

As if she could have resisted him.

She shook her head and welcomed the hot fury raging inside. She didn't know how to handle this physical craving she had for him, but anger was familiar. Her fists clenched. "I am my own person."

Leif glowered. "You belong to me. If your wants endanger you or my people, you will adjust them accordingly."

Before she had a chance to reply to his ridiculous statement, the door opened and Harald entered. He was also dressed completely in black. The bushy beard had been trimmed close to his face. His green eyes shone with excitement. "*Min kung*, the hour grows late. We should confiscate the truck before it moves to a new place." He bowed quickly to Naya.

"We'll continue this discussion later," Leif shot over his shoulder as he strode across the room to join Harald. "You *will* be here when I return."

Naya stared after him as the door slammed behind them. She'd arranged to go with Holden in the morning. The arrogant Viking king would just have to deal. She sank down into one of the chairs flanking his desk.

She'd hoped her last memory would be of making love to Leif, not wanting to knock some sense into his thick head. Now that he knew the true connection between herself and the wolverines, it was not likely he'd ever take her to his bed again.

Chapter 17

LEIF STOMPED DOWN THE HALLWAY, FOLLOWING HIS *stallare*. Harald adjusted the scabbard hanging off his belt and glanced over his shoulder, quirking an eyebrow. "Did you fill your boots with lead?"

"Mind your own business," Leif snarled, easing up on his footfall.

"I would, but you're broadcasting yours to everyone." He shot a cocky smirk over his shoulder.

Leif opened his mouth to give him hell, but shut it when he found three Vikings and two Valkyries in the foyer, staring at him wide-eyed. "What the fuck is your problem?" he said instead.

Everyone avoided his gaze. What *was* their problem?

He took one more step down and studied his warriors. Per and Ulf avoided his gaze, but Torvald stared at him, defiance glittering in his eyes. "How can you bond with a human?"

"Watch your tone, old man." Harald took a step toward him, hand on his sword hilt. "Show your queen the respect she deserves."

Torvald ignored him. He stared at Leif. "A non-Valkyrie as queen, it's not done."

Leif took the last step down and strode toward his oldest warrior. "I am your king. You do not question me." He felt Harald's presence at his side, slightly behind him. "And you do not question Freya. Naya is my *själsfrände*."

Torvald straightened, but still had to look up to meet Leif's eyes. "She is not a warrior. She is not one of us."

Leif widened his stance.

Torvald flinched.

Ulf stepped forward. "She saved the king's life. Killed four wolverines on her own. She's as good of a warrior as any of us. Better than some. You liked her well enough when she installed the surveillance and computer system."

"Know your place, *pojke*. That was before I knew she bonded with the king." The old Viking sneered.

Ulf pulled his sword. "I'll show you what my place is, you grizzled fool."

Leif's berserker responded to the heavy tension lacing the air. His nostrils flared and his right hand clenched, searching for the hilt of his favorite weapon. Behind him, he heard Harald pull his sword halfway out of the scabbard. The warriors had all collected their favorite weapons from the armory.

"Everybody calm the fuck down," Astrid growled.

Leif glared at her. She held her head high and something wild glittered in her eyes. She clenched her jaw so hard, her teeth ground against each other.

Her berserker was close to the breaking point.

She startled him by walking up to him and grabbing his wrist like a vise. "Calm down," she whispered. "Your berserker's rage is feeding ours."

"It's true," Per whispered as if in awe. "I feel my connection to the king growing. His anger is fueling mine."

"A human queen is not right," Torvald muttered.

Astrid turned. "Get used to it, old man," she spat out. "Your queen tracked down where our enemies grow their poison."

Ulf cleared his throat. "Actually, I tracked down the truck."

Wild-eyed, Astrid swiveled around.

He blanched. "Okay, the queen showed me how."

"She saved Sten," Per said quietly.

"Louder," Astrid commanded.

Per turned to Torvald, squaring his shoulders to confront his mentor and teacher. The young Viking rarely contradicted the older warrior and was the only one who ate his cooking. "Sten was dying until Irja injected him with the queen's blood."

The older warrior raised a skeptical brow.

Irja's black hair gleamed in the light. She looked at Torvald. "I couldn't save him. The king's mate gave him life."

Torvald's shoulders slumped. "She is not a Valkyrie." He surveyed the room for support.

"Who the fuck cares?" Harald bellowed. "The bond makes our king stronger, which makes all of us stronger." He slipped his sword back in its scabbard. "Now can we please get the fuck out of here and go kill some wolverines?"

"Please do." Astrid rolled her eyes. She appeared calm again. "I've had enough antiquated testosterone-driven posturing to last me a lifetime or two."

Torvald muttered something under his breath, but quieted when the blond Valkyrie glared at him. The others put on their jackets, adjusted the sword scabbards on their belts, and slipped a gun or two into holsters. They lined up shoulder to shoulder, sword hands on their hilts.

Harald turned to Leif and handed him Arngrim in its

scabbard. The broadsword bore the name of a berserker featured in the old sagas. His father had given him the weapon on his fifteenth birthday.

Leif took the sword and pulled it out of the scabbard. The ring of steel brushing against leather resonated through the air as he held the sword up high, its weight balanced comfortably in his grip. He'd wielded this weapon for so long it felt like an extension of his arm. His warriors pulled their own swords, holding them above their heads. The broadswords were hard to conceal and not very effective against modern weapons, so these days they used them mostly in training and for ceremonial purposes. The sword connected them to their past, strengthening their bonds with their berserkers and the bond they shared as battle brothers.

Harald led them in a war cry. Leif's berserker howled and he felt his Vikings' inner warriors join. The energy of all those war-ready berserkers resonated within his chest. The power almost overwhelmed him. He had never connected with his warriors this strongly.

The looks of wonder on his brothers' and sisters' faces showed that they experienced it as well.

Harald took a deep breath and stepped forward. "Will you join your king in victory?"

"*Ja!*" Their shouts echoed in unison through the foyer.

They sheathed their weapons and Harald handed Leif a gun. Swords were the honorable choice, but that didn't mean modern weapons didn't have their usage. "Here," he said then turned to bark at the others. "It takes you longer to get ready than a gaggle of women braiding their hair with *midsommar* flowers. Are we going to discuss how pretty our dresses are or are we going to fight?"

"Fight!" Ulf shouted, and the others echoed.

En masse, they spilled out the front door and loaded up into the SUVs parked in the courtyard.

———

Naya peered at the monitor in front of her. She needed to leave the Vikings, but worry about Leif had her dragging her feet. What if he didn't survive this battle? She'd stay just long enough until she knew he was safe. Until then, she'd work on an encrypted email she'd intercepted by monitoring the wolverines' email traffic from the farm.

Frustrated, she tapped the keyboard. The lines of numbers and letters of the short message changed, but still didn't combine into anything readable. She'd run an algorithm comparing the message to all the world's languages. None had matched.

She stretched in the chair, arching her back like a cat. She needed to work out. Even though her enhanced senses gave her the advantage in most fights, she preferred to train to keep her skills sharp. Especially now that she seemed to be fighting monsters every other day.

She'd just try one more time to decode the message. A knock on the door interrupted her typing.

Astrid entered and flung herself in the other office chair. Her muscles twitched and her blue eyes glittered. "I'm bored." She sounded like a teenager.

"I'm busy," Naya retorted. "Go bother someone else."

"Come fight with me." The Valkyrie widened her eyes.

"No time." Naya turned back to the screen.

Astrid leaned forward. "What's Batch 439?" she asked, staring at the screen.

"You can read that?"

The Valkyrie pointed at the screen. "It's Old Norse. Of course I can read it."

Excited, Naya stood. "What does it say?" Damn, she'd only compared to living languages, not historical variations. She needed to update her encryption database.

Astrid shot her a calculating look. "How much is it worth to you?"

Sighing, Naya sat back down. "What do you want?"

"If I tell, you'll spar with me?"

"Fine." She could always pull back on her hits and slow down her reaction speed.

"I pick the weapons?"

"Yes." She clenched her fists to keep from shaking the woman. "What does it say?"

Astrid shrugged. "Something about a Batch 439."

"Please read the full text," Naya said through gritted teeth.

The Valkyrie sighed theatrically and pulled her chair closer to the screen. "I didn't know you were interested in Old Norse. I have some books I could lend you." When Naya impatiently waved to get her to continue, she cleared her throat. "It says, 'Encouraged by the success of Batch 439. Inject all old models immediately. Keep them isolated until desired effect is observed.'"

Naya carefully kept her face neutral while her heart pumped faster than a jackrabbit's on speed. The government agent had called her an "old model." Batch 439 could be an antidote. It could also be some new poison. Shit. To know for sure, she needed access to the camp's computer records. She'd managed to break through their firewall, but not well enough to dig around in the records undetected. Their tracers always found her, and she had to disconnect in order to not be tracked.

Astrid waved her hand in front of Naya's face. "Hello, earth to Naya."

She shook her head. "I'm sorry, what did you say?"

The tall blond sighed dramatically. "I said, time to pay up."

"I need to figure this out." Naya gestured toward the computer.

The Valkyrie shot to her feet, grabbing Naya's arm and making her rise. "Nope," she said, dragging her out of the room. "You promised me a fight…a sparring, and I need to get rid of some energy. Can't wait any longer."

⁓

The rubber mat under Naya's bare feet cooled her soles, a contrast to the rest of her overheated body. For the last hour, the Valkyrie had punched and kicked like a demented kangaroo. Even though Naya had blocked most of them, some had made contact with various body parts. She'd be black and blue in the morning.

Naya tried to blow her bangs out of her eyes, but the sweaty strands remained plastered to her forehead. Wiping them away would leave an opening for Astrid, and Naya's ribs already ached enough. She kept her hands in front of her face, protecting her nose and eyes.

The tall, blond woman smiled. "You fight pretty well for a shorty."

She tuned out the taunting, concentrating on what Astrid's hands and feet were doing. The Valkyrie was a master of advertising one move while executing a completely different one. Soon, Naya would have to stop pulling her punches.

Her opponent bounced her weight to her left leg a little more.

Naya watched both of Astrid's legs and prepared a comeback kick of her own. The overhand punch took her by total surprise. Stars flashed briefly behind her eyelids as she fell down on all fours on the mat. "Shit, that hurt."

"Sorry." Astrid grinned, not looking contrite at all, her eyes glittering mischievously.

Naya pushed herself off the floor, shaking her head. Sweat flew in all directions, like a dog shaking itself after a swim. "I thought we were sparring, not fighting for real." Astrid's maniacal energy woke something within Naya. Her nostrils flared.

Astrid laughed. "If we were fighting for real, you wouldn't be just bruised—you'd be dead."

"Well, I am black and blue." She found her footing on the mat. She faked a jab and crouched down when Astrid moved to block it. She quickly bounced back up, executing a semicircular spinning kick to the Valkyrie's kidney. The tall woman fell like a lodgepole pine.

If this had been a real fight, Naya would have followed up with an overhand punch or a front kick. Instead, she jumped back, bouncing on the front of her feet a safe distance from her opponent.

Astrid took a deep breath, pushing off the mat with her hands to stand up straight again. "Good delivery," she wheezed.

Naya made a little mock bow, but kept her hands in ready position in front of her face.

"Even Torvald would approve of that blow."

She frowned. "What does Torvald have to do with anything?"

"Nothing." Astrid's gaze cut to the left.

A classic sign of lying for right-handed people. Astrid's dominant hand was her right, but this could be another fake.

Naya cautiously lowered her hands. "Seriously, what does Torvald have against me?"

Astrid sighed. "I shouldn't have said anything. He just doesn't think a human should rule over the Vikings and Valkyrie."

For all that was holy, these people would not give up. She laughed out loud.

"What's so funny?" Astrid tilted her head.

"I'm not going to be your queen. There's no way I'd marry Leif."

Astrid studied her for a few heartbeats. "But you *are* our queen. Leif introduced you as his mate at the ceremony beneath the ash tree."

Naya dropped her hands. *Shit.* That's what standing by his side had meant. He snuck that one by her. "I don't want to be your queen."

Astrid tilted her head. "You have no choice. The gods picked you as Leif's mate and that automatically makes you our queen."

Naya sat down on the mat with an ungraceful thud. "Bond or no bond, it's just sex between us, nothing deeper than that." *Liar,* the little voice in her head whispered. She ignored it.

Astrid stared at her incredulously and then rich laughter bellowed from her mouth. She sat down, wiping her eyes. "The sex completed the bond."

Heat flushed Naya's cheeks, but her insides were as cold as Antarctica. "Why is this bond so important?"

"The bond between two *själsfrände*, soul mates, is sacred." She punched her lightly on the shoulder. "Dang, girl, you guys are really going at it in bed if you didn't even notice Leif's tattoo completing itself."

Ice water trickled through her veins. So Astrid also believed that the tattoo had somehow completed itself. A forgotten memory from the night Leif first made love to her rose in her mind. "The tattoo," she whispered. "It glowed and tingled."

Astrid nodded. "When you make love, the tattoo might glow. I've never heard about tingling though." She pushed Naya's shoulder, leering at her. "Was it in a good spot?"

In a daze, Naya shook her head.

If Astrid and the others thought she'd made a commitment by sleeping with Leif, it would be harder to slip away unnoticed. She turned to face Astrid. "Tell me everything about this bond and the freaky tattoo." Leif had explained, but maybe Astrid knew of a loophole.

"Hey." The other woman frowned. "This is a good thing. The bond only works between people who have the potential to truly love each other. Once it is completed, it makes the two *själsfrände* physically stronger and enhances their connection."

Naya startled. "What do you mean, 'enhances their connection'?"

Astrid fidgeted. "Maybe you should be talking to Leif about this."

Naya grabbed the blond woman's hand. "Are you telling me that this…this bond thing is messing with my emotions?" Astrid pulled on her hand, but Naya refused to let go. "Tell me!" she shrieked. "You say I'm your queen. I demand you tell me."

The Valkyrie's eyes cooled. "Very well, Your Highness." She executed a small bow. "What is it you want to know?"

"Have I been given something that alters my emotions?" She already knew her blood had been altered. Had they been putting stuff in her food? Was it in that broth Irja brought when she was sick?

Astrid tilted her head. "Nobody's given you anything." She jerked her hand free. "You started the process when you first touched Leif. Saving his life might have enhanced the connection. It's not always clear how the bond is triggered, but the *själsfrände* bond must be completed or the warriors are called back to Valhalla."

The room spun. "What do you mean, our connection got stronger?" She put both hands on the mat to anchor herself.

"I've heard of *själsfrände* who could read each other thoughts, but that's unusual. Most couples pick up on the other's feelings, especially if they are strong. And when they are near each other, they influence the other's emotions." She glared at Naya. "Are you okay? Has Leif not explained this to you?"

No, she was not okay. Would never be okay. He'd explained some ancient Norse tradition that was connected to the tattoo. He hadn't explained that it influenced her emotions. Maybe she should have suspected something when she learned about the altered blood. But how could she ever have suspected that the strong connection, the attraction between her and Leif, had been nothing but a trick of manipulated neurochemistry? She'd felt safe among these people, but it was no different than when she was imprisoned in the lab.

Her feelings were not true. They were a by-product of whatever had been done to her body. She couldn't trust her emotions.

Her friendship with Irja and Astrid wasn't real.

Her affection for Leif was a lie.

Bile rose in her throat. "I have to get out of here." Unsteadily she rose and stumbled to the wall for support.

Astrid took a step toward her. "Hey, let me help."

Naya flinched. "Don't touch me."

The other woman backed up. "I won't, but let me help you. You look sick."

She had to get out before Leif decided she was the enemy and made her a prisoner. Before he looked at her with disgust and contempt. She shook her head. He may feel that already. He probably lied when he said he wouldn't hurt her. The connection between them was manipulated. Whatever he may have felt for her could be turned on and off. If there were any feelings at all. He'd never shared anything deeper than sexual attraction. Her head spun. Maybe this had all been a game. A way to lure the wolverines to come out in the open. Had she been his bait all along?

She dragged herself across the courtyard to the main house.

In her room, she stuffed her laptop into its bag and threw everything else into her duffel. She shrugged into her leather jacket as she surveyed the room for anything forgotten. Her gaze lingered on the bed, and she furiously blinked. She'd been such a fool.

Downstairs, she grabbed the keys to Sten's bike from the wooden cabinet by the door. Once she reached the city, she'd ditch the bike so they couldn't track her through its GPS. Without looking back, she opened the huge front door just enough to slip outside. The door closed behind her with a soft click.

Tears streamed down her face as her heart broke. There was no "home" for her, no deep connection with the Viking king. Only altered neurochemistry that tricked her into feeling normal affection for another.

But she was not normal. Hadn't been for a long time and would never be again. It was time she stopped deluding herself by thinking she was anything but a freak.

Chapter 18

LEIF BOUNDED UP THE STAIRS TO NAYA'S BEDROOM. HIS vision blurred and he couldn't draw enough oxygen into his lungs. His heart raced like a deer on the first day of hunting season.

The berserker howled inside him, clawing to get out and take control of his body. It demanded to find its *själsfrände*.

The berserker had surfaced while they fought the wolverines and burned the truck with the poisonous plants. Battle fever had raged through his body more intensely than usual, but he had known Naya would calm the warrior spirit as soon as he returned to the fortress.

Where was she? The bed hadn't been slept in. Maybe she was in the computer room. He turned, but before he could leave Astrid glided through the door.

"*Min kung*, are you okay?"

"Naya," he growled. "Have to find Naya."

Astrid shook her head. "She left. I don't know where she went, but she took one of the bikes." She looked around the room. "She packed her stuff."

His berserker spun out of control. Howling, it clawed at the mental barriers keeping it in check. Leif's vision bled crimson. He pulled out his dagger from his boot and pressed the tip into his palm until blood trickled through his fingers. Ice-cold pain centered him. Breath by breath, he calmed his panting. Slowly, the berserker receded and Leif took a shallow breath. "Why didn't you stop her?" he wheezed out.

Astrid took a step back, her face registering alarm. "As your *själsfrände*, she is my queen. I have no right to stop her."

The berserker bellowed in rage. She'd left them. The beast inside him was dangerously close to taking complete control of Leif's body.

He needed to find her. To reason with her. He needed her to soothe and comfort his inner warrior, to comfort him.

He banged his fist on the dresser, smearing the wood with blood.

"Fuck!" he shouted, feeling marginally better.

Astrid disappeared into the bathroom and came out with a towel that she used to wipe up the blood.

Harald entered the room. His second-in-command was still in battle gear. He took one look at Leif's hand, then hastily glanced away and cleared his throat. "Did I come at a bad time?"

"Fuck you," Leif snarled. "We have to find Naya." At the thought of Naya, the berserker paced faster in his cage, running in tight circles. Leif pressed the dagger into the wound on his palm again.

Harald flinched when blood dripped on the floor. He took the towel from Astrid and used it to wrap Leif's hand and forced him to sit down in one of the blue chairs. Harald then took a seat in the other. "What did she tell you before we went to battle?"

Leif tried to think through the red haze of anger filling his mind. "She has a client she's visiting."

"Luke Holden," Astrid said, leaning against the wall. "He owns Desire, the nightclub."

"Find him." Leif wasn't sure if it was his voice or that of the berserker growling out the words. They both wanted to get their hands on the man who had their woman. Preferably wrap them around his neck. That Naya was going with Holden of her own free will didn't matter.

"We will." Harald leaned forward in the chair. "I'll have Ulf track down all property registered to Holden."

Leif nodded. The berserker demanded to hunt, to fight. The chair toppled when he stood. "Check for her name on any passenger list. Buses, trains, and planes." He wanted to wring Naya's neck for leaving. He wanted to yell at her. But what he wanted most was for her to be back where she belonged. With him.

Harald stood. "I'll take care of it." He watched him for a few moments. "You need to calm down. We'll do everything we can."

Leif ignored him. "What was the name she used when she first came here?" He pressed his hands to his head as if the pressure would spit out the answer he wanted. "Daisy something. Ask Irja."

"Daisy Driscoll," Harald said. "We'll search that name too."

"She may use other aliases." Desperate, he looked up. "How do we find her other aliases?"

"We will find her." Harald grabbed Leif's hands and lowered them. "You need to try to remain in control."

"I won't be able to for much longer." He tugged free from the red-bearded Viking's gentle grip. "In another day or two you will have to lock me up."

Harald's gaze slid to the side. "Irja will prepare a sedative."

"Even drugged, you have to lock me up." He paused. "You need to send for one of the other kings."

Astrid made a sound of protest. Although Odin spoke to all Viking and Valkyries, only the kings could contact the god unbidden. Only a ruler of one of the other warrior tribes would be able to tell the Wise One to call Leif back to Valhalla.

Harald shook his head. "We don't have to make that decision now."

Leif grabbed his shoulder, smearing blood on Harald's tunic. "Promise me you will send for one of them." Without Naya, he'd live the rest of eternity as a drugged animal in a cage. Unbearable. He shuddered.

"I promise," Harald whispered, not meeting his gaze.

The door swung open and Irja marched in, lab coat billowing in her wake. "*Min kung*, I have news." The healer had returned early to the fortress once it was clear they would beat the wolverines.

Leif's head jerked up. "About Naya?"

The Valkyrie stopped a few feet away. "Yes, somewhat."

"Don't dawdle, *jänta*. Tell the king," Harald said gruffly.

"I started some processes on the wolverine blood before we went to battle. In case we had injuries or someone got poisoned," she explained. "I wanted to know as much as possible about the creatures."

"And?" Leif said when she didn't continue.

"I found nanoparticles similar to Naya's." She looked away.

"What are you saying?" Harald insisted. "Is Naya related to Loki's monsters?"

Leif rubbed his eyes. "We knew of the connection

between Naya's kidnappers and Loki's minions." And Naya had told him the wolverines had been created in the same lab.

"Yes," Irja whispered. She coughed. "The nanoparticles show that whoever created the wolverines are the same people who trained and enhanced Naya."

"That doesn't necessarily mean anything. She told us she was a prisoner in the lab," Harald said.

Leif appreciated his *stallare*'s loyalty to his queen, but it was time to face reality. He couldn't believe there was the same evil in her as in the wolverines. Surely the berserker would have picked up on it? But why had she left if it wasn't to weaken him? "She could have been created by Loki to be a weapon against us, just like the wolverines." She'd left on purpose. He'd explained how the bond worked. Hadn't he?

"She wasn't like that." Harald looked to Irja for confirmation.

The Valkyrie flushed. "She…didn't always tell us the whole truth."

Was his *själsfrände* an enemy? Had he bonded with one of Loki's monsters? Leif's heart thundered in his chest.

―――

Naya tottered up to the rental car counter on stripper heels, making sure she put enough swing in the hips to make her short skirt flounce. Her boobs were pushed up to just below her chin thanks to some silicon cutlets, and she made sure she leaned over the counter far enough for the clerk to get a generous glimpse of her cleavage.

"How can I help you today?" His sleazy smile

matched his gelled hair. The name tag on his chest said "Chuck."

"I need a car, please," she said in her best breathy Marilyn Monroe impression and handed over her driver's license. It had a fake name worthy of her outfit.

"Of course"—his eyes left her chest long enough for a quick glance at her license before returning to her boobs—"Miss Mystique."

Naya gave him what she hoped was a flirty smile. "I'd like something with four-wheel drive. I'm planning a trip to the mountains." She leaned over a little farther. Her hastily purchased driver's license was a cheap fake. The ID would not have worked for air travel, but luckily she'd caught a lift with Holden's private jet to Colorado. Private airfields did not ask for identification. She was supposed to draw up the plans for his ski lodge in Aspen while he was there on business, but she'd talked him into postponing for a few days so she could stop by and visit Scott.

"I'll see what we have available." He cleared his throat and took another peek at her cleavage before tapping the keyboard. "The Rockies are beautiful this time of year." He typed some more. "Denver also has a lot to offer. If you are in town for a few days, I'd love to show you the nightlife." He flashed another smile as he jotted down his cell phone number on the rental contract of a brand-new BMW X5.

"I don't have a company credit card yet," Naya said. "Is cash okay for now?" She lightly touched his arm.

The clerk faltered in his typing, but recovered quickly. "Of course, I'll just need a larger deposit."

Naya counted out the bills on the counter. She

grabbed the keys and gave Chuck a little wave before sauntering out of the rental office.

Five miles outside of the Denver city limits, she tore off the itchy cheap blond wig and lobbed it out the open car window. Sighing contentedly, she ran her free hand through her own hair, digging her fingers into the scalp until the itching stopped.

A few miles later, she popped the silicon cutlets out of her bra and threw them on the passenger-side floor. They were more expensive than the wig and had proved quite useful. She might need them again. She needed to change at the next rest stop. The heels were too hard to walk in and left her vulnerable. She'd drive barefoot if it wasn't so cold in the mountains. Hopefully she wouldn't need to fight in her current getup. The new name should have thrown off any handlers on her trail.

The thought of fighting exhausted her. Her aching head refused to stop throbbing, no matter how many ibuprofens she popped. She had trouble swallowing because of a sore throat.

A honking horn yanked her back to reality. *Shit.*

She'd forgotten she was driving and swerved over the center line. Jerking the wheel right, she pulled over on the shoulder. She took slow, deep breaths. Her vision darkened at the edges. Panicked, she grabbed the supersized soda she'd purchased from a gas station and poured the sticky liquid over her head. Chunks of ice slid off her hair and down her now-deflated cleavage. They traced a cold trail on her skin. She concentrated on their icy path until her vision slowly returned to normal. She ignored the ruined clingy top and dripping hair.

She dug her cell phone out of her bag and popped

the Bluetooth earpiece in place before dialing Irja's number. She tried to ignore a stabbing ache in her chest. She was not missing Leif. It was fake. It would go away. It had to.

She concentrated on the phone's screen. She'd prefer to avoid any contact with the warriors in the mansion, but if Irja had cured Sten, then she may have suggestions for how to treat Scott.

The medical officer answered on the first ring. "My queen, you have to return right now." The pitch of her voice was higher than normal, panicked. "Leif is…sick."

"I'm not your queen." She swallowed. Had Leif been injured during the fight? "I called to find out if you figured out how to remove the nanoparticles from Sten's blood."

Irja's voice broke. "You hurt our king with your absence. The bond weakens him." Her anguish sounded sincere.

"Why would the bond make him sick?"

"He's losing control of his…his rage. He's going insane. Just come back," she pleaded. "If you don't, we…I will have to sedate him and then…"

Guilt rippled through Naya's chest, then she steeled herself. "My brother needs me. Did you find out how to remove the nanoparticles?" She hated how cold she sounded, but Scott had to come first, and they were running out of time. She suspected her fatigue was related to the time-ticking nanoparticles in her blood. Maybe they had been accelerated by whatever manipulations she'd experienced through the bond.

Irja's breath hitched. "Please, come back, and I'll tell you what I've discovered."

Excitement made her hands shake. "So you

found something? Do you know how to remove the nanoparticles?"

"I'll tell you when you get here." So Naya could be used as their bait again?

A wave of anger washed over her. She wanted to rip the steering wheel out of the console. She'd kill the Valkyrie for resorting to blackmail—after she'd squeezed the details about the cure from her. The violence of her rage surprised her. Forcing herself to breathe evenly, she released the death grip on the steering wheel. "Irja, tell me."

"Come back and I'll tell you."

She bit back a curse. "If this was about your brother, if you had the chance to save his life, would you return?"

"My loyalty is to my king first and foremost, as yours should be." The Valkyrie's voice wavered.

"Leif has all of the warriors by his side," Naya ground out. "My brother has only me. If you ever cared about me, you will tell me if you have found a way to help my brother." Tears ran down her cheeks. Irritated, she wiped them away with the back of her hand, coating it in sticky soda.

"If I tell you, will you promise to come back to Leif?"

Naya could scarcely breathe. She had waited so long for this moment. She weighed her words carefully. "I will return after my brother gets better." She would risk a visit with the Vikings if her brother would be healed.

"I want your promise to return, even if my method doesn't help you or your brother."

She bit back a scream of frustration. "Fine. But only after I try whatever you have found on Scott."

The line stayed quiet for several heartbeats. "This

may not help, but I managed to attach the free-floating nanoparticles to a particular kind of white blood cell. I injected Sten with extra basophil cells, the white cells that release antihistamine and respond to inflammation."

"Does it work?"

Irja sighed. "It's too soon to tell, but Sten says he feels better, stronger."

Naya swallowed her disappointment. She had hoped for a miracle cure, but this was better than nothing. "Can you email me the details of your treatment?"

The line went quiet again. "When will you return?" Irja finally asked.

"After I help Scott."

"I want your word as our queen that you will return."

She clenched her jaw. "I give you my word."

The Valkyrie sighed. "I'll email you the details as soon as I get to the lab."

Naya wiped her cheek and got more sticky soda on her hand. "Thank you," she said before hanging up.

His knuckles split open as he hit the sandbag in the gym, but Leif welcomed the pain. He'd left the gloves off and only taped his hands before taking out his frustration on the inanimate object. Sparring with one of his warriors would be a better workout, but he didn't think he'd be able to hold back the berserker if it smelled blood other than his own.

Sweat trickled down his bare back and chest and into his eyes. He closed them and kept hitting the bag. Each hit reverberated pain through his arm and up to the shoulder. He didn't care. He'd beat his body into a bloody heap if it would calm the berserker. He'd do it every day and twice on Wednesday, Odin's day.

The hairs on his neck rose. Someone else was in the gym, watching him. He swiveled and opened his eyes, raising his hands before jabbing a right hook at whoever had been stupid enough to sneak up on him.

Irja parried his hook easily, grabbed his wrist, and used his momentum to swing his arm underhand.

He flipped over, dropping to the floor face-first. Humiliated, he spit blood from his split lip. "Fight or get out," he snarled.

Irja's pupils widened as her body became attuned to the presence of his warrior spirit so close to battle rage. "I will not fight you." Her nostrils flared, a sure sign her berserker was responding to the challenge of his.

Shit. Even his most stoic Valkyrie couldn't control her warrior spirit around him. "Then get the fuck out." He rose from the floor, wiping his mouth and nose, smearing blood on the white tape on his hand. He straightened.

Irja's six-foot frame made her tall for a woman, but he loomed over her by a few inches. A small part of him felt ashamed for intimidating his medical officer, the one warrior he trusted the most after Harald.

The rest of him didn't give a crap. He just wanted a fight. He took a step forward.

Irja widened her stance, holding her hands loosely by her side. Black streams swirled in her dark irises. Her berserker had surfaced.

His warrior spirit howled, happy to find a willing opponent, a willing victim. He faked a left hook and instead followed through with a right uppercut.

Irja sidestepped both and landed a right overhand between his shoulder blades.

He went down, flat on his face again. Snarling, he jumped up.

The Valkyrie held out her palms in the universal sign of surrender. "I will not fight you. I came to talk."

"Fight," he snarled in a voice so different from his own he thought a third person had entered the gym.

Her eyes widened in surprise. "*Min kung*, I spoke to your *själsfrände*."

He went still. Even the berserker stopped pacing, anxiously waiting for news of Naya. "Tell me," he growled.

"She is well." She paused. "But her brother is not."

The brother.

"She is with her brother? Where are they?" He took a step closer.

Irja stood her ground. "I do not know, but she will take care of her brother and then return to us. She gave me her word."

He forced himself to breathe deeply. Naya had not trusted Leif enough to tell him where her brother was. Even after he'd offered to protect and treat him. Maybe their bond was not a true *själsfrände* binding. It carried the sexual connection and the separation dangers, but the trust and companionship had not developed between them.

Had he failed his people in his choice of queen? He could not meet Irja's gaze.

Naya had called one of his people, but not him. Another sign that they were not truly connected. Perhaps she fought on Loki's side after all. "How long?"

"I don't know," Irja repeated. "Can we track her through her cell phone?"

Leif shook his head. "Ulf tried. Her phone does not have GPS or she has somehow disabled the signal." She was a fucking genius. Of course she'd find a way to block her signal.

How could she be a weapon of Loki's when all her actions while in the fortress had been aimed at helping the Norse warriors? She might not be in love with him, but she felt something for him. The connection he had with her through the berserker told him so. Surely he'd notice if she'd been intent on betraying them? He buried his face in his hands.

The distance between himself and his *själsfrände* muddled his mind. He could no longer think clearly and he very much needed to come up with a strategy.

Irja reached out to touch him, then changed her mind and pulled back her hand. "The important thing is that she will return."

"If I get worse before she does"—he looked up— "you must sedate me and lock me in the prisoner cell."

She paused for a few moments. "I give you my word. But when the queen returns, you will be well again."

Leif tried to muster up a smile. Naya might never return. A *själsfrände* should not be able to leave so easily without looking back. And even if she did return, their connection might not be strong enough to leash his berserker.

Chapter 19

NAYA CROUCHED BY HER BROTHER'S SIDE, STROKING his hand. "Scott, I'm here to make you better."

His gaze was empty and a slight sheen of sweat covered his upper lip and forehead. She blotted his face with a tissue. "I've been working with…a friend in a different lab. She may have found a way to clean your blood. The injection Dr. Rosen just gave you contained extra white blood cells."

She rested her head on Scott's thigh and closed her eyes. She was so tired. Exhausted from worrying about Scott—and about Leif. The Viking king was constantly in the back of her mind, thoughts of him beating the same dull rhythm as her headache. She tried to force them out, but it was impossible.

Irja had sounded frantic on the phone. She didn't think the Valkyrie could have faked the worry in her voice, no matter how much she wanted Naya to return.

Scott's head jerked. He moaned.

She stood and cradled his head in her palms. "Take it easy, little brother." Would the treatment backfire and make him worse?

His eyes popped open and rolled to the back of his head. Convulsions shook his torso and legs.

She held his head, pressing her body to his to make the spasms stop. Normally it would be no effort at all, but her weakened body broke out in a cold sweat from her effort. She punched the alarm button on the headboard.

To her relief, feet thundered down the hallway and the door flew open. Two scrubs-clad nurses rushed to the bed with Dr. Rosen on their heels.

One of the nurses gently, but firmly, moved Naya aside. He tilted Scott's head back, checking his eyes with a small flashlight. "He's seizing."

Dr. Rosen grabbed the statoscope hanging around his neck. "Give me two milligrams of Ativan."

Naya grabbed Dr. Rosen's sleeve. "What are you doing to him?" Her voice sounded sharp in her own ears.

The doctor turned. His eyes widened as if he'd just realized she was in the room. "Ms. Driscoll, please wait outside."

"I'm not leaving until you tell me what you're doing."

"We're giving him an anticonvulsant to stop the seizures. I'll join you outside as soon as we have him stabilized." The doctor's green eyes implored her to cooperate.

"I'm not leaving this room," Naya said. She trusted the medical team, but her nerves were too frayed to keep a door between herself and her brother.

Dr. Rosen hesitated, then shrugged. "Fine. Just stay out of the way."

Naya watched from a chair in the far corner of the room. She nibbled her lower lip. Irja had emailed the dosage she had used on Sten. But what if it was wrong? Naya had thought it safe to use on Scott.

Another of the nurses left the room and returned with a rolling monitor that he hooked up to a small clamp placed over Scott's index finger. The machine would measure the oxygen saturation in his bloodstream and his heart rate. She'd often been hooked up to one herself after new injections in the lab. The familiar piece of equipment made bile rise in her throat.

Dr. Rosen walked over to her. "We've stabilized your brother for now." He crouched down by her chair and touched her arm. "You need sleep. Your brother won't wake up for at least six hours. Go rest."

She shook her head. "I'll stay here."

The doctor touched her forehead and frowned. "You are running a fever. If you won't rest for yourself, think of your brother. With his compromised immune system, an infection would be devastating."

Dr. Rosen walked over to the cabinet on Scott's side of the bed and removed a small white jar before returning to the chair. "This is a fever reducer that will also help you sleep. I insist you take care of yourself before returning to your brother's side."

Naya wanted to protest, but couldn't find the energy to argue. She put the pills in her pocket.

She said a quick thank-you and dragged her tired ass out of the room and to the rental car. On the drive back to the motel, she kept her mind numb. She couldn't deal with the thought of Scott permanently unconscious.

The diner reeked of overheated grease and unwashed bodies. Naya glanced away from her laptop screen long enough to reach for the cup beside her computer. She reconsidered and set it back down when the smell of burnt coffee assaulted her nose.

After eight hours of sleep, she didn't need caffeine anyway.

Naya was still running a slight fever and wasn't allowed back in the clinic until her temperature was back to normal. Dr. Rosen had insisted on it. She sighed and brought up her email inbox. Irja had responded to her message about Sten. Again, the Valkyrie implored her to return to the mansion. Naya typed a terse reply, letting the healer know Scott still wasn't doing well.

Irja insisted Naya being separated from Leif made him ill. She almost believed her. If the bond could manipulate intense feelings of attraction and out-of-this-world orgasms, it probably could make someone sick. Eventually, the effects would wear off. Maybe the flu-like symptoms she was experiencing herself were a combination of the ticking bomb and the bond wearing off.

She'd give anything to have her normal strength back. Operating at half-mast sucked. She rubbed her eyes with the heels of her hands and looked back at the computer screen. The failed injection therapy made her more determined to find out what "Batch 439" referred to in the intercepted email from the wolverine ranch. She'd scoured every underground forum and database she could find, but found nothing. The only thing left to do would be to hack back into the lab's servers and see how long she could hide from their tracers. But she wouldn't do it here, in Colorado. If the lab tracked her IP address, they may be able to get a lock on her location. She didn't want to leave a track that could be used to find Scott.

She closed her laptop and fished two ibuprofens out of her bag. They went down with the last of the water in her glass. The computer slid easily into the pocket at the back of the bag. She threw enough money on the table to cover the coffee and tip, looped the shoulder strap over her head, and strode out the back door.

The parking lot gravel crunched under her boots as she headed for the motel and her rental car. She should exchange it for a new vehicle before she set off north. Since she'd paid cash, dumping the car and renting a new one under a different name wouldn't even require a trip back to Denver. First, she needed to check in with Dr. Rosen. Even if he wouldn't let her see Scott again, she wanted to speak with the doctor in person before leaving the state. She might not be coming back from this hacking mission, and she needed to leave a message for her brother.

~~~

Exercise no longer worked to keep the berserker in check. Neither did alcohol or *feberandas*, Leif's old methods of calming the inner warrior. The berserker's rage boiled his blood. *Mine*, it screamed inside his mind, its voice overpowering all other thoughts. Irja had given him a sedative, but even that didn't counteract his restlessness, the need to fight, to kill.

He kept to his room, the curtains drawn, the lights low. He couldn't risk interaction with his warriors. Couldn't risk inadvertently hurting them if the berserker's full-on rage took over. Despair lay heavy in his heart. He had no choice but to go back to Valhalla. He was a danger to his people. Odin would have to find a different Viking king to save the world—Leif was no use to the Wise One now.

A knock sounded on the door and Harald entered

the room. Through Leif's crimson-colored vision, he appeared a blurry shadow just inside the door. "What do you want?" Leif roared.

"*Min kung*, I've come to see if you would please take some food." Harald held up a bowl of soup.

"I'm not hungry." Leif hadn't eaten since the day before, but there was no need. When he slept the eternal sleep back in Valhalla, his body would need no earthly sustenance. Besides, the berserker's rage obliterated all other needs. He hungered only for his *själsfrände*. The one thing he could not have.

"If you would just eat something, it may give you the energy to withhold a little longer." Harald sounded desperate.

"Silence!" Leif roared. "I have no need of food. Where is the king I asked you to bring here? You have to send me back."

Harald hesitated. "I have not yet sent the message. There may still be a chance—"

Leif lunged toward his *stallare*, stopping only because he pressed the tip of his dagger into his arm. The pain cleared the fog of anger for a brief moment. "I gave you an order. Fetch another king now. There's not much time left. I might kill someone." He gazed at his second-in-command, trying to urge him to understand his despair. "I might kill one of my battle brothers or sisters."

Harald took a step closer, but then checked himself. "Irja will sedate you fully before that happens. Just give us a little more time to track down Naya."

Leif dragged his body over to the bed and lay down. "It's no use. She will not come back to us and we cannot trust her."

"I don't believe she would betray us. Nor do I believe she's an instrument of Loki's." Harald's voice was firm. "You should have more faith in your berserker's choice."

Leif didn't bother answering. On some level he knew there was no evil in his soul mate, but she had left him. She didn't love him. Their bond, already weakened, would break either way.

Another knock on the door sounded and Harald turned to answer it. Leif debated on scolding him for turning his back on what was essentially a wild animal, but he couldn't be bothered. He closed his eyes, trying to sleep despite the berserker's roaring in his mind.

Ulf entered the room. "My king, I have good news. Your queen emailed Irja, and I was able to track down where the message came from."

Leif's eyes flew open. "Where is she?" His voice sounded guttural, the berserker and himself speaking as one.

Ulf's eyes widened. "She is in Colorado."

Chapter 20

THE COMPOUND LOOKED THE SAME FROM A DISTANCE, but as she drove closer, she saw some of the buildings had newer exteriors. Courtesy of her bomb, no doubt. Naya grinned grimly. This time she had no explosives, no blueprints, not even a plan or a getaway car.

She'd managed to hack into the lab's servers and found out that Batch 439 was something called a "scrubber." She'd tried to find out what that meant, but came up empty. In the end she got out of the network before they could trace her. Naya had to find out what the substance was and, if it could possibly help Scott, she absolutely had to get her hands on some of this Batch 439. Her only option was to get into the compound. Inside the lab's firewall, she could dig through the ultra-secured files. If she had to, she'd walk through the front door and rip the compound to pieces to find out what Batch 439 was.

She felt flushed, her fever spiked at odd intervals, and her vision had remained tinted red since she left Colorado. She'd slept once on the side of the road, but only for a few hours. And still she felt alert and ready, her body pumping with adrenaline.

At the guard kiosk, she rolled down her window and gave the uniformed man her most winsome smile. "I'm Naya Brisbane. I believe I'm expected."

The guy went on full alert so quickly he almost jerked straight out of his uniform. She must still be on the most-wanted list. He fumbled when reaching for the machine gun slung over his shoulder. "Don't move." Pointing the barrel at her, he reached for a phone and spoke hurriedly into the receiver.

She couldn't make out the words, but the reply was brisk and the gate opened immediately. Saluting the guard, she drove through the massive gates. A few minutes later, she reached the main building.

Two armed soldiers greeted her when she stepped out of the car, machine guns following her movements as she slowly walked to the door.

"Keep your hands visible!" one shouted.

The front door opened and a man in a white lab coat stepped out. His salt-and-pepper hair and straight nose reminded her of an older version of Richard Gere, but a large port-wine stain covered most of his upper left cheek.

Naya stopped mid-stride. She remembered the birthmark. Dr. Trousil. A growl rose in her throat.

He took a step toward her. "I see you remember me fondly."

She ignored his offered handshake.

"Shall we?" He stepped aside, sweeping his arm to indicate she should precede him through the door.

Naya shook her head. "Oh no please, after you. I insist."

Dr. Trousil's jaw clenched, but he walked ahead of her. At the door, he nodded to the leader of the two guards. "Search her," he said.

The soldier handed his gun to the other. "Raise your hands," he directed.

Naya complied and gritted her teeth as the man patted her down with more force than necessary. He confiscated her sidearm, the switchblade from her boot, and the hunting knife in her bag.

"Still packing a small arsenal," Dr. Trousil tsked. "Your predictability is uninspiring."

Naya kept quiet, grabbed her bag from the soldier, and followed the doctor.

"I can take it from here," Trousil said, closing the door.

She hitched the bag higher on her shoulder, appreciating the heft of the hollowed-out laptop shell and the gun hidden inside.

The doctor strode down a drab hallway and opened one of the doors. "Step into my office," he shot over his shoulder. "We'll complete the intake forms and then those two good men will show you to your quarters."

He sat on the couch and crossed one leg over the other, brushing an invisible piece of lint off his pants leg. "So, what made you visit when you've worked so hard to avoid our…invitations?"

She sat in a nearby chair. "Why do you want to keep me alive when you executed the other older models?"

His eyes widened and a small part of her, deep down, gloated.

"Why am I so special?" She leaned back in the chair. "Don't get me wrong, I appreciate the effort and attention."

He studied her with a feral grin. "I'm going to enjoy breaking you again."

She suppressed a shudder and moved her foot a smidgen, nudging her bag on the floor. The contact helped her find her center. "Again?" she asked, eyebrow quirked.

"The twelve-year-old you was stubborn. I wonder what it will be like for you now, after being out in the real world. I bet you'll fight the process even more this time."

She traced a pattern on the arm of the chair. "You never broke me. Plus, this time you don't have my brother to use as a bargaining chip."

A shadow fell across his brow before he smoothed his expression. "What makes you think we haven't already found him?"

She ignored his taunt. She would have been notified by Dr. Rosen if they'd found Scott. "Is that why you created the wolverines? To track Scott and me down?"

Dr. Trousil's eyes momentarily narrowed. "Not everything is about you. A client asked for some creatures with special skills. The fee he's paying helps our research dollars stretch further." He settled more deeply into the couch. "The wolverines are a new direction we're exploring. The compulsion to find you was an added bonus feature." He smiled again. "Added bonus for us that is."

She kept her face passive, but relief flooded through Naya's body. Leif and his people were safe from her. Slowly she nudged her bag open with her toe. The sight of her laptop calmed her even more. "So why go to all that trouble when I have already killed several of your expensive wolverines?" She smiled sweetly. "Why do you need me alive so bad?"

He paused for several seconds, "Who says we do?"

An ice-cold shiver shot down her spine.

Dr. Trousil's smile showed he enjoyed her discomfort. "You'll be dead soon anyway, all of our older models self-destruct eventually."

She played the trump card. "Then why develop Batch 439?"

The doctor smirked. "I wondered if you'd found out

about that." He angled his head. "You were actually not created in our lab. You're the genetic offspring of one of our super-soldiers."

Naya swallowed. "My parents were created here?"

"Only your dad, but that still makes you the find of the century. If we can reproduce your genetic code, there are no limits to what we can do."

Naya's mind reeled from the revelation about her dad. But she couldn't think about that now. She had to stay on mission. Save Scott. She reached for a nearby pillow and put it on her lap. "Why don't you tell me about Batch 439 and maybe I will share how I know about the formula. You'd be able to plug a security breach."

Dr. Trousil frowned as if he was disappointed she didn't react to the bomb he'd just dropped. "The only thing I want from you is the location of your brother."

"Why do you need Scott when you have me? He's in a coma, remember?"

The grin stretching his thin lips radiated pure evil. "We developed Batch 439 for your brother. He needs to stay alive for a little longer."

She quirked an eyebrow to get him to continue, squelching the need to knock the smile off his face.

"Haven't you guessed yet?" He leaned back again. "A brother and a sister. A male and a female. We need his Y chromosome to create beautiful test-tube babies, using your DNA."

Swallowing the nausea rising in her throat, Naya nudged the pillow off her lap. She leaned down on one knee, unsnapping the laptop shell. The gun cooled the hot skin of her hand as she shielded it from the doctor's view with the pillow.

Dr. Trousil caught on that something was amiss and half stood, but it was too late.

She shot him through the pillow and straight through the ugly birthmark on his cheek. The pillow silenced the gun, and she'd made sure to angle the trajectory of the bullet to pierce the doctor's brain. The despicable man crumpled to the floor.

She remained crouched, holding her breath as she listened for footsteps in the hallway.

None came.

Nudging the doctor's body with the tip of her toe, she slipped the gun into her waistband at the small of her back.

She walked over to the door and placed an ear against its cold wood. Not a sound from the corridor. Just in case, she turned the lock before grabbing her bag and crossing the room.

The doctor's desk took up most of the room. She sat down and concentrated on opening the doctor's laptop. While the password retrieval tool worked, she drummed her fingers until Trousil's code appeared on the screen.

She quickly scanned the folders, looking for anything with the word "batch" or number sequence 439. A few minutes of searching led her to an inventory list. A serum called Batch 439 was stored in lab number seven. Additional information described it as a serum that cleaned self-destructive nanoparticles out of the bloodstream. Jackpot.

A few more seconds of searching found two large directories labeled with hers and Scott's names and designated numbers. She uploaded them to a cloud server together with all of the information on Batch 439 and then mirrored the hard drive.

She hesitated a moment, but then emailed Irja a link to the server. Since the wolverines were created in this lab, Leif and his people might have use for the information. She'd promised them she'd return, but she might not survive the exit from this compound. Thinking of never seeing Leif again made her fingers stumble on the keyboard. She forced herself to concentrate. Find Batch 439 and get it to her brother. Her only mission now, maybe her last.

She clicked through a few more files to find a floor plan of the building. Lab number seven was on the other side of the complex, close to where Scott had been housed when she rescued him. She closed her eyes, reviewing the blueprints in her mind, and overlaid them on the floor plan from Trousil's computer. Together with her real memories, she should be able to find her way.

She returned to the doctor's body and searched for a security pass. She found his ID clipped to a retractable cord attached to his belt.

She listened at the door again, gripping her gun while slowly unlocking and opening the door. The corridor was empty. She slipped out and jogged lightly in the opposite direction of the front entry.

A few turns later, voices and footsteps bounced between the walls down the path she wanted to take. She tried the handles of the doors closest to her, and panicked before finding one unlocked. Quickly, she slipped through the opening just as a boot tip appeared at the end of the hallway. The door closed behind her with a soft click, but whoever strode down the hallway spoke loudly enough with their companion to cover the sound.

A bigger problem faced her in the lab tech staring at her with wide eyes, syringe raised. Naya's focus narrowed.

A drop of liquid fell in slow motion from the tip of the needle as the woman opened her mouth to scream.

Before so much as a squeak left her lips, Naya lunged across the floor and slammed the butt of her gun against her temple. "Sweet dreams," she whispered as she caught the unconscious tech and slowly lowered her to the floor. She quickly bound and gagged the woman using the lab coat.

A red-eyed white mouse stared at her from the bottom of a wire cage, whiskers twitching. Behind him or her, another twenty or so cages held other mice and rats. She took pleasure in opening all of them and leaving the window of the lab ajar before continuing on her way.

Three minutes later, she reached lab number seven. The door looked like the others she'd passed on the way, but a card reader lock barred entry. She slid Trousil's security badge through the slit. A short hum and a click signaled the electronic lock granting her access.

As she opened the door, vapors of antiseptics and disinfectant triggered an assault of memories. She'd spent so much time in labs just like this one, tied to a gurney or a chair. People in white lab coats prodding and poking her with needles.

Shaking her head, she stepped through the doorway and closed the door behind her. A lab coat hung on the back of the door, and she slipped it on, stuffing the gun in one pocket and the security card in the other. Darkness engulfed the lab, but she could make out the shapes of cabinets and counters with what little light slipped through the slats covering the window.

Against the opposite wall, a larger construction loomed, creating a checkered dark void in the gloominess. She couldn't make out what it was. She turned the dead bolt before flipping the light switches on the panel next to the door. Bright overhead light blinded her for a second and she blinked rapidly to clear the bright spots dancing in front of her eyes.

Finally her vision cleared and she peered across the room. Familiar black eyes stared back from the inside of a human-sized cage.

Chapter 21

HER HEART JUMPED INTO HER THROAT AS SHE STARED at the cage. "Irja," she whispered, but knew it was wrong as soon as the name left her lips.

The eyes were the same pools of darkness, but the cheekbones' angle was more pronounced, and the hair brushed only the top of the person's shoulders. The nose protruded at a slightly crooked angle, broken and not set properly before it healed. A large bruise bloomed across the right cheek. The jawline was wider and more squared than Irja's.

Naya blinked and the pieces snapped together.

A man stared back at her from the cage, a male version of Irja.

She slowly walked across the room, stopping just outside arm's reach of the cage. "Who are you?"

The man didn't answer or rise from the cage floor. He sat with one knee up at an angle, his arm resting casually on top. Everything about his posture said relaxed and friendly, but in his eyes suspicion glittered as he watched her warily.

She crouched down to his eye level. "Do you know Irja?"

His nostrils flared and his lips thinned. She felt the tension coiling in his muscles. Still he didn't speak.

Voices drifted in from the corridor. Naya froze and turned toward the door. They passed by and grew fainter before disappearing altogether. She stood and surveyed the room for the most likely storage site of the serum she'd come to retrieve.

Two floor-to-ceiling refrigerators flanked one of the walls. Their glass doors revealed hundreds of vials and bottles.

She grabbed a pair of scissors from one of the lab benches and walked over to study them. Simple key locks secured the doors. She quickly popped them out by jamming the sharp end of the scissors into each one and twisting.

Rifling through the vials, she spoke over her shoulder. "If you want me to let you out, I need your promise that you won't fight. I don't have time to kill you." She didn't bother turning around when only silence met her statement.

In the middle of the second refrigerator, she hit the jackpot. Small brown bottles labeled B-439 were lined up like brave little soldiers. She found a small plastic cooler on the bottom shelf and filled the container with dry ice from the cylindrical freezer unit next to the refrigerators.

Chilly steam obscured her view of the cage as she shoved as many bottles as she could fit into the cooler. When the steam dissipated, the man was standing on the other side of the wire mesh. She hadn't heard him move.

He watched her intently. "How is Irja?" he croaked, as if he hadn't used his voice in a while.

She took a step closer, but stopped when he jerked back. "She's well. She healed me when I was injured."

A ghost of a smile flittered over his lips. "I haven't seen her in almost a century, but she is still a practicing *noita*."

Naya frowned. "I have no idea what that means."

"It means my twin sister is a witch."

His twin. It rang true. The two appeared so alike, it couldn't be a coincidence. "Would you like me to take you to her?"

"Who are you?" He leaned toward her. "I sense your berserker close to the surface, but you don't act as if the warrior spirit is in control, and you don't look like a Valkyrie."

Naya didn't understand half of what he said. "I'm not a Valkyrie." She walked over to investigate the lock on the cage. "I'd love to chat more, but how about we do a walk-and-talk?" She rattled the hanging lock. "I'm kind of in a hurry." Damn, the lock contained a series of interlocking gear wheels. With some time, she'd be able to figure out the combination.

She scanned the room again, her gaze landing on a cylindrical tank. No bigger than an old-fashioned milk pail, she carried it over wearing the triple insulated gloves she found on top of the lid. "Stay back," she said before opening the container and lifting it up to the lock.

"What's in there?" Irja's brother asked.

"Liquid nitrogen." She tipped the tank and a stream of super cold liquid hit the lock, evaporating immediately with a low hiss. Naya grabbed the lock in one glove and jerked downward. The metal shattered into three pieces and took a large chunk of the wire mesh with it as it clanked to the floor. She opened the cage and peered in at the man. "You coming?"

Without waiting for an answer, she turned and walked to the lab door. She felt rather than heard him following closely behind her. At the door, she turned off the lights and listened for any movements on the other side.

The lock had made quite a racket, but it was evening and most of the personnel had probably gone home. She closed her eyes and concentrated on the map she'd created of the facility in her mind.

Irja's twin moved up behind her.

She slipped into the corridor with him close on her heels. Rather than heading back toward the entrance, she opted for an emergency exit in the opposite direction. Skirting the outside of the building to get to her car would attract less attention.

Before they exited, she ditched the white lab coat, stuffing the contents of the pockets into her bag. Irja's brother waited patiently by her side. His presence had the same effect as his sister's. Her shoulders relaxed and her breathing slowed down. "What's your name?" she asked.

"Pekka," he said but didn't ask for hers before opening the door and melting into the evening shadows.

She quickly followed, working hard to copy his stealth. "So, Pekka, do you know where you're going?" she hissed through the darkness.

A flash of teeth glimmered. "No," he whispered back.

"Then how about letting me lead?" She slipped past him, careful to keep close to the wall. They flanked the building soundlessly until her car was in view.

Naya cursed under her breath in the dark corner where she and Pekka stood close to the main entrance. Several streetlights illuminated the shiny blue exterior of the rental car still parked in the courtyard. Two armed guards, probably some of the soldier boys from before, stood by the front door, her car straight in their line of vision.

Pekka touched her shoulder. "Wait here," he whispered.

She turned to answer him, but he had vanished. A quiet scratching on the roof made her look up just in time to catch his boot disappearing over the edge.

Shit.

They didn't have time for whatever covert spy game he was playing. She glanced at the two guards. They stood on each side of the door, chatting quietly.

Naya gasped as Pekka appeared on the roof just above them. He stared straight at her, signaling a throwing motion. She picked up a rock from the ground and threw it across the courtyard. The projectile bounced and landed a few yards in front of the guards. On immediate high alert, they raised their machine guns and took a step forward, leaving the cover of the roof overhang.

Like a liquid shadow, Pekka spilled from above with his arms stretched out. He grabbed the side of the guards' heads and knocked them together.

Naya winced at the bone-on-bone and teeth-rattling sounds. The two soldiers crumpled.

Before they hit the ground, she shot out from her hiding place and sprinted toward the car.

Floodlights lit up the courtyard like the Fourth of July. Armed men streamed out of every building, their guns pointed straight at Naya and Pekka.

She raised her arms at their shouted commands. Four soldiers surrounded her, three keeping her in their gun sights while the other patted her down and removed her gun.

Naya desperately searched for Irja's brother behind them. He'd armed himself with the two guns from the felled men. "Put down your guns!" someone shouted at him. "Put down your guns or we kill your friend."

Killing the head researcher must have scratched her off the "keep alive" list.

<center>~~~</center>

The sterile room reeked of antiseptic. Naya avoided looking at the hospital bed in the corner. It brought up too many bad memories.

The lab must be in a tizzy with Dr. Trousil dead, because the guards had dumped Pekka and her in this room together. Prisoners were always kept separate according to the textbook Naya had learned from during her training. The quality of instruction in the lab was obviously lacking. Or maybe they didn't need to separate them because they would both die anyway.

The worst part was that they'd taken away her cooler. She'd lost Scott's last chance.

She turned to Pekka. "Why didn't you shoot and run?"

"They outnumbered me."

She snorted. "You would have had a good chance of making it out alive."

He shrugged. "I couldn't leave a friend of my sister behind. She'd never forgive me."

"You told me you hadn't seen Irja in a hundred years. Why?"

Pekka picked at a small scratch on his hand. "She's hard to track down," he finally said.

She shot him a quick glance, but he hadn't cracked as much as a hint of a smile.

Another minute passed before he opened his mouth

again. "She thinks she betrayed me, and I was too immature and too proud to set her straight."

Naya opened her mouth to ask more questions, but he shook his head. "Not my story to tell. You must ask her."

"I will." But that wouldn't happen unless they escaped, and stayed alive. "How did you end up trapped in the lab?" she asked to distract herself. They'd examined every crevice of the room. The only way of escaping would be to overpower their captors when they came to move them. If they decided to move them.

She didn't want to think about the alternative.

Pekka studied the top of his other hand. "I was hunting in Montana when someone shot me with a tranquilizer gun."

"Why did they capture you?"

He shrugged. "I don't know. But they're using a lot of my blood for something. They took samples every day."

"That's all you know?" Naya purposefully didn't look at him. He seemed more comfortable not making eye contact.

"I've been imprisoned for several months. Long enough to figure out they're running some sort of genetic experiments." He turned toward her. "Why are you here? And how do you know my sister?"

Naya told him an abbreviated version of escaping the lab and meeting Leif and his tribe of warriors. "I need the Batch 439 serum to cure my brother," she finished up.

Pekka studied her for several seconds. "If you are not a Valkyrie, why is there a berserker pacing inside you?"

"What's a berserker?"

He waved his hand in the air. "Your warrior spirit. Didn't anyone explain while you lived with the warriors?"

Another secret the Viking king had omitted. "Why don't you explain it to me?"

"Every Norse warrior has a berserker inside them. In battle, it rises up and makes them almost indestructible. If a Viking or Valkyrie allows the berserker to completely overtake them during battle, the warrior spirit needs to be calmed down afterward. If it isn't, the berserker may take over the warrior's psyche and he or she succumbs to permanent battle fever."

"How do you calm down this warrior spirit?" Were the uncontrollable anger and her red-washed vision related to this berserker-thingie?

"This is one of Freya's secrets, but one way to completely control your berserker is to have a *själsfrände*."

"The bond that makes the serpent tattoo complete?" Naya turned toward him.

Pekka glanced away. "Yes. Very few of us are lucky enough to meet our soul's true mate." Pekka tilted his head. "Most Valkyries wouldn't allow their warrior spirit as close to the surface as you have without close proximity to their *själsfrände*."

She was so sick and tired of this soul-mate crap. "You say 'lucky enough,' but why would anyone want to subject themselves to something that manipulates their emotions and makes them do things they don't want to do?"

His eyes widened. "The bond doesn't make anyone experience emotions not already there. A warrior can't manipulate the *själsfrände* to do something against their will."

To her embarrassment, tears filled her eyes. "Are you sure?"

He studied her carefully. "To be with your *själsfrände* is to experience the most authentic connection possible. When two souls recognize each other and trigger the bond, they connect with the gods and goddesses."

Naya thought about the silver-haired woman she'd seen the last time she and Leif had made love. Had that been a goddess? Thinking about Leif filled her mind with images of him and her in bed together, and her restlessness increased. She squelched thoughts of Leif and concentrated on what Pekka had told her. Was it possible that Leif had no more control over this bond thing than she had? Hope rose in her chest. "What happens if the two *själsfrände* split up?"

"Once bonded, the two partners need to stay close together. The bond gives them incredible strength and energy reserves, but if they are separated, they are weakened and become physically ill. Sometimes, a warrior can lose control over the berserker if their *själsfrände* is separated from them or dies."

"How do they regain control again?"

"They don't. A berserker out of control will have to be put down. Odin or Freya will call the warrior back to Valhalla and induce the eternal sleep."

She swallowed hard.

Irja had said Leif was sick and that Naya was the cause. She'd hurt Leif. Her stomach clenched.

She'd never see him again. Never feel the warmth of his body surrounding hers. Never have a chance to tell him how sorry she was. Or that she loved him.

The door to the room flew open. Pekka sprung up, placing himself in the path between the entrance and Naya.

Chapter 22

LEIF PAUSED IN THE DOORWAY. HIS BERSERKER panted, sniffing the air.

As soon as the Norse warriors had entered the compound, it had known his *själsfrände* was somewhere inside this building. Finally, it had found her, but an unknown male stood in the way.

Tall and gaunt, the man appeared to not have eaten or trained properly for months. His long, dark hair hung matted to his shoulders. Despite not carrying any weapons, coal-black eyes challenged Leif. He growled out his anger and raised his gun, ready to kill.

"Leif, no!" His mate jumped in front of the male, shielding him with her body.

He forced his muscles to freeze but kept his weapon ready. His female approached.

"Step back." The dark male grabbed her arm, trying to push her behind him. "His berserker is in control. You can't reason with him now."

Leif took a step toward the male. He sniffed the air and detected an unearthly essence around the other. Maybe he had been sent back to Midgard like his Vikings. Didn't matter.

If he touched Leif's *själsfrände*, he would die.

Raising the gun again, he bellowed a battle cry.

"Stop!" Naya shouted, holding up a hand. Her slight body hesitated before coming closer.

Blood pounded in his ears, overpowering all other sounds. The berserker howled—the sound coming out as a growl through Leif's mouth.

Her eyes widened, but she slowly walked toward him.

The gaunt male grabbed her arm, but she shook him off.

She smelled of other men. Others had touched his *själsfrände*. He dug his nails into his palm to keep from throwing her on the bed in the corner and claiming her as his.

She'd been away for too long.

Blinded by anger, he grabbed her shoulder with his free hand, shaking her. "Mine!" he roared.

The gaunt man grasped Leif's arm, but he hit him with the barrel of the gun. With a satisfying thud, the body hit the wall.

His mate gasped but didn't resist his grip. Instead, she reached up and cupped his face.

Calm power flowed from the spot where she touched him, radiating through his body. The berserker soaked up her energy like a healing balm, almost purring as it relinquished some of its control of Leif's body and senses. He shook his head as the red haze cleared from his vision. He felt stronger now and more in control. Appalled, he carefully caressed where he had grasped her, touching his forehead to hers. "I'm sorry," he whispered. "I didn't mean to hurt you."

"I'm not hurt." She stroked his jaw. "I didn't know about your berserker or how the bond affected your control. I would never have left if I did." Naya paused. "Or at least I would have tried to talk to you instead of just leaving the fortress."

He closed his eyes, breathing in her soothing scent, feeling her presence through his skin. "I know." He caressed her cheek. "I should have explained it better."

She opened her eyes, gazing deeply into his. "I see colors again." She smiled. "I liked my rose-colored vision, but I'd miss your ice-blue eyes," she whispered. He started to ask her what she meant, but stopped when she shook her head. "It's a long story."

He couldn't wait any longer. He had to taste her. Palming the back of her neck, he pulled her toward him. When her lips met his, he sighed contentedly. Another kind of restlessness spread through his body.

She pushed back against his chest. "We have to get out of here."

He held on tight.

"I need to check on Pekka." She squirmed to loosen his hold.

"Who?"

"Irja's brother. The guy you just backhanded into the wall."

He remembered the man who'd been blocking his path to Naya. "Irja's brother?" He turned to the body lying on the floor. The man was a mirror image of their medical officer. "Fuck." He let his *själsfrände* go.

Naya rushed over to the man, kneeling by his side. "I think he might be coming around." She looped his arm around her neck. "Help me get him up." She stood, her height so slight the man lifted only three-quarters of the way off the floor.

Pekka's eyelids fluttered, but he didn't wake. Leif took the arm Naya held and hoisted the unconscious body over his shoulder. Reaching for his *själsfrände*, he

turned toward the door. "Let's go. The others are keeping the soldiers busy."

She jogged to keep up with his longer stride down the
hallway. "How did you find me?"

"Ulf figured out how to track you through the emails
you sent to Irja."

"Shit, that was sloppy." She stopped mid-stride.

He tugged on her hand to keep going. "If it makes
you feel better, we were headed to Colorado before Ulf
corrected our course at the last minute."

The last couple of days' mad dash across the country
to find her had made him dizzy. At times he didn't think
he'd survive. The berserker had wanted to tear limbs
from bodies, pushing him into a rampage when they
changed direction and headed to North Dakota.

Irja'd had to sedate him.

"I'm sorry," Naya mumbled.

They reached the front door of the building. "Let's
talk later." He slid Pekka's body to the ground. "Get
ready to fight."

Tossing her hair out of her face with a flick of her
head, she eagerly smiled back at him. "Hell yeah."

He shook his head and flung the double doors open
to pandemonium.

Thuds and grunts echoed across the courtyard where
his warriors battled the camp soldiers. Heavy boots
crunched the gravel as feet fought for traction. Battle
cries rose in air dense with the smell of blood. Every one
of his warriors had insisted on coming with him.

He'd tried to keep Sten at home, but the young
Norseman argued that since Irja was going, he'd have
medical care during the trip. In the end, he'd allowed

Sten to be one of the drivers, but with strict orders of staying in the van when the fighting started.

Of course, Sten hadn't listened and was in the middle of the melee, kicking ass with the best of them.

Irja stood back-to-back with the young Viking, her long dark hair a whirlwind around her head as she swept and hook-kicked her opponents.

Leif heard her laughter from where he stood on the stairs. Thank the gods they'd positioned Ulf and Torvald as sharpshooters on the roof. They fired every time a soldier tried to exit the building through any of the doors.

His mate jumped down the steps, leaping into the air, executing a perfect ax kick.

The soldier holding on to Astrid's hair hit the ground with a heavy double thud as his head bounced on the ground.

"Stop pulling hair!" Naya shouted. "We're not in elementary school anymore."

The Valkyrie grinned and jabbed the man's windpipe. "Good to see you again, Your Highness." She bowed, adding a little hand flourish to the gesture.

Naya grinned and bowed back before twisting around to punch another solider. He too fell to the ground.

A soldier rushed Leif with a knife held high. A quick elbow thrust to the man's sternum stopped the attack effectively. Leif used the Glock to shoot two more guards storming toward him, before he jogged over to Naya. "The vans we came in are about fifty yards from here." He pointed. "Fight your way toward them."

She nodded. "What about Pekka?"

Leif turned toward the stairs. The tall, dark man had

recovered enough to stand on his own. "I'll grab him."
He strode toward the house.

Pekka backed away, hands lifted palms out. "I'm on
your side."

Leif flushed. "I know. Sorry about the slap. The berserker didn't take kindly to you touching Naya."

"Slap?" Irja's brother quirked a dark eyebrow, the
gesture so much like his sister's. "My ears are still ringing from hitting that wall."

Leif grimaced, holding out his hand for the other man
to shake. "You want to chat or fight?"

White teeth glimmered in Pekka's dark face. "I've
been wanting to kick these fuckers' asses for a while."
He grabbed Leif's hand.

Harald rushed up, gun in hand. "Are you girls finished
gossiping?" He peered over Leif's shoulder, aimed, and
shot. A weak grunt and dull thud signaled another solider down. "The rest of us would like to get out of here
now that we have the queen secured." Blinking rapidly,
he stared at Pekka. "What the fu—"

"Irja's brother," Leif explained and turned around,
looking for Naya. His berserker kept calm, so she must
not be in danger. He finally spotted her several yards
from where he'd left her.

Facing two armed men, she disarmed one of them
with a semicircle kick. The weapon flew across the
gravel, landing a distance away. While the soldiers'
eyes followed the arch of the projectile, she grabbed the
other's gun and quickly shot both of them.

His berserker hummed low with approval.

Naya gazed down at the bodies and shook her head.
"Who trained you?" she shouted. "You are a disgrace."

She must have detected his warrior spirit's pride, because she faced him and fired off a brilliant smile.

Only a few enemy soldiers still stood to fight. Leif marched across the graveled lot to reach his *själsfrände*.

Harald shouted over the ruckus. "We've secured the queen. Head for the vehicles, Norsemen."

"Wait!" Naya bellowed. "I have to get my cooler."

Leif ushered her toward the vans. "I'll buy you a new cooler."

She resisted as he tried to make her move. "The antidote for Scott is in that cooler."

The brother. The one she sacrificed everything for, even her own happiness. Their happiness.

He tugged on her arm again, but she held firm.

"I need it as well, or I will die."

Leif swore under his breath. He turned to Harald. "Think you can keep things under control for a little longer?"

Sten took a punch and barreled into Harald. "Sorry," the young warrior threw over his shoulder as he lunged for his opponent.

A front kick later and the soldier fell to the ground.

Right behind Sten, Irja ducked a jab and used a cross-counterpunch to dump another body next to the one Sten had taken care of. She wiped sweaty bangs out of her face with the back of her hand. "Greetings, my queen." Her eyes widened when she discovered who stood beside Naya. "Pekka," she whispered, eyes brimming with tears.

"Hello, *Sisko*." The male mirror image of Irja hesitantly took a step forward.

Irja pushed Harald out of the way and threw herself at her brother, wrapping her arms around him in a bear hug.

Leif tore his eyes from the happy reunion and inspected the battleground. Per and Astrid kept the remaining soldiers busy across the courtyard but would need some help to completely neutralize the threat.

Naya tilted her head. She was about to run into the building without him. At least she'd paused long enough for him to catch up.

"We're going back in." Leif directed the comment to his *stallare*. "Take care of the last of the opponents and don't let anyone else leave the building."

Harald nodded and turned to Irja, Pekka, and Sten. "You're with me. Let's finish these fuckers." He ran toward Astrid and Per.

Surprised that his second-in-command allowed him to enter a hostile building without backup, Leif studied his warriors. When his berserker had run amok, the Norse men and women in the fortress had been on edge. He mentally reached for the connection to his warrior spirit. Warmth and excitement flowed from the berserker, but nothing like the overwhelming heat and panic he'd felt over the last days.

He closed his eyes. The berserker remained alert, but was calm and content.

He reached further beyond his warrior spirit and forgot to breathe when he connected with each of his Vikings and Valkyries. They glowed like beacons in a huge interconnected web. Although each bright light glimmered as a shapeless ball of energy, he could tell his warriors apart.

Sten's light shone dimmer than the others, but still strong. Leif startled when he realized that his *själsfrände* pulsed with a deep red glow. Her light felt different, but somehow she was connected to the other warriors through him. Did she have an inner warrior?

Naya tugged on his sleeve. "Let's go." She rushed up the steps to the door. "We'll get more of the drug where I first found it. I have no idea where they stashed my cooler."

Leif blinked and the spiderweb of shining flames disappeared. He rushed after his *själsfrände*.

"Lab number seven!" she shouted. "It's where I found Pekka."

He followed Naya and drew his gun, releasing the safety. Two soldiers rounded a corner, surprise on their faces. He shot them both between their eyes without stopping. "The sound will probably attract more armed guards. Hurry," he encouraged his mate.

Not that she needed any. Naya's stride ate the floor in a pace he'd be stretched to maintain for longer distances. "Here," she said, stopping outside a closed door. "Stand guard while I get the formula?"

Leif opened the door to do a security sweep. Empty. He waved Naya inside and positioned himself with his back to the door.

Shouts and loud footsteps announced another patrol. Leif shot the four guards barreling down the hallway. The magazine held seventeen rounds. He still had plenty of ammunition should more guests care to join the party.

Naya returned with a clear bag filled with small glass vials. "This is all they have. Let's go." He turned to make for the building's entrance, but she grabbed his arm. "There's a closer exit."

Leif followed her to a back door where she poked her

head out. Normally his berserker would have protested and insisted on taking the lead. Leif felt it paying attention, but it seemed to trust Naya's reconnaissance.

Head still outside the door, she gestured with her hand behind her back. "Give me the gun."

The berserker twitched, ready to hand over the weapon to their magnificent mate, but Leif resisted. "Step aside and let me—"

She turned, hot impatience reflected in her beautiful eyes.

He handed over his gun.

She quickly fired four rounds.

Soundlessly, she slipped outside. He copied her movements, closing the door with a soft click. "I want it on the record that I rescued you from captivity," he said as she returned his gun. "Anyone watching would think backup unnecessary."

A smile lit up her face. "If anyone asks, I'll make sure to mention your heroics."

He grabbed her head and claimed her mouth in a deep kiss. "Good. Let's get back to the crew." He set off for the courtyard, his lips stretching into a satisfied grin when it took her a few beats to get moving.

They rounded the corner to find the two vans filled with Norse warriors and ready to go. Bodies of camp soldiers littered the courtyard.

Ulf and Torvald stood sentinel on roofs of opposite buildings, rifles ready to take down anybody else entering open ground. "King and queen incoming!" Torvald shouted.

The engines of the vans revved as Leif and Naya sprinted toward one of them. He arrived first and pulled his mate into his lap as he closed the sliding door behind her.

Torvald and Ulf jumped down and ran backward to the other vehicle, keeping the buildings in their gun sights. They got in the van and the two vehicles careened down the road.

Naya squirmed on his lap, but he held her still, needing her body against his until he knew for sure all danger was over. "Just let me hold you for a little while."

She tensed, but then finally relaxed in his arms. "I'm okay with making it a long while."

He touched his forehead to hers and tucked his arms around his *själsfrände*, pulling her closer and breathing the essence of her deep into himself.

His berserker approved. *Ours*, it whispered. *Ours* always.

Naya fingered the bandage on her arm as she looked around Leif's bedroom—their bedroom now. The Viking king had asked her if she'd consider sharing his room. Since she planned on spending her nights in his bed, she'd agreed.

During the two days they'd been home, Ulf and Per had helped her move the desk from the guest bedroom she'd slept in previously into an office in the mansion and added the two sky-blue chairs. Handlers might still be hunting her, so Astrid and Irja had fetched the rest of her belongings from her apartment.

Whatever reservations the warriors had had about the connection between her and Loki's wolverines, the fighting at the lab seemed to have squelched any remaining hostility. Killing the chief scientist apparently proved her loyalty—that and rescuing Irja's brother. Torvald had grumbled a little, but was quickly silenced by the others. Ulf had pointed out that Naya's biology may give them clues to how the creatures had been created.

The bandage came loose. She patted it down again. She'd heal without it, but the injection site itched, and covering it kept her from scratching. Irja had tested Batch 439 first in test tubes and then on Naya through several small doses. The amount of nanoparticles in her blood had significantly decreased, even the ones that had merged with blood cells after the *själsfrände* bond activated. As soon as Naya was in the clear, Irja would send samples of the drug to Dr. Rosen in Colorado to test out on Scott. The two medical professionals had already exchanged test results and hypotheses via email and phone.

The door opened, interrupting her reverie. Leif walked toward her. His powerful stride sent all kinds of good tingles through her body. She grinned at him so he would smile back and show off the dimples she couldn't get enough of. He didn't disappoint.

When he reached her side, he slid a hand around her waist and pulled her close. "I like you ready for bed," he said, lifting the hem of her short silk nightie.

"Can't a girl wear something pretty without you getting ideas of bedding her?" Naya reached up, putting her hand behind his neck to pull him down for a kiss. She'd never get enough of touching him. Of trusting him.

He explored her mouth thoroughly and placed his other hand on her hip to draw her body against his. His hardness nudged her stomach and he slipped his hands to her buttocks to lift her. "I'm always thinking of bedding you," he said before moving his hot lips lower, sucking on her clavicle.

His hard shaft pushed at her entry and she gasped into his mouth. Even through her panties and his denim jeans, she could feel him throbbing. A satisfied groan rumbled through his chest, vibrating her nipples.

Like good little soldiers, they perked to attention immediately. She rubbed the hard nubs against him, savoring the sensation of silk sliding over her hot skin.

He released her mouth to trail kisses down her cheek and then nibble on the sensitive spot behind her ear.

Naya shivered with need, moaning as she tried to move closer. She swung her legs around his waist and crossed her ankles behind his back. "I like the way your mind works," she panted before losing herself in the sensation of his hardness rubbing against her core.

Leif took the few steps across the room to the bed in record time and flung her down on the covers. He leaned back to tear his clothes off. "My mind hardly works at all when you are near."

She chuckled and leaned back on her elbows, enjoying the view of naked flesh being revealed. She rose up on her knees and traced the ridges on his chest and abdomen. As her fingers trailed down toward his proud shaft, he captured her wrists.

"Be careful." He smiled down at her. "I'm loaded and might go off any minute."

She laughed. "You've been watching too many old Western movies with Harald."

With a light push on her shoulder, Leif pushed her

back on the bed and followed her down. He hovered over her body, bracing his weight on one arm, while he pulled down the strap of her gown to reveal a breast. His lips captured her nipple. He sucked and then gently bit the tip of the peak when it puckered under his attention. "Just stating the facts, ma'am," he said, his lips hot against her skin.

She squirmed under him, impatiently grasping the hem of her gown to pull it over her head.

Chuckling, Leif eased back to help her and then made quick work of her damp panties as well. He leaned back down and touched her forehead with his. "I love your strength, your independence." He smiled. "I love your stubbornness. Basically, I love you more than life itself," he whispered.

Naya froze. The words ricocheted in her mind as her own feelings threatened to blow a hole through her chest. She gasped for breath.

Leif pulled back to gaze into her eyes. "Are you okay?"

She nodded. To her horror, a tear slid down her temple. Through their bond, she already knew how he felt, but hearing it out loud was different. Trusting him enough to believe his words was overwhelming. "I love you too."

The Viking's satisfied grin showed off his dimples to their full advantage. He captured her hands in his and pulled them behind his neck before devouring her mouth. She opened wide to let his tongue tangle with hers. With his knee, he nudged her legs apart. He positioned himself between her legs and grabbed the backs of her knees.

With one forceful thrust, he plunged deeply into her wet tunnel.

Her arms fell back as the pleasure made her back arch. Leif captured first one nipple, than the other between his lips. Sucking and gently biting while thrusting his hips faster and faster.

Naya squeezed her thighs around his waist to hang on and matched his feverish pace.

He released her breasts and arched, forcing his hips forward, driving himself deeper.

Someone screamed his name and she realized it was her. She placed her hands against the bed, pushing her groin against his. Their tempo increased.

He twisted his hands, hooking thumbs behind her knees and lifting her ankles onto his shoulders. Entering her deeper than she'd ever thought possible, the tip of his shaft hit the very back of her, creating a vibration deep in her womb with each thrust.

Again, he increased the pace and she lost the ability to breathe.

He climaxed shouting her name while pulsing inside her.

She clenched her inner core muscles around him and wave after wave of pleasure washed through her body. She felt light and free as she flew past the now familiar circle of white lights and into the balmy darkness of complete stillness that she'd visited before.

The silver-haired woman appeared, illuminated by a light from within. She regarded Naya with strange dark eyes, deep pools of glittering darkness. "Welcome."

"Freya?" Naya hadn't moved her lips to utter the word.

"It is I," the woman said, reaching out to caress Naya's cheek. Icy fingers trailed over her skin, and yet warmth radiated from where they touched.

"You have endured much, and yet it only made you stronger." She captured Naya's chin with her fingers. "You will be a wise queen and a worthy Valkyrie."

"I'm not a Valkyrie," Naya said…thought.

Freya's smile held infinite wisdom. "Daughter of my heart. Loyal and fierce warrior. You have always been like my Valkyries." She touched her forehead to Naya's. "You will be a true daughter of mine after the handfasting."

Before she had a chance to answer, Naya drifted out of the stillness and away from the goddess. She came to in her own body with a gasp. She turned her head. With eyes the color of an icy sea, Leif studied her.

He reached out and traced his finger along her jaw. "You okay?"

She nodded, wanting to tell him about meeting the goddess, but not sure how to put it into words.

"I love you," he whispered, leaning forward and nibbling her lower lip. "You belong to me."

She pushed gently on his chest to create some space between them. Meeting his ice-blue gaze, she corrected him, "I belong *with* you."

He hummed his agreement before pulling her closer, engulfing her in his arms.

She breathed in the scent that was uniquely him. Her heart slowed its frantic beat and she relaxed in his embrace.

The Viking king belonged to her.

Epilogue

A month later

NAYA TRIED TO STAND STILL WHILE ASTRID ATTACHED flowers in her hair. "Ouch, that's the third time you have poked me with a bobby pin."

"If I wanted to be a hairdresser, I wouldn't have learned to fight," the blond Valkyrie shot back, but her broad smile took the sting out of the words.

"I think we need Irja to help with this."

"Help with what?" the Finn asked as she entered the room. Her rose-colored, ankle-length chiffon dress complemented her pale skin. Her dark hair, twisted into an elaborate updo, was sprinkled with wild roses of the same color as the dress.

"I can't figure out where these freaking pins go," Astrid complained. Her dress, the same color and material as Irja's, reached only mid-thigh and draped across one shoulder, leaving the other bare. She had refused flowers in her hair, but wore rose-colored thigh-high leather boots.

Irja dumped the bouquet of wild roses and baby's breath she carried into a chair and joined the other two in front of the floor-length mirror. "Here," she said, taking the hairpins from Astrid, "let me do the hair."

Naya studied their reflections. A sash in the same rose color as the Valkyries' dresses bisected her white dress. The three of them, so different in stature and complexion, were perfectly color coordinated. Irja caught her gaze in the mirror and smiled while expertly twisting tendrils of Naya's hair and braiding flowers into them. "You are beautiful, sister."

Naya swallowed the lump in her throat and smiled back. The last month had been interesting. Leif and she had navigated how to live together without killing each other. Compromising was hard work.

She had dug through most of the files she'd stolen from Dr. Trousil. Her dad had escaped the compound and met her mom while on the run. All of the other soldiers in his unit had eventually gone into uncontrollable rage and been executed, as had the ones in hers and Scott's unit. Her brother and she were the only ones left. Maybe they'd lasted longer because they were the natural offspring of another super solider. Irja was studying the data in the files, but it wasn't likely they'd ever find out exactly why Naya and Scott were different from the others. The more important reason to study the files was to gain an advantage on the wolverines.

Their attacks had escalated after the warriors burned their mobile herb garden. She had refused to miss out on the fights in which the other warriors participated. After a couple of heated discussions, the Viking king no longer tried to stop her when she patrolled with the Norse fighters. He'd actually added her to the rotating schedule and put his own name down on most of her patrols.

The king and queen joining their warriors strengthened everyone's fighting skills, but also seemed to enhance the communication between battle brothers and sisters.

She pushed the thoughts of combat out of her mind.

Today was her Valkyrie initiation, and after that, her handfasting to Leif would happen as an extra bonus. They would be engaged for a year and a month, like the old tradition dictated. Next summer they'd be married.

"Time to go," Astrid said as Irja put the finishing touches to Naya's hair.

"Before we go downstairs"—Irja grabbed Naya's hands—"I want to thank you for bringing Pekka back to me."

"You've thanked her every day for the last four weeks," Astrid said. "We have a Valkyrie initiation and a handfasting to perform. Let's go." She handed the bridal bouquet to Naya.

"With everything that you have done for Scott, we are more than even." Naya kissed Irja's cheek.

Irja smiled. "I only wish your brother were here."

"Me too," Naya said. After extensive testing of Batch 439, both on Naya's and Scott's blood, Irja had come up with a treatment for her brother. Although he was improving every day, his body tolerated only small increases of the dose, and he was not yet fully conscious. It would take some time to completely eliminate the destructive nanoparticles from his system. "He'll be here soon though. As soon as he's fit to travel, I will go and get him." He'd be at the traditional wedding next year.

"I'm making progress on resynthesizing the formula." Irja straightened a flower in Naya's hair. "Soon I'll be able to produce it on my own."

"That's fantastic." Naya kept tabs on the research facility in North Dakota, but Dr. Trousil's death and the deaths of dozens of compound soldiers seemed to have stopped its activities.

"Let's go." Astrid gestured from the door. "If we don't finish the Valkyrie initiation soon, Torvald will have drunk all the *mjöd* and eaten all the *sill* by the time we get to the handfasting."

Naya liked the sweet honey mead that Per and Sten brewed in one of the sheds, but didn't mind missing out on the pickled herring. "We're coming," she told Astrid as she and Irja followed the tall blond down the hall and the stairs.

The women led her to the clearing where the giant ash stood, tall and majestic behind the stone throne. The ash tree symbolized Yggdrasil, the sacred mythological tree that held together the nine Norse worlds.

Naya followed the Valkyries behind the tree. A small altar stood nestled among the ash's roots. A figurine of a gold chariot pulled by two blue cats stood on top, with a gold goblet next to it.

Irja and Astrid knelt on a blanket in front of the altar and gestured for Naya to do the same. She knelt, careful not to wrinkle her dress.

"This is the gold chariot driven by our mother Freya," Irja said.

Naya swallowed a nervous giggle. "Why the cats?"

Astrid smiled. "Thor gave them to her. When the god of thunder gives you steeds to pull your wagon, you know they're going to be strong no matter what animal they are." She reached for the goblet. "Clasp your hands together and hold out your arms."

Naya did as told and the two other women both held the goblet, raising it through the circle formed by Naya's arms.

"Sister of Valkyries. Daughter of Freya," Irja said. "Share our wine." She leaned forward, placing her lips on the rim of the gold cup.

Astrid gently pushed on the back of Naya's head until she also had placed her lips on the goblet. Astrid then added her own mouth to its edge.

While very carefully tilting the cup and their heads, the Valkyries orchestrated a simultaneous three-woman sip, Naya receiving most of the wine. Although the liquid was cold when it entered her mouth, heat trickled down Naya's throat as she swallowed.

Irja returned the cup to the altar and pulled out a long, gold blade that had been hidden in the folds of the cloth covering the small table.

Naya reared back, but Astrid shot her a reassuring grin. "We don't do the whole sharing-of-blood thing when it's just us girls."

Irja cut an inch of her hair before handing the blade to Astrid, who hacked off a good chunk of her blond curls before handing the strands to Irja. The blade then passed to Naya, who copied Astrid, probing her hair carefully so she wouldn't upset any of the flowers adorning her head.

Irja rolled the three bunches of hair between her palms until they were mixed together. She placed the strands in the gold chariot and reached for two small metal pieces. Striking them against each other caused sparks to fly and lit the hairs on fire.

The acrid smoke hit Naya and she instinctively closed her eyes as the fumes burnt her nose. The Valkyries grabbed her hands when she swayed backward.

Naya zoned out, but remained anchored by the other

two women holding her. Inside her head she heard a loud whisper. "Daughter mine. Valkyrie Mine. Warrior Mine." The touch of a cool hand brushed across her forehead. Freya.

The skin of her left bicep stung and she came to, rubbing her arm. She looked down to discover a tattoo encircling the top of her arm. Instead of the Nordic design the Vikings and Valkyries wore, her snake's runes swirled around each other, forming patterns similar to a Celtic knot.

Naya traced the pattern.

"Beautiful," Astrid said.

Irja nodded and smiled. "You are truly our sister now."

"What does that mean?" Naya asked.

Astrid shrugged. "It's different for everyone. Only Freya knows."

Irja touched Naya's arm carefully, tracing the design. "The goddess has a purpose for each of her Valkyries. If you are lucky, she will tell you yours."

Astrid snorted. "Or you'll be like me and still, after hundreds of years, wonder what your true destiny is." She rose. "Let's get back to the fortress while there's still *sill* left."

The three women strolled back through the forest. In the garden behind the main house, several chairs had been lined up in front of a tall arch decorated with green leaves and traditional midsummer flowers of daisies, bachelor buttons, and poppies. The white, blue, and red of the wildflowers were echoed in colorful streamers hung from the trees, under which long tables bowed from platters of food. The Vikings wore tunic tops over slim leather pants tucked into knee-high boots. Wool cloaks were slung over their shoulders, secured by large metal broaches.

As Naya and her new sisters stepped into the garden, Ulf and Torvald cheered and thumped Leif on the back where the three stood together under the flowered arch. The king radiated power and understated sex appeal, dressed completely in black with an intricately patterned silver broach keeping his cloak in place.

Naya forced herself to walk slowly across the lawn. She wanted to run and take her place beside him. As she strode down the aisle, the seated Vikings smiled encouragingly.

Pekka gave her a wink and a thumbs-up. She returned both gestures.

When she finally reached the flowered arch, Leif grasped her hand and smiled down at her. "Ready?"

Her stomach fluttered when his familiar dimples appeared. She'd never grow tired of seeing them. "Ready as I'll ever be." She returned his smile.

He traced a finger along her new tattoo, quirking an eyebrow. "You do know that by pledging yourself to me, you also bind yourself to this whole group of rowdy men and women?"

"Yes," she said as warmth spread through her chest, "I know that by pledging myself to you, I'll finally be your warrior queen." They didn't know if completing the bond would alter her aging process. Maybe she would become as invincible as the other Valkyries. Maybe she would only live a normal human life span.

However much time she had left, she wanted to spend it with Leif.

A cheer rose in the audience when Leif claimed her lips.

"Save those for after the ceremony!" Harald, who had the honor of officiating, bellowed over the ruckus.

The king released her lips, his grip on her elbow steadying her as they turned toward the *stallare* to recite the vows that would bind them closer.

Leif bent down. "And I'll be your Viking king," he whispered close to her ear and then grinned wider as her breath caught.

Acknowledgments

I have been gifted with amazing support and generosity from so many people that thanking them all is going to be impossible, but I will do my best.

So, a huge thank you from the deepest parts of my heart to:

My editor, Cat Clyne, for fishing my manuscript out of the slush pile and guiding me through the process of making it a much better story. And to the entire Sourcebooks team for making me feel welcome and for being as excited about this book as I am.

My agent, Sarah E. Younger, for answering millions of questions, calming me down when I stress out, and always knowing exactly what to say to support and encourage me.

My writer pals who read parts of early drafts and showed me how to make them stronger: Holly, Erin, Teresa, Jeré, Melissa, Scott, and Geneva.

My RWA community for educating, encouraging, and always supporting me: IECRWA, GSRWA, RCRWA, KOD, The Contemporary Chapter, TGN, and FF&P. And to the Dreamweavers, who are the very best part of being a Golden Heart finalist. Also, special thanks to Cherry Adair for running the Finish the Damn Book challenge—without that Leif and Naya's story would still be on chapter 3—and to Rebecca Zanetti for being generous not only with great advice, but also unwavering support.

My instructors in the INCW MFA program, especially to Rachel Toor and Natalie Kusz for showing me that good writing happens when I push out of my comfort zone.

My family and friends for being understanding when I disappeared for many months and for always asking, "When is the book out?" Here it is!

My bestie, Jeré, for going way out of her way to support me, whether that involves house and doggie sitting, a long talk, or an inspiring card.

My incredible, amazing, award-worthy husband who has endless patience and puts up with me being absent-minded, stressed out, and sometimes discouraged. Your support and encouragement means the world and none of this would matter without you by my side.

And lastly, a very grateful thank-you to you for reading this story. Without you, these amazing people's support would have been in vain.

Wolf Trouble

SWAT: Special Wolf Alpha Team
by Paige Tyler
New York Times and *USA Today* bestselling author

He's in trouble with a capital *T*

There's never been a female on the Dallas SWAT team and Senior Corporal Xander Riggs prefers it that way. The elite pack of alpha-male wolf shifters is no place for a woman. But Khaki Blake is no ordinary woman.

When Khaki walks through the door, attractive as hell and smelling like heaven, Xander doesn't know what the heck to do. Worse, she's put under his command and Xander's protective instincts go on high alert. When things start heating up both on and off the clock, it's almost impossible to keep their heads in the game and their hands off each other...

Praise for Paige Tyler:

"A wild, hot, and sexy ride from beginning to end! I loved it!" —Terry Spear, *USA Today* bestselling author of *A SEAL in Wolf's Clothing*

"Hot, action-packed, and sexy as hell!" —Sara Humphreys, award-winning author of *Vampire Trouble*

"Wow, just wow!" —*Fresh Fiction*

For more Paige Tyler, visit:

www.sourcebooks.com

In the Company of Wolves

SWAT: Special Wolf Alpha Team
by Paige Tyler
New York Times and *USA Today* bestselling author

The new gang of thugs in town is ruthless to the extreme—and a pack of wolf shifters. Special Wolf Alpha Team discovers this in the middle of a shootout. When Eric Becker comes face to face with a female werewolf, shooting her isn't an option, but neither is arresting her. She's the most beautiful woman he's ever seen—or smelled. Becker hides her and leaves the crime scene with the rest of his team.

Jayna Winston has no idea why that SWAT guy hid her, but she's sure glad he did. Now what's a street-savvy thief going to do with a hot alpha-wolf SWAT officer?

Praise for Paige Tyler's SWAT series:

"Bring on the growling, possessive alpha male… A fast-paced and super-exciting read that grabbed my attention. I loved it." —*Night Owl Reviews* Top Pick, 5 Stars

For more Paige Tyler, visit:

www.sourcebooks.com

The Good, the Bad, and the Vampire

by Sara Humphreys

—~~—

Trixie LaRoux is a pink-haired, punk rock, badass vampire with mad bartending skills. Everyone in the coven thinks she's as tough as nails, but only her maker knows the truth; underneath the sultry eye makeup and neon hair is a woman haunted by a past full of troubled relationships.

Dakota Shelton is a vampire with deadly, dangerous skills. But with a penchant for Johnny Cash, he's a good ol' Southern boy at heart. Thrown together by mutual friends in New York City, Trixie has no idea what to do with Dakota's old-fashioned chivalry. But after her tumultuous dating history, Trixie just may be ready for the one man she never expected...

—~~—

Praise for Sara Humphreys:

"Ms. Humphreys continues to possess the gift of storytelling and gathering the hearts and souls of her audience." —*Night Owl Reviews*

"Sara Humphreys writes an intelligent, inventive, and spirited series where the impossible seems possible." —*The Reading Cafe*

For more Sara Humphreys, visit:

www.sourcebooks.com

A Silver Wolf Christmas

by Terry Spear

USA Today Bestselling Author

—⁓⁓⁓—

Wolf-shifter C.J. Silver is more than happy to help the new female shifters in town renovate an old hotel for the holidays—especially if it means opportunities under the mistletoe with the tempting Laurel MacTire.

But renovations become a lot more difficult when the hotel attracts the attention of human ghost hunters. Determined to keep their visitors from discovering that werewolves live in town, C.J. and Laurel have to work together to protect their community. As they sneak around the old hotel to keep an eye on the ghost hunters, C.J. and Laurel are in for a much hotter holiday treat than they expected…

—⁓⁓⁓—

Praise for Terry Spear:

"A masterful storyteller, Ms. Spear brings her sexy wolves to life" —*Romance Junkies*

"Ms. Spear is one of my go-to authors when I want to escape with a book guaranteed to entertain." —*Long and Short Reviews*

For more Terry Spear, visit:

www.sourcebooks.com

SEAL Wolf in Too Deep

by Terry Spear

USA Today Bestselling Author

~~~

Debbie Renaud is a police diver working on criminal cases with SEAL Allan Rappaport. She admires him greatly for his missions in the navy, plus he's just plain HOT. Allan seems to share her attraction, but what she doesn't know is that her partner is wolf shifter.

Allan is really hung up on his smart, beautiful dive partner, but he can't get involved with a human outside dive duty. Yet when she gets between a werewolf hunter and his intended victim, one of the members of Allan's pack, they run into real trouble, and their lives are altered forever.

~~~

Praise for Terry Spear:

"Nobody does werewolf romances like Terry Spear. The romance sizzles, the plot boils, the mystery intrigues, and the characters shine." —*The Royal Reviews*

"Ms. Spear brings her characters to life, both old and new... Each story she brings us in the series is fresh and new." —*Night Owl Reviews*

For more Terry Spear, visit:

www.sourcebooks.com

About the Author

Asa Maria Bradley grew up in Sweden surrounded by archaeology and history steeped in Norse mythology, which inspired the immortal Viking and Valkyries in the Viking Warriors series. She came to the U.S. as a high school exchange student and liked the country so much she stayed. Asa holds an MFA in creative writing from the Inland Northwest Center for Writers at Eastern Washington University and an MS in medical physics from the University of Colorado. She lives on a lake deep in the pine forests of the Pacific Northwest with her British husband and a rescue dog of indeterminate breed. Visit her at www.AsaMariaBradley.com.